FATED DESPAIR

ANGEL'S FATE: BOOK 4

TESSA COLE

Gryphon's Gate Publishing

Fated Despair

Copyright © 2020 Tessa Cole

Cover Design by Melody Simmons

Gryphon's Gate Publishing

550 King St. N.

PO Box 42088 Conestoga

Waterloo, ON

N2L 6K5

ebook ISBN: 978-1-988115-82-5

Print ISBN: 978-1-988115-81-8

CHAPTER 1

SEBASTIAN

Deaglan's demon-vampire hybrid slid his katana into Amiah's chest and my world froze, the horrific moment burned into my mind.

It happened so quickly. One moment she was desperately trying to save Cassius by channeling an enormous amount of power stolen from the men around us—since her own reservoir had been mostly depleted—and the next, the hybrid had stabbed her.

I stumbled, caught my balance and pushed myself to run faster and reach her. I couldn't stop. I had to get to her. I'd been running since Cassius's throat had been slit and she'd started screaming, a soul-deep desperate wail.

Her eyes widened with surprise at the blade in her chest, her mouth open on a gasp, then the hybrid yanked his blade out and her impossible power exploded into a blazing golden light. It overwhelmed her unnatural full-body fae glow and blazed from her eyes with the unmistakable magic of an angelic mating brand.

For a second, I hoped that somehow, even though the brand was newly formed and she wasn't supposed to be able to, she'd be able to draw life force from her mate and it would save her.

I didn't care which one of us she bonded with, so long as she survived. I didn't even care if it was me.

But then she cried out and the golden light blazed in the hybrid's eyes.

Oh, fuck.

He was her mate?

How the fuck was he her mate?

"What did you do?" the hybrid gasped, his expression as stunned as hers.

The brand's magic swelled. The leash spell binding me and Amiah shattered in my chest making me stumble, and another, more powerful spell exploded between the hybrid and Deaglan.

Just like the last time I'd seen a vampire get branded, the power of the forming angelic mating brand severed any other bonds that weren't soul bonds between the two recipients.

Guess the hybrid wasn't a part of Deaglan's team of his own free will. Which was good, because if he was well and truly Deaglan's man, we were fucked.

Deaglan snarled, his expression a mix of rage and shock, and flew out of the hole in the roof. His men, those who were still alive, ran screaming from the cavern.

I dropped my light spell, throwing the Summer Court's luminous cave garden into deep shadows. The glow from the luminescent rocks and moss and algae was weak in comparison to the light I'd summoned to prevent Deaglan's shadow fae assassins from jumping between shadows, but I kept running, trusting my vision to quickly grow accustomed to the darkness.

I knew agony burned through me. It had for the entire fight with Deaglan and his men because I'd had to maintain the light spell, but I couldn't feel anything. All of me—all of my senses, my thoughts, my soul—was focused on Amiah, her hands pressed to her chest, her blood rushing between her fingers and soaking into her beige cotton shirt, and her eyes wide with horror.

It didn't matter that her soul was now bonded to the hybrid. I had to get to her.

Hawk screamed and bolted toward her, and Titus was close at his heels.

She crumpled to the ground, and the hybrid continued to stare at her, his expression still shocked, her blood dripping from his katana.

"What did you do?" he asked again, as if he couldn't get his mind to move past their sudden, horrifying soul bond.

Titus snarled and swiped at him with his claws and my heart leaped into my throat.

"Don't kill him," I yelled. "She's branded him. They're soul bonded. You kill him, you kill her."

Titus's golden gaze jerked to me, then he closed his hand at the last second and slammed his fist into the hybrid's face instead of ripping out his throat.

The hybrid didn't even defend himself. I wasn't even sure if he was aware Titus was there. He never looked away from Amiah until Titus's punch knocked him down, and, even clearly dazed from the blow, he strained to keep his eyes on her as the big dragon pinned him to the ground, the hybrid's body under Titus's knees and the hybrid's head captured under a big hand.

Amiah gasped, the pool of blood shockingly large for the few seconds she'd been down. She needed to heal herself. Why wasn't she healing herself?

Right. Fuck. Cassius. She'd been channeling all her magic and the magic she'd torn from Deaglan's men into Cassius.

Hawk dropped to his knees beside her and cupped her face in his hands, forcing her to look at him, although I was too far away to actually tell if she was able to focus on him.

"Come on, Amiah. Heal yourself. You've got a bit of power left. Use it. Please use it," he begged. "Please heal yourself."

I barreled past them and scrambled up the three shallow jagged shelves at the back of the cavern where the key to unlocking Faerie's Heart had become empowered, and where Cassius was bleeding out—

Please let him still be alive. God, please. Don't do that to her.

I dropped to my knees beside Cassius, not caring I was in a pool of his blood or that the agony in my body was making me shake, and pressed my hands over his heart. I just needed to sense a glimmer of magic inside him. That's all I needed to keep him alive.

I couldn't heal him. But I could cast a hibernation

spell and freeze him in time until Amiah could save his life.

But only if he was still alive.

And only if I could survive channeling that kind of magic.

There. A small, barely lit glimmer of power in his heart. It would take Amiah a massive amount of magic just to bring him back. She'd need to be fully recovered to save him, but she could save him.

I'd make sure of that.

So long as I didn't kill myself.

"Amiah, please!" Hawk cried, his voice breaking with desperation, making my heart clench.

I didn't know how he'd managed to fall in love with her so quickly. They barely knew each other. But the impossible had happened and Hawk's heart belonged to Amiah. And no one knew if an incubus who'd lost his lover could remain sane. Being in love was thought to be genetically impossible and on those extremely rare occasions when it did happen, it was considered a mental disorder.

What I did know from his heartbreaking pleas was that if she didn't save herself, he'd let himself starve to death. Yes, he'd known she and Cassius were going to end up in a traditional angelic monogamous relationship, but she'd still be alive. She'd be happy and have what she desired. That might have been enough for him to keep on living.

But her death was going to break him and he was one of the strongest people I knew.

"Come on, Amiah. Please."

Convince her. Please, God, convince her to live.

Because I could save Cassius. I had to save him. I just needed to focus.

I shut Hawk out. I shut everything out, all the pain, the fear, and the anger, and reached for my connection with Faerie's primal magic.

The demonic magic that wasn't supposed to be inside me, that I couldn't get out, blazed the strongest it ever had, and scorched through my magical channels and veins, setting every nerve on fire.

Everything within me begged me to stop, and yet my soul begged me to keep going.

I was in love with Amiah, too.

It was crazy. I swore I'd never fall in love again, thought she was frustrating and annoying and uptight—

Until she hadn't been any more. Until she'd let down her walls and let me in, and God, I wanted to keep what we had. Her, me, and Hawk. Hell, if Titus and Cassius wanted to join in, that would be great too, but all of it would be gone if Cassius died.

His death would shatter her and I didn't know if the rest of us would be enough to get her through that, especially with her unwanted angelic mating brand permanently bonding her with someone who'd tried to kill her at least once and who she knew nothing about.

God, she'd done everything, had a chunk ripped out of her soul to get rid of it, and it had still formed.

Maybe it wasn't a real bond. Maybe all the power she'd been impossibly channeling had bonded her to the hybrid when he'd stabbed her and, once I'd regained my full power—*if* I ever regain my power—I'd be able to break it for her.

I captured the small thread of fae magic that should have been a torrent coming through my connection and spun it into the hibernation spell, twisting my intention over and over again, creating the spell from scratch because I didn't have it tattooed on my body.

It needed to be strong. It needed to hold without me having to keep pushing power into it, because after this, I was summoning the man who'd failed Amiah and owed her for a job he apparently hadn't done, and casting that would likely be one spell too many.

Already the fire of uncontrolled magic burned in my chest, my will weakened from constantly fighting the demonic magic and having to keep casting spells day after day.

I strained to stay in control.

Just a little more. I could do this. I could survive this. I could have my Amiah, the Amiah who wasn't heart-broken over the death of a man she loved, the one who wanted to explore her desires, and who somehow magically connected with me during sex.

My willpower stuttered and the weak thread of fae magic stuttered with it, losing shape and burning into my body.

I gritted my teeth and yanked the thread back into the ball that only I, and maybe Hawk because he was a Sensitive, could see. I was almost done.

The spell and my focus.

I just needed a little more.

Another stutter and another flash of fire that threatened to consume me from the inside out.

Almost.

There.

I pushed the last bit of power into the hibernation
spell, making it flare to life, and released it in Cassius's
chest before my power burned me up. The spell activated
and I let go of my magic.

Smoke billowed from my hands and forearms like
Cassius with his fire, except I wasn't fireproof like the
angel. I sagged forward, gasping, the demonic magic
screaming through me. But it hadn't killed me.
Thank God.

Just one more spell. That was all I needed to do and
she'd be safe... or rather safer.

God, Deaglan knew she had one of the keys to freeing
the powerful magic of Faerie's Heart. He'd be coming
after her, and I could only pray the others would be able
to hide her long enough for her to recover. Because after
this, there was no way I'd be able to protect her.

"Hawk, is she stable?" I asked, dragging my attention
back to the horrific scene, her laying in a pool of blood, Hawk
staring into eyes only partially open, and Titus pinning her
newly bonded mate to the ground, his teeth bared.

"She will be," he said, and he pressed his lips to hers.

The pressure of his power, the weight I felt because of
my magical sensitivity, swelled, and he shoved his magic
in Amiah.

Oh, fuck.

He was giving her his life force, something she told

him never to do again. Incubi and succubi consumed life force through a person's sexual energy and, unbeknownst to most people, could also give it back.

He could give her enough magic to maybe heal her, in the very least stabilize her, but if he gave too much, he'd kill himself.

And I needed him to help get all of us out of there. Titus had a hold on the hybrid for now, but if he decided to fight back it would be a struggle to contain him and move both Amiah and Cassius. Especially since my next spell could incapacitate me.

Amiah gasped and her fae glow flared, but she didn't open her eyes, and Hawk trembled, the pressure of his power rushing out of him, weakening his essence.

He was going to give her everything.

Of course he was. He was in love with her.

"Hawk, stop." I staggered off the shelves and, with a strength I didn't realize I had left, yanked him away from her.

We both fell back, landing on our butts, and the demonic magic snapped and sliced into me.

"Did I save her?" he gasped before his eyes rolled back, and he collapsed.

My sense of his power flickered and vanished.

Fuck fuck fuck.

He'd given her too much. He needed an infusion of sexual energy or he'd die, and I was God damned not going to let him or anyone die. I crawled to him, pressed my lips to his, and imagined I was kissing Amiah, since while I found Hawk attractive—everyone in all the realms would find him attractive—he didn't turn me on like a woman did. Like Amiah did.

Except thinking about kissing her made me glance at her and her too-pale skin and her barely-there breaths, and chilled any desire I might have had.

Think of something else. Anything else.

The demonic magic sliced deeper, making my breath short sharp pants.

I struggled to focus. I needed to forget everything and get turned on. Just for the duration of the kiss.

Hell, this would probably turn Amiah on. She'd just love to see this. Me lip-locked with Hawk when I'd been adamant he wasn't my type. Everything else with her and sex had been surprising, I'd bet she'd be into this too. She'd loved it when Hawk watched me make love to her. Hell, she'd loved it when I'd watched her give me a blow job.

Her pupils had dilated, turning into dark bottomless pools surrounded by brilliant blue, glowing sky. I bet they'd go big and dark again, eager to watch us kiss, eager to explore this new dynamic. I had no idea how she'd managed to keep her vow of celibacy for over a hundred years. I think I would have lost my mind. But now that her self-imposed drought was over, it was clear she wanted it all, and I wanted to give it to her.

The memory of her face when I'd first pushed inside her tight slick sheath filled my mind. Her eyes had rolled back, her lashes had fluttered shut for a second, and her expression had been pure bliss. Her cold angelic mask and her desperate need to control everything had been forgotten and she'd let me glimpse the real her. The Amiah I'd fallen in love with.

Hawk groaned into my mouth and captured the back of my head, deepening our kiss and sending a sliver of magic into me to strengthen my desire and give him a bigger hit of sexual energy.

I clung to the memory of Amiah, determined not to pay attention to who I was kissing or the acidic burn of the demonic magic consuming me for fear I'd lose some of my desire.

I focused on all of the delicious sounds she'd made, her cry of release, my name on her lips, and her gasps and moans as she drew closer to the edge. From the first time I'd had her, I'd fantasized about having her again. I hadn't had a lover release her hold on everything like that in a long time, and coming from Amiah, it had been shocking and amazing. And then when we'd had sex to save Hawk's life, I'd started fantasizing about the three of us, but hadn't really thought she'd be into that. I hadn't thought she'd be into blow jobs either.

She just kept surprising me. I wanted more surprises. I wanted to get through this mess with the Heart and have her naked in my bed. With or without Hawk. I didn't care. Hell, I didn't even care if she was naked. I just wanted her, wanted her around, wanted her determination and caring.

Except that would never happen. It wouldn't even happen with Hawk or Titus or Cassius added to the mix.

Her soul had bound her to the hybrid, giving me serious doubts about the belief that an angel's soul mate wouldn't be fundamentally different from her.

What if that was just a myth, like how beautiful the bond was? Amiah had been terrified of it, saw it as a prison that she had to escape from where all other angels thought it was beautiful and sacred. What if being bound to her perfect match was also a lie?

Hawk pulled away from me, his chest heaving with rapid breaths, his hellfire blazing in his eyes. "I didn't think I was your type."

"If it'll get Amiah out of here, everyone is my type," I groaned, the pain of the demonic magic flaring. "Did you save her?"

Hawk ripped open the cut in the front of her blood-soaked shirt to get a better look at her stab wound. She didn't react, her eyelashes didn't even flutter, but she was breathing. Barely, but she was.

"She's still bleeding, but it's no longer gushing. Hope-fully my magic has healed the worst of it." He turned a furious gaze on the hybrid, jerked to his feet, staggered then caught his balance.

I grabbed Hawk's wrist, stopping him, sending agony screaming through me. "We'll deal with him later. Get Cassius."

Hawk's expression turned grim.

"Did she save him?" Titus asked, his pupils slitted and his canines extended. He trembled, and from his expres-sion it was from barely contained panic and rage.

"He's barely alive and I've put him in hibernation. She'll need all her power to heal him." I gasped in a painful breath and met Titus's gaze then Hawk's. "We don't tell her about him until she's fully healed herself."

"But thinking he's dead will crush her," Hawk replied,

heaving to his feet and heading to the shelves where Cassius lay.

"And we all know she'll kill herself trying to save him. She ran into the middle of a fight for fuck's sake." The demonic magic flared and the cavern got even darker.

Fuck. Just stay conscious. Just a little longer.

"Cassius is safe," I said through gritted teeth. "Even if I die, the hibernation spell will hold."

"You're not fucking dying," Hawk said. "No one is dying."

"We still need to get out of here." I turned to the hybrid, the little bit of movement shooting agony through me. He still wasn't fighting Titus's grip and he still looked stunned. "Hey, hybrid. Does Deaglan know about my apartment in the mortal realm?"

"No," he replied, his voice barely more than a whisper, his attention never leaving Amiah.

The always-on intention glyph tattooed on the inside of my right thigh didn't respond. Shit. The spell needed an emotional lock on him to work and he was either really good at hiding his emotions, or I was in too much pain to know if he was lying or not.

God damn it.

"If you're lying, I'll put you in hibernation and forget about you," I said, trying to get enough of an emotional reaction for my glyph to work.

"Yes, your highness," the hybrid replied.

Nothing.

Titus snarled and put more pressure on the guy's head.

Still nothing.

Just fucking great, and we really didn't have the time to keep pressing him. I wanted out of Faerie before things got worse, and in Faerie things could always get worse. Even if Deaglan didn't know about my apartment, it still wasn't guaranteed to be safe, but it was the only place where I knew for certain there was a circle with a barrier strong enough to keep the hybrid captive until we could figure out what to do with him.

"If I pass out, demand Karthick portal you back to my apartment and put Talkative here in my clean room and activate the barrier glyph on the circle," I said as Hawk climbed the shallow shelves to Cassius, his movements not nearly as nimble as usual, meaning he wasn't even close to having gotten his power back from our kiss.

I dragged in a painful breath and turned away from Titus and the hybrid.

This was going to hurt. A lot. I pressed my hands to the ground and grabbed the barely-there thread of fae magic inside me.

The connection was even weaker than it had been a few minutes ago. Every time I used my magic the demonic magic got stronger and pushed out more of Faerie's magic, and I had a horrible feeling this final spell was going to push all of Faerie out of me. If I didn't burn up right away, I'd die the drawn-out, painful death of a fae cut off from his realm.

And it didn't matter. Amiah had to get out of Faerie.

I tugged on my connection and the demonic magic surged, tearing through my body and threatening my hold on my power and my consciousness. Fire burned under my skin and I started to smoke.

Come on. Just one last spell.

Just one more.

I heaved everything I had into my hands and with a scream, shoved the power into the ground and demanded Faerie, not just one of its courts, but the entire realm, summon Karthick. He would come and he would come now. I was a royal and a sorcerer. My connection to Faerie was stronger than most fae and so was my ability to command it.

Please work. Please, God, work.

The burning darkness of the demonic magic roared into my cells and flames burst over my forearms. My blood rushed over the ground around my hands as my skin blistered, burst, and blackened.

One of the guys yelled, but with the roaring in my head and the agony in my body, I couldn't tell which one.

I tipped forward, gasping, and the inferno inside me burned up my biceps and across my chest, drawing closer to my heart even though I was no longer pushing power into the spell.

It was cast. I could only hope Karthick wouldn't resist and would answer. He'd be pissed. No one, not even the monarchs of any of the courts, dared summon him like that, but I was out of options.

It hurt to breathe or move or hell, even think. Somehow—I had no idea how—I was still alive. Barely, but I was alive. Every inch of me blazed with agony, and while not all of my outside had second- and third-degree burns, most of my magical insides did.

Please come. Please help us.

"What the fuck is wrong with you?" Hawk demanded, his voice close and yet far away at the same time.

The power of a portal popped against my senses, and a pressure that had been squeezing around my heart released.

Oh, thank God.

I forced myself to sit up and face what was sure to be an angry sorcerer. The room darkened and each breath, each miniscule movement of my muscles, sliced agony through me. I fought to stay conscious. I just had to make Karthick help us. That was all that was left to do.

"You actually summoned me?" Karthick asked his voice thick with disgust at receiving a royal summons. "Oh, high and mighty prince of the Winter—"

His gaze landed on me, and the short, squat summer fae's eyes widened, and his attention jerked to the cavern around him and the shadow fae bodies littering the ground.

The cavern's weak illumination grew even darker and I clutched at my consciousness.

Just stay awake. Just long enough to save her.

"You owe her," I forced out before Karthick could ask for an explanation. I didn't have enough in me to answer questions. I just needed to get her safe. "She paid you to take her brand and she's still soul bonded. With Deaglan's hybrid."

She was God damned bonded with a stranger. The very thing she was terrified of.

Karthick frowned. "Well I can't remove an angelic bond once it's formed."

"Which was why you were supposed to have gotten

rid of her fucking brand." And now it was going to make her fall in love with the hybrid and not me. Fuck. "Pay your debt, Karthick. Portal us to my apartment in the mortal realm."

Karthick's attention turned to Amiah and the pressure of his magic crushed inside my chest, adding to my agony.

I clenched my jaw, but a whimper escaped, jerking Karthick's gaze back to me.

"I don't know if Faerie will let her go through a portal to another realm," Karthick said. He almost sounded apologetic.

Well he should. And while I recognized it wasn't completely fair to be angry at him, that angelic mating brands were a magical force all their own that no one really understood, I couldn't help myself. Everything had gotten worse because he hadn't gotten rid of her brand. She wasn't even going to fall in love with Cassius. I might have been able to get over that. But the hybrid? How the hell could she be soul bonded to the hybrid?

I heaved my thoughts back to the real issue. "She can't stay in Faerie. It's not safe."

The demonic magic sliced deeper, cutting into the core of my being and my connection to Faerie shrunk to a miniscule pinprick. I was running out of time.

"You owe her." I gasped. "I'm calling in your debt. Break her connection... and get us... all of us... the fuck out of here."

"She's too weak. Breaking her connection will kill her."

God damn it.

"Then block it."

"Blocking it will only buy you so much time. Faerie will summon her back and she won't be able to resist."

I knew that, but it was all we had. "Just fucking do it."

I couldn't force Karthick to do anything. On a good day, if I got lucky, I might have been a match for him, but this wasn't a good day. It hadn't been a good day for a long fucking time.

And if we stayed in Faerie, we were dead.

CHAPTER 2

TITUS

THE METALLIC SCENT OF BLOOD AND THE CHARRED REEK OF burned flesh filled my nose, making my beast rage inside me. Amiah barely breathed and I knew she was only clinging to life because Hawk had given her his. She was so pale, her small, fragile body in a terrifyingly large pool of blood, and Seireadan looked like he was about to pass out—and from the horrific burns on his hands and arms, I was shocked he wasn't howling in agony.

It took everything I had to fight my clawing, howling beast and stay where I was. I *had* to go to her. She needed me. Even if I couldn't heal her, she needed my soul, needed flesh to flesh contact.

Except I couldn't. I was the only one in any kind of condition to hold the hybrid—my rapid healing having already healed most of the injuries I'd gotten during the fight. And while he lay perfectly still beneath me, I didn't know if it was because he was still stunned from my punch or waiting for a moment to attack, or if he knew that if he moved even an inch my beast would tear into him.

And I would. The bastard had tried to kill Amiah. Both my beast and I were in agreement on that.

Except Seireadan had said hurting him hurt Amiah.

Because they were soul bonded.

My pulse picked up, and my beast snarled at that.

She couldn't be soul bonded with the hybrid. She was mine.

Mine!

I didn't know how the hybrid had soul bonded with *my* mate, but if Seireadan said he had, then it was true. Seireadan had been just as horrified, and if he was married to her—which was still a possibility that neither him nor my beast wanted to admit—then a soul bond with the hybrid destroyed everything for both of us.

And if we didn't get Amiah to safety and healed, none of it would matter.

The strange Summer Court sorcerer, Karthick, pursed his lips—and it better have been in concentration to form a portal to get us out of Faerie and not trying to decide if he should actually do it. Seireadan had risked burning himself up to summon this guy, he had to have believed the man would help us even if his words to him had been angry and demanding.

Amiah's fae glow fluttered brighter for a second, but she didn't react, making my pulse pound faster, and my beast dig deep rents in my soul.

Go to her. Hold her.

No. She'll take a deeper breath any second now. She'll wake up. Something. Anything. Please.

"Her connection to Faerie is blocked, but I don't know how long it will last," Karthick said as Hawk, staggering with Cassius slung over his shoulder, carried the unconscious angel back to us, leaving a trail of blood on the uneven rocky ground. "Deaglan can't be allowed to get the Heart, and I know that bastard will figure out she has a key."

"He already... has," Seireadan groaned and his head lolled forward as if it was too heavy to hold up. "Why do you think... I'm trying to get her... out of Faerie."

"Call me when she needs to come back." Karthick knelt in front of him and raised a finger to Seireadan's forehead.

"Don't," Seireadan said before Karthick could touch him. "Give the summoning spell to Hawk or Titus."

Karthick's expression grew grim. "Fine." He turned to Hawk and pointed at the ground. "Kneel so I can reach you."

Hawk knelt, still holding Cassius, and Karthick pressed his finger to the middle of Hawk's forehead.

"Decide you want to summon me. That will activate the spell, and I'll pull you back into Faerie."

Hawk shivered and his hellfire flared. "Why don't you just come with us?"

Smart thinking. I should have thought of that. Inviting another sorcerer who wasn't seriously injured to join us would help ensure Amiah's safety.

"Faerie won't let me leave and it isn't anything I can solve with my magic," Karthick replied, making me wonder just what he'd done to make Faerie trap him like that. You had to really piss off the realm or be a monarch without an heir for Faerie to stop you from going through a portal to a different realm. "Now think about where you want my portal to take you. Imagine it in your mind."

Hawk closed his eyes and Karthick clapped his hands.

The air around us shimmered and thickened. It clogged my nose and ears, filling me with the unnerving pressure of a portal, then *popped*, releasing us in the middle of Seireadan's dark living room, the portal shoving his couch and the low table in front of it aside to make room for us.

We'd arrived positioned exactly as we'd been in the cavern with Hawk and Seireadan kneeling, Amiah behind them, and me a few feet away holding down the hybrid. A glimmer of strange purplish-orange light shone through one of the windows at the back of the room, but other than that, it was dark outside.

"Get the hybrid in my clean room and in the circle and touch the lock glyph at the circle's edge," Seireadan said and he collapsed face first onto his floor, drawing my gaze to the growing dark stain of Amiah's blood oozing across the white marble floor toward him. She was still bleeding.

"Crap." Hawk set Cassius on the floor and stood. "Let's get the hybrid in the room."

My beast snarled at Hawk. It wanted to go to Amiah. Now. She needed help. Now. But I wrenched one of the hybrid's arms behind his back instead, moved my hand from his head to his neck, and hauled him to his feet. As much as I needed to go to Amiah, the hybrid was still a potential danger.

And I wasn't stupid enough to tell Hawk I could

handle the hybrid on my own so Hawk could take care of Amiah. For all I knew, the hybrid was just biding his time, waiting for us to take him with us wherever we retreated to before trying to finish murdering Amiah.

I shoved him toward the hall where the bedrooms and the clean room were. All the doors stood ajar, with the exception of the guestroom door that I'd ripped off its hinges.

Everything was as we'd left it when we'd raced to save Amiah from Balwyrdan. The sheets on Seireadan's bed in the room at the end of the hall were bunched to one side. He'd been naked when I'd wrenched the door open and drenched in the scent of Amiah's arousal. My bed also had crumpled sheets, the door, half on the floor and half leaning against the bed, while Amiah's room was untouched, the bed perfectly made with a pile of olive green clothes neatly folded at the foot... because she hadn't had a chance to sleep in it that night... because she'd slept with Seireadan... and then been abducted by Balwyrdan.

Had that only been a few days ago? If I thought about it, I'd known even then that she was my mate. I just hadn't wanted to admit it because I'd thought she was Seireadan's or Cassius's.

And she still might be. She might be mated to all of us.

Or none of us—

Or rather, just the hybrid.

I shoved him into the center of the clean room, a white, windowless space with nothing in it except a large circle of glyphs carved into the white floor where

Seireadan could protect those around him when he cast dangerous spells.

Hawk waited until I was outside the circle then pressed his hand against the lock glyph. A blue-white light flashed from all the glyphs and a pale bubble, only visible from the corner of my eye, burst around the hybrid. Anyone on the outside could touch the lock glyph and remove the barrier, but only Seireadan would be able to go in or out of the barrier.

The hybrid sank to his knees, rested his hands on his thighs, and closed his eyes, all sense that he was stunned gone. All sense of any kind of emotion gone.

My beast snarled at him. Neither of us could believe this cold lifeless man was Amiah's mate. She was life itself. Passion and compassion and love. Even Cassius who was cold and hard at times, was really trying to contain his powerful emotions.

"Come on," Hawk said, stepping into the hall. "Bane built that barrier before the demonic magic fucked him up. No one's getting through that."

My beast huffed and I stormed after Hawk, yanking the door closed, remembering at the last second how weak the hinges were, and managing not to break it.

With a groan, Hawk headed back to the living room, his bare shoulder bumping against the hall wall and leaving a blood smear before he regained his balance. "Cassius is in hibernation. He'll be fine on the floor until we can find time to get to him. I'll get Bane to bed and see what I can do about his burns. You take Amiah, clean her up, and pack that wound. I doubt she has much power, so we'll have to wait a few hours for her to get some back before she'll be able to stop her bleeding."

"Will a few hours be enough?" I asked. It took more power for her to heal herself than it did us, and I had no idea how much magic Hawk had given her and how well it would help heal her.

"I hope so." Hawk knelt in front of Seireadan, who was out cold. "I'm not going to be able to watch her bleed for more than that."

Neither would I.

The muscles in Hawk's jaw clenched, then he hefted Seireadan onto his shoulder, staggered to his feet, and headed back toward the hall.

"Hawk," I said, carefully gathering Amiah in my arms, my beast howling at her pale limp form. *Mine mine mine.* Her breath was so shallow. I had to strain to hear it. Her lashes didn't even flutter when I picked her up. *Mine.* "Thank you."

"You were only going to be able to hold your beast back for so long. You need her."

"And she needs us." I'd seen it in her soul. "All of us."

Yes, my beast believed she was my mate, but it also recognized what it had seen in her eyes back in the aerie. There was something in her soul that needed to connect not just with me but with the others. She thought that meant we weren't mates. Hawk thought it might mean we all were. That would certainly explain why my beast *knew* she was mine while at the same time the Winter Court behaved like she was Seireadan's.

I carried her into the guestroom I'd first woken in, kicked the door off the bed, and went straight into the bathing room. The other guestroom still had its door, but I didn't want to dirty up the bathing room or the bed just in case she wanted some privacy when she was better.

My beast hated the idea. That would mean she wouldn't want to be near me, and right now my beast never wanted to let her go. But she wasn't just mine, and she'd been held against her will before—twice now—and I wanted her to feel like there was a space that was all hers, where she could be with the others or just be alone if that was what she needed.

But that's not what she needs. She needs me.

Right now. Yes.

Because she's mine.

And possibly theirs as well—

Except the horrible truth was that she wasn't mine or even theirs. She was soul bonded with the hybrid. He was her soul's mate. Which didn't make any sense. He was the one who'd stabbed her.

I set her on the floor, propped up between the wall and non-magical rain-shower stall, which was a tight fit for just me, let alone both of us. Not to mention, if I couldn't get her to wake up—and I wasn't sure I wanted to wake her given everything she'd just been through—it would be challenging to shower her while she was completely limp.

I carefully cut off her bloody shirt and pants with a sharp claw, dampened one of Seireadan's small white cloths in the sink, and gingerly wiped the blood from her body.

The hybrid's sword strike had gone all the way through her and both the front and back wounds still wept blood. The only positive was that at least they were no longer gushing. I didn't know if that meant that Hawk had given her enough energy to fully heal her and she'd be fine in a few hours or not.

When she was clean, I wadded up more small clean clothes against her wounds and tightly wrapped a large towel around her chest to hold them in place. The next step was to put her in bed, but both my beast and I had to hold her and I was also covered in blood—hers, mine, and the blood of the shadow fae I'd killed. I needed to clean up, but I couldn't bring myself to let her out of sight for the few minutes it would take to shower.

I moved her out of the mess left from cleaning her up to the other corner in the bathing room by the door, stepped into the rain-shower stall and quickly scrubbed away the blood on my already naked body—because the last time I'd shifted, I'd destroyed my clothing and I hadn't had a chance to replace them.

Once clean, I took her to bed, curling my body around hers, holding her tight, and giving her as much flesh to flesh contact as possible.

A few minutes later Hawk staggered into the doorway, his gaze instantly jumping to Amiah. His hellfire was barely-there smoldering red pinpricks in his eyes and his expression was filled with longing and exhaustion and fear. It was clear he wanted— no, *needed* to be close to her too, but was afraid of my beast.

And my beast was snarling at him for just standing in the doorway looking at her. But it also recognized that Hawk had been willing to sacrifice himself to save her. She'd told him to never do an energy transfer again because it could kill him and he hadn't hesitated. That and he'd been desperate and hopeful at the thought that we were all her mates. I hadn't thought incubi took mates, but his need for her was clear, possibly as strong as mine... which couldn't be, because she was *my* mate—

Except she wasn't, damn it.

"Get cleaned up," I growled. My voice was darker, my beast closer to taking over than I liked, but there wasn't anything I could do about it. My mate was hurt. And I couldn't even give her vengeance and kill the hybrid for hurting her.

Hawk frowned at me as if he didn't understand what I was saying.

"You're not getting in this bed looking like that."

His gaze slid down his body as if he hadn't realized he was covered in grime and blood.

"She needs you, too," I said. And Seireadan and Cassius.

My beast heaved and snarled inside me. It didn't matter that she was soul bonded with the hybrid. I'd seen her soul. She needed all of us.

She has to need me.

And I wasn't going to think about the new horrible possibility that finding her soul's mate changed that. She wasn't a dragon. Her soul wasn't like ours even though she seemed to need the same physical contact to soothe her soul.

She would still need me when she woke.

She would. Please.

CHAPTER 3

AMIAH

I DRIFTED TOWARD CONSCIOUSNESS, FIRST BECOMING AWARE of a searing agony slicing through my chest and then the wild ferocity of Titus's life force along with the fiery darkness of Hawk's life force thrumming against my senses.

From that, I knew Titus was in good health—if exhausted—and lay behind me in bed, both of us under the comforter. His massive body was curled protectively around me, my back to his chest, his muscular arms holding me tight, while Hawk lay close in front of me, also under the comforter, his forehead pressed against mine. He was also physically fine, his magic having rapidly healed any injuries he'd taken during the fight with Deaglan, but he was still exhausted and his magic was dangerously low.

Despite that, it felt good to be in bed with them, even if it was odd to be with Hawk and Titus instead of Hawk and Sebastian. My soul sang with their nearness. This was right. The way it was supposed to be. I was steady with them near. It didn't matter that I wasn't a shifter, that

I wasn't supposed to need flesh to flesh contact like this. I needed them. Needed all of them to ground my soul within me.

And then I remembered.

Cassius was dead.

My throat and chest tightened, and my heart rushed into a rapid, desperate pulse.

Oh God oh God oh God.

Dead.

I'd just gotten my best friend back, just realized that I was in love with him. We were just starting to figure ourselves out and now... now...

My breath turned sharp, slicing agony through me.

Please, God. Please.

It had to be a bad dream. A horrible dream. I'd wake up and he'd be angry with me for running into the middle of the fight... to save him...

But I hadn't saved him.

And my soul knew this wasn't a dream. His life force was missing. I hadn't even been aware that I'd been sensing it all this time. But now it was gone and his absence in my soul was as painful as the literal hole in my heart.

Except the physical hole was mending. Given time and power, I could heal my body. I couldn't heal my soul. Not even time would heal the hole left by Cassius's death. It was like I was missing a limb that I hadn't known was there in the first place, and now that it was gone, I realized I needed it, depended on it, couldn't live without it.

My soul started to tremble and it didn't matter that Titus and Hawk were close.

Cassius was gone because of me. Because I hadn't tried harder, hadn't pulled magic faster from those men—

The pressure in my chest clenched tighter, and I couldn't breathe.

I'd killed those men. I'd purposefully taken their lives to save Cassius, and I'd do it again in a heartbeat. I should have killed more of them, gotten more power, gathered it faster, pushed it into Cassius sooner. I should have held on and finished saving him even with the hybrid's sword in my chest and saved Cassius.

All those years trying to convince Cassius and myself that I wasn't weak and when it really counted, I'd failed.

I hadn't even told him I loved him.

God, why? Why? Why hadn't I told him?

But I'd been afraid he'd demand I give up Sebastian and Hawk, and I wasn't ready to make that kind of a commitment. Which was stupid. He'd said he'd wait for me. I could have told him how I felt. It was just three simple words. And it was the truth. He would have given me the time to figure out why I connected with the others during sex. He'd said he would. And now it was too late.

Now the damage to my soul was deeper than anything Karthick had done when he'd ripped out my ability to create a soul bond.

I bit back a bitter huff.

And more permanent.

I'd suffered excruciating agony for him to tear away my partially formed mating brand, but fate was cruel. It took away the man I loved and bound my soul to a monster.

Except I'd used my healing magic to take life. I'd done the one thing I vowed I'd never do. Maybe I deserved to be bound to a monster. An angelic mating brand didn't bind incompatible souls together, which meant I deserved to have my life permanently connected to that lifeless, emotionless man...

Unless of course that was also a lie. The soul bond wasn't beautiful or sacred. Perhaps it didn't care what souls were bound together, it just happened when it happened. Which had to be the case because how could a man who was the antithesis of life be my soul mate? He wasn't even alive. He was half vampire. He didn't have a heartbeat.

And maybe the bond wasn't a real bond. I couldn't feel it.

Except that didn't mean anything.

The connection formed with an angelic mating brand could develop slowly. An angel might not even know who she was bonded with for days, sometimes even weeks. That, and I couldn't feel much beyond the pain in my chest and Hawk's and Titus's life forces. And even then, all of that was a barely-there sensation compared to the pain in my soul.

But maybe all that power I'd been channeling when the hybrid had stabbed me had accidentally connected us like the leash spell had connected me and Titus. Maybe Sebastian would be able to remove it.

My pulse pounded faster.

Sebastian had been in rough shape before we'd even started the fight. The demonic magic infecting him that he couldn't get out of his system had been consuming him from the inside out, and every time he used his magic it burned deeper into his magical channels.

At the thought, my senses jumped beyond Hawk and Titus and connected with Sebastian. A breathtaking agony swept through me and not just the agony of the demonic magic consuming him. It seared my hands and arms and chest with a nauseating mix of fiery pain and numb nerve damage from a combination of second- and third-degree burns.

My need to heal overwhelmed me and I jerked up, making the room darken and lurch. I was exhausted and low on magic, but it didn't matter. I had to go to him. I had almost enough to heal the burns to ugly, tender scars. He'd still have some nerve damage, but I had enough to ease most of his pain until I could regain more magic. I couldn't let him suffer. I couldn't lose him too.

Which didn't make sense. He wasn't dying. But I needed him now more than ever. I needed all of them, needed them near, needed to feel their life forces. I wouldn't survive another amputation like I'd suffered with Cassius. I didn't know why I needed them or even how they fit into my soul. I wasn't soul bonded with them. I knew that for certain. All I knew was that my soul was weaker without them.

God, I needed to tell them I loved them before it was too late, even though I wasn't supposed to have fallen in love with Sebastian and Hawk. Even though neither man would love me back. It didn't matter. They had to know.

Titus's arm around me tightened, keeping me from scrambling off the bed, and Hawk's eyes flew open.

"I have to go to him," I gasped. Sebastian needed me. Now.

Tears rolled down my cheeks. I'd been silently sobbing this whole time and hadn't realized it. The pain in my soul had been overwhelming with my grief for Cassius and for Sebastian's agony and because I couldn't lose anyone else. And because Hawk and Sebastian were going to eventually leave me.

"Heal yourself first. He can wait." Hawk said.

"Hawk, please. He needs me. I have to."

His hellfire flared and his eyes filled with sadness.

Did he think I was talking about Cassius?

Who was dead.

No. God, no.

Focus. Sebastian was in pain. He wasn't dead and he needed me. This was something I could do. I could help him like I hadn't been able to help Cassius.

My compulsion to heal squeezed around my heart even as my thoughts jumped back to Cassius.

Dead.

I never got to tell him I loved him.

More tears streamed down my cheeks. They had to know. All of them. Even if it didn't make sense, even if I'd only known them for a few days. I didn't want to let them go. I didn't want to be without them. Somehow falling in love with them was the only explanation for how I felt. And something could happen to them too. I could lose any one of them. I could lose all of them.

I cupped Hawk's face in my trembling hands and met his gaze. "I love you, and I know you can't love me back, and that's okay. I don't expect you to. But I never got to tell

Cassius, and—" My throat tightened. "I never got to tell my best friend that I—" The pressure in my chest squeezed, making it hard to breathe. "I didn't get to tell him and I can't lose you too. I love you."

Titus pressed his lips against the back of my head, and curled his body tighter around me. I tried to turn in his embrace, but he wouldn't let me move.

"I've fallen in love with you too."

"You don't really know me," he said, throwing back the words I said to him when he'd begged me to be his mate. "You don't really know any of us except Cassius. You're upset and mourning. That's all. Your soul needs something from ours, but that's not love. It can't be. We're not your soul's mate."

His words sent cold rushing through me and more tears welled in my eyes. It didn't matter if I loved any of them. If my bond with the hybrid was real, then eventually I'd love him and only him.

No. I wouldn't let that happen. I'd fallen in love with Hawk and Sebastian and Titus, and I was going to stay in love with them. I'd already lost one man I loved, I wasn't going to lose anyone else. I'd fight my bond, find a way to get rid of it. There was always a way. Everything else about the angelic mating brand had been a lie. Its permanence had to be a lie as well.

My need to heal Sebastian squeezed tighter.

"Please, Titus," I begged. "Let me go."

"You have to heal yourself first, gorgeous," Hawk said, wiping a tear from my cheek, the sadness in his expression darkening into a heartbreaking grief. "My magic healed you more than I thought it would, but you're still bleeding. We've had to replace the washcloths twice now and it's only been a few hours."

His magic?

Horrific realization flashed through me. He'd done an energy transfer to save me and given me enough to mend the hole in my heart. It was barely mended, leaving me with deep puncture wounds on either side, but I wasn't rapidly bleeding out. I could have lost him too.

"Hawk—"

"Heal yourself," he said, fear sharpening the grief in his expression. "Please."

Except I couldn't. My compulsion to heal Sebastian was growing stronger. I'd survive a few more hours without medical attention. I'd be weak from blood loss and having spent my magic, but I'd survive.

"I'll be okay for a few more hours. I have to ease Sebastian's pain." And the moment the words came out, I realized I also needed to be closer to his life force, too.

More tears rolled down my cheeks. I wasn't strong enough to withstand the pain of Cassius's missing life force without their help.

"I'm too weak to fight the compulsion, and I'd rather not waste power healing him from a distance. I'd barely make a dent in his burns that way."

Hawk's gaze jumped past me to Titus.

"I'm not even sure my magic will let me heal myself," I added. Which was the truth. If I was at full power, if I didn't have a gaping hole in my soul, if my heart wasn't shattered, I might have had the willpower to turn my magic inward. "Don't make me fight myself, too."

"Okay," Titus said, his voice heartbreakingly soft.

He tugged the towel wrapped around my chest tighter and pushed back the comforter. With the exception of the towel, we were both naked and so was Hawk, and neither man seemed to care. Even with us being in bed with an incubus there hadn't been anything sexual about it. We'd been more like a small shifter pack, piled together needing the soul-steadying comfort of flesh to flesh contact in our time of grief.

Titus picked me up, the movement shooting agony through me and making the room whirl. I pressed my face against his broad chest and squeezed my eyes shut, praying the sensation would stop, praying I'd wake up from this nightmare, praying for everything to be different. Why couldn't it have been different? Why couldn't I have saved Cassius?

We headed to the door at the end of the hall, Sebastian's bedroom, and Hawk opened it for us. Inside was a room about the same size as the room we'd just left decorated in the same white, silver, and blues. A huge painting of a winter forest hung on the far wall, reminding me of the Winter Forest in the Winter Court that Sebastian loved so much, and books were stacked on every piece of furniture as well as on the floor.

Sebastian lay asleep in his bed with only a thin sheet pulled up to his waist, his full-body fae glow barely alight, his complexion gray, and his expression tight with pain even though he was unconscious. Blood stained the strips of white sheet someone had wrapped around his hands, arms, and chest, and the rest of his torso was covered in the scratches and bruises I hadn't healed when I'd healed his shoulder after the fight at the waterfall.

His life force snapped cold and bright against my senses, fighting the overwhelming darkness of the demonic magic inside him, and for a second all of my pain and exhaustion and grief was gone. There was just Sebastian and his injuries and the fact that I could do something to help him.

"Set me down beside him," I whispered, not wanting to wake him.

Titus set me down and stepped back, taking his ferocious life force with him.

"No, stay." I reached out my hand to him. "Both of you." My throat tightened and my grief for Cassius swelled. "Steady my soul."

Titus didn't hesitate. He eased onto the bed propped up against the headboard and pulled me into the V between his legs letting me lie on his chest while still able to touch Sebastian, and didn't seem to care when Hawk pressed the length of his gorgeous sculpted naked body against his leg and draped his arm across my chest, resting his palm against my cheek.

"What the hell... are you doing?" Sebastian gasped and his eyelids cracked open.

Then his gaze met mine and my pulse stuttered. His pale, almost colorless blue eyes were filled with a pain and darkness that I couldn't do anything about, no matter what I wanted. I could heal his burns, but I couldn't do anything about the demonic magic infection.

"Let me... guess. You're healing me... first."

I released a thread of power into him, straining to hold what little magic I had back so I didn't cause him more pain. My power heaved against my control. It wanted to heal him, needed to. Now now now. It didn't understand how painful it was to have your cells yanked back together to the way they were before. It just healed. That's what it did. And in that moment, I felt more like a vessel, a means for the power to release itself than someone in control of it.

I wasn't in control. I never really had been. If I had, I would have saved Cassius.

"I'm sorry," I said as the last drop of power slipped out of me into him and the peaceful darkness of unconscious dragged me under. "I promised I wouldn't fall in love with you."

But the darkness wasn't peaceful. It was filled with ice and pain and fear.

I was trapped. Again.

God again and again. I was never going to be free. I would always be someone's prisoner.

The Winter Court had claimed me and I could feel it calling to me, its frozen power muffled and far away, but still there, still straining to possess me, and my angelic mating brand had awoken and bound me to a monster.

Why couldn't it have been any of my guys?

My guys.

But they weren't my guys... and yet they were. Except if they weren't my soul mates what were they to me? Why did I need to connect with their life forces?

My life force could have saved Cassius if our souls had been bound together with an angelic mating brand. Why had I waited until I'd had the brand removed to have sex with him? I could have saved him. He could have taken life and strength from me even when my magic failed me.

But now I would save Deaglan's demon-vampire hybrid. The man who'd tried to kill me the first time we'd met and who'd decapitated one of Balwyrdan's men with one emotionless swing of his black katana.

And yet he'd told me to run when we'd met in the illegal market and had given me a knife when Balwyrdan had held me captive.

He'd also been filled with an excruciating pain when he'd hesitated to obey Deaglan's command to bite me.

Except if he hadn't stabbed me, Cassius wouldn't be dead.

I jerked awake, sending fiery pain slicing through me, and found myself alone in Sebastian's bed.

Cold, heart-stopping panic added to my pain, and the profound absence of Cassius's life force filled me, making my throat tighten and my eyes burn.

He was dead.

And I was alone.

A sob broke free and I staggered out of bed. It was foolish. I was still bleeding and should heal myself first, but I couldn't focus on anything past finding my guys and easing the pain in my soul.

Clutching the towel around me, I stumbled out the door. The dim hall whirled around and around and I leaned against the wall to keep standing, heading toward the living room, the direction from where I could sense their life forces. Surely they were there or in the kitchen. They wouldn't have just left me.

I reached the first door, Sebastian's clean room, and

my senses leaped to the strange cold and fiery, alive and dead life force inside.

The hybrid.

My mate.

The man who'd killed Cassius.

And while he hadn't slit Cassius's throat, he'd shattered my concentration by stabbing me. If I'd just had a few more seconds, I could have saved him. I wouldn't have a hole in my soul. But I'd still be trapped.

CHAPTER 4

RIN

THE DOOR FLEW OPEN AND THE ANGEL WHO'D IMPOSSIBLY freed me from the King of the Shadow Court staggered in. She was wrapped in a towel that barely covered her, her hair was a tangled mess, her eyes were red from crying, and she was absolutely stunning.

She stunned me every time I saw her with her powerful determination and her sensual body—which I'd gotten an amazing view of in that dress she'd worn to the party where she and Prince Seireadan were to formally consummate their marriage—and her unusual, heady magic. A magic that was unlike any other magic I'd sensed before. It called to a primal part of my demonic nature, urging me to feed on her, while the rest of her called to the man whose desires had only been satisfied when his king allowed it, and infrequently at that.

But all those desires were overwhelmed as the metallic scent of her blood slammed into me and shattered my tenuous hold on my hunger. My fangs fully extended and I couldn't stop them, and I instantly knew, not even needing to see the bloodstain on the towel at her heart, that she was still bleeding from the wound I'd given her.

"You killed him."

She trembled—I was surprised she was able to stand—and her breathtaking blue eyes were unfocused and barely lit with her angelic glow indicating she was low on power. Even her impossible high fae full-body glow which King Deaglan had said meant she really was Prince Seireadan's wife was weak.

She should have recovered more power in the time I'd been locked in the circle... unless she'd used what she'd regained to heal her husband, a man who obviously cared for her. He'd been willing to burn himself up by channeling too much magic to summon that Summer Court sorcerer to portal us to the mortal realm. The horrific burns on his hands and his collapse the minute we were through the portal was proof of that.

Recklessly using her magic when she was injured and weak would go with what I knew about angels with powerful healing magic. They often died young, a good couple hundred years before other angels, even angels with weaker healing magic. They drained themselves to death because they were unable to fully control the compulsion that came with their powerful innate magic. And I'd known what she was the moment I'd seen her in that forest in the mortal realm where we'd found the dragon. I hadn't even had to sense the flavor of her power to know.

I had no idea how the others hadn't figured it out. It had been obvious by how she knelt over the dragon. But if they weren't going to say anything to the Shadow King, neither was I.

If King Deaglan knew what she was, he'd want her, and I couldn't let him have her. She wouldn't last fifty years as his prisoner. He'd use her in all the horrible ways he used his women until she'd drained herself or killed herself to end the torture, and then he'd toss away her corpse without a second thought.

Except maybe not. Maybe she would last. Maybe she'd be able to escape. Somehow she was more powerful than just an angel with healing magic. Healing angels, no matter how powerful, couldn't break spells, and King Deaglan's spell holding me captive had exploded the moment I'd run her through.

Maybe it had something to do with her marriage to the heir of the Winter Court. He felt powerful, but he also had demonic magic inside him that was blocking his power. Maybe she could channel what he couldn't through their marriage bond.

And none of that really mattered.

I was free. Sort of.

But so was my hunger. Completely.

That had been the only good thing to come out of being taken by King Deaglan. His spell keeping me a prisoner and in constant pain had also held back some of the gnawing, desperate hunger inside me. A hunger that was more powerful than the vampire's who'd made me because my demon half also hungered for magic. Dying and becoming a vampire hadn't changed one hunger to another. It had doubled it. And the little bit of magic inside her, both angelic and fae, called to me as powerfully as the blood leaking from her body.

"You killed him," she said again, one hand clutching the towel around her and the other clenched in a fist. "You killed him."

Power sparked in her eyes, a taunting glimmer of what I craved, and a tear rolled down her cheek.

"I could have saved him. I could have—"

Her breath grew sharp and fast and her heart pounded faster, making her blood rush and my mouth water.

My stomach growled and her eyes widened with horror as if she were finally really seeing me for the monster that I was. I had no control right now and I could feel my hellfire burning across my cheeks. I was starving. King Deaglan had seen to that. And now that his spell was gone, there was nothing holding me in check.

I don't think I'd ever been so grateful to be locked up behind a magical barrier before. I had no idea how I was going to convince Prince Seireadan to let me go, especially after attempting to kill his wife. Hell, I had no idea how I was going to convince him to let me live.

Except he hadn't let the dragon kill me, which meant he had plans for me.

A shudder swept through me. Once he recovered from the fight with King Deaglan, he could still draw enough power to bind and starve me just like King Deaglan. Even with the demonic magic consuming him.

"Oh, God." The angel took a staggering step forward,

the look in her unfocused eyes horrified and heartbreaking. "What did he do to you?"

Then her eyes rolled back and she crumpled to the floor. The towel fell open, giving me an indecent view of her beautiful body, and my gaze jumped to the delicate gold lines swirling over her left hip and sparkling with a strange magic I didn't recognize.

The urge to leap to my feet and go to her surged inside me and I forced myself to stay kneeling. I couldn't help her and I needed to keep what little hold I had on myself. I wouldn't let myself become a raging wild hybrid when there was a chance Prince Seireadan would keep me alive. And if I was alive, there was always a chance—be it a slim one—of being free. This angel was proof. I was no longer King Deaglan's assassin.

Besides, with my heightened hearing, I knew the others had heard her talking to me and were on the way.

Footsteps pounded down the hall and Prince Seireadan, the dragon, and the incubus rushed into the room. The prince and the incubus both wore loose pants while the dragon had a sheet tied around his wide hips. All were shirtless, all well-built, all were dangerous in their own way, and all three gazes instantly jumped to the angel as if they were all drawn to her. Like I was.

"Fucking hell." Prince Seireadan ran a hand over his spikey white and silver hair. The burns on his hands, arms, and chest, now partially covering the glyphs tattooed on his body, were still an angry red, but they were no longer weeping blood. She *had* healed him.

He jerked forward a step, glanced at his hands, then moved out of the way so the others could get to her.

But she hadn't had enough to give him full use of his hands which meant her healing magic was either weaker than I thought or the prince's burns were more serious.

"I told you we shouldn't have left her alone," the incubus said, kneeling to grab her, but the dragon got to her first, tugging the towel closed and lifting her into his arms.

She looked broken and fragile nestled against his broad chest, and he looked even more muscular and imposing than before.

He glared at me, his gaze more ferocious than it had ever been even when he'd gone crazy and shifted into his dragon form in the Winter Court's ballroom or at the waterfall in the Autumn Court.

"The woman is impossible," Prince Seireadan snapped. "She couldn't just stay unconscious for ten fucking minutes while we dealt with Cassius? And why the hell didn't she heal herself first before dealing with *him*?" He jerked his thumb toward me.

The dragon's glared deepened and he bared his teeth and snarled.

"Come on." The incubus placed a hand on the dragon's biceps, drawing his attention away from me. "Let's get her back in bed."

The dragon headed out the door and the incubus followed, pausing on the threshold to look back at the prince.

"You need sleep too."

Prince Seireadan looked longingly at his wife then ran his hand over his hair again and drew in a ragged breath. "I need to have a conversation with buddy here first."

The incubus's eyes narrowed. "He doesn't have a tracking spell on him, and the binding spell Deaglan had on him shattered when Amiah branded him."

Branded?

So that's what they thought happened? That was how she freed me from King Deaglan? The prince's wife had branded me with an angelic mating brand? But that didn't make sense. She'd taken the fae marriage vow and bound her soul to Prince Seireadan's. The Winter Court responded to her as if she were already its queen. She wouldn't have been able to create a mating brand... would she?

My thoughts jumped to the delicate gold lines in her pale skin. If that was an angelic mating brand, then she'd definitely branded someone, but it couldn't have been me. She didn't know me. She must have branded her husband as part of taking her vows and for some reason they thought I'd been added to the bond.

Except I didn't feel like my soul was bound to either her or the prince. It felt free. Finally. The pain of King Deaglan's spell that I'd lived with for hundreds of years was gone. Mostly.

Of course the fight hadn't been that long ago and my hunger was ferocious. Maybe the bond wasn't strong enough, maybe my hunger was too overwhelming for me to feel it.

My hellfire snapped with a sharp *crack*. Had she freed me from Deaglan to keep me for herself as a second subservient mate? An angelic mating brand couldn't be broken and when one mate died the other died or went insane, so her death and the death of Prince Seireadan wouldn't free me.

God, I was still a slave, trapped to the whims of a royal from Faerie.

Panic twisted in my chest and my hellfire snapped again.

I narrowed my focus to the still nothingness in my heart, determined to rise above the turmoil inside me. *I* wasn't the hunger. *I* wasn't the fear. They were just sensations in my body. I might not even be branded. They had no proof. *I* had no proof.

Of course if I was branded, the mark would be on my hip, a match to the one on hers.

The need to check surged inside me.

No, I didn't need to check right now. And I certainly wasn't going to check while they were in the room with me.

"We still need to have a conversation," the prince said to the incubus. "I won't let Amiah be blindsided again. She's barely holding on as it is, and she's headstrong as hell. She's going to come back to him, probably the second we all fall asleep."

"Fine." The incubus turned to the dragon. "We'll join you in a few minutes."

Prince Seireadan rolled his eyes at him. "I'm perfectly capable of having a conversation with a barrier between us. You need her as much as Titus does. Go."

"And I haven't been able to figure out what kind of demon he is," the incubus replied. "If you weren't so exhausted you'd know no one should talk to him alone even with a barrier between you."

He talked back to his master as if he were an equal, and I didn't know if that spoke to the kind of man Prince Seireadan was or the nature of their relationship—since the prince had passionately kissed the incubus after the incubus had saved his wife.

Prince Seireadan turned his attention to the dragon. "If she wakes, don't let her leave the bed until she's stopped bleeding."

The dragon huffed, a strangely dragon like snort in a human body, and took the angel, Amiah— No. I corrected myself. She was *Princess* Amiah, Prince Seireadan's wife. The dragon took her away while the prince and the incubus sagged to the floor in front of the barrier.

"How about we start with your name?" the prince said.

I glanced from him to the incubus whose gaze was ever-so-slightly out of focus. He'd said he knew I didn't have a tracking spell on me and that Deaglan's hold on me was broken. He had to be a Sensitive and was looking for any other spells on me. Or maybe he was using his sensitivity to figure out what type of demon I was. Which he wouldn't be able to. Some half demons, like me, gave off muddy essences, making it impossible to figure out what exactly we were. And now that I was a vampire, the only things that gave me away as a demon were my eyes.

Prince Seireadan sighed. "I'm Sebastian. This is Hawk. We both think Deaglan is an asshole."

"Way to just lay all our cards on the table," Hawk said,

but he didn't sound particularly upset just exhausted.

"Yeah, because he hasn't already figured out who we are or what we think of Deaglan." The prince rubbed his face. "Who are you?"

"Rin." It was just my name. There was no point in holding back that information, especially since I had no idea if this prince would torture me for refusing to say my name like my last master would.

The only positive in this situation was that Prince Seireadan—and I wasn't foolish enough to call him something so personal as Sebastian—was too weak to properly bind me this very minute. He could leave me in this barrier and let me continue starving, but at least there wouldn't be sudden moments of blinding agony in the near future. I'd finally gotten a reprieve.

Of course, that might only be for so long. I'd nearly killed his wife. He'd want justice for that.

"How did you end up in Deaglan's employ?" the prince asked.

"He bought me." He'd paid to have me murdered and turned into a vampire on the off chance that I'd inherited my mother's short human lifespan, because he'd thought I was more valuable and powerful than I actually was.

My father had been a sin eater, able to eat magical energy and, more importantly, the energy that powered spells. Unfortunately, after Deaglan had taken over my connection with my vampire sire and bound me with a carefully crafted spell that was next to impossible for a sin eater to consume, he realized I'd only inherited half of my father's abilities. I could only consume raw magical energy before it had been manipulated into a spell.

I think the only thing that had saved me was my skill as a warrior... either that or it amused him to keep me. He certainly got pleasure out of my hunger, both denying it and, when it was too much to bear, watching it force me into a frenzy.

The prince raised a white eyebrow. He clearly wanted more information, but I wasn't going to offer up anything extra. He might look like King Deaglan's opposite, pale and cold, but that didn't mean they were different. Prince Seireadan was a prince of Faerie, and I had yet to meet any royal who didn't have a hidden agenda.

"How long ago?" the incubus, Hawk, asked.

"The end of the Sengoku period."

Hawk frowned.

"That would be Japan," the prince said to him, "about five hundred years ago."

"Didn't he have Titus for about five hundred years?" Hawk asked. "That seems awfully coincidental."

"Too coincidental. Which means your demon half is something really interesting." Prince Seireadan turned his pale, almost colorless winter fae gaze back to me. "What would Deaglan actually spend money on instead of just taking?"

"What would be easier to buy instead of take?" Hawk shifted right to the edge of the barrier without touching it and stared at me. His hellfire sparked, a sign of frustration... or great concentration... and then his eyes flashed wide. "Holy shit, you're a sin eater."

I clamped down on my own surprise. No one had ever been able to tell what I was. I didn't think anyone was sensitive enough to tell. Deaglan only knew about me because he'd seduced my mother—something else he liked to tell me about—and had learned about my father.

"Well that's just great," Prince Seireadan said. "So you've just been sitting here behind a barrier you could easily take down, waiting for what? You could have escaped at any time. With your magic, you know the only one capable of putting up any kind of a fight right now is Titus. Your odds of getting out of here are good."

I glanced from him back to Hawk, who still looked at me with a slightly out of focus gaze. Would he be able to see the whole truth about me? Was he that sensitive? And if he couldn't, what did I tell Prince Seireadan?

I'd have to tell him the truth. If he bound me, he'd expect me to be able to break spells for him. Of course, if he knew the truth, he might not bind me, he might just kill me—

Except he thought I was soul bound to his wife. If he killed me, he'd kill her.

"He isn't biding his time. He didn't get the full power. I don't think he can break the spell," Hawk said, his expression turning grim. "Your demon parent just gave you the hunger with none of the benefits of being a sin eater."

I gave a tight nod. There was more to this incubus than met the eye. There was more to all of them. The other angel had a fire magic that was so out of control I couldn't grasp onto it long enough to take a sip, and Prince Seireadan radiated the promise of extraordinary power. The most normal person in the group was the dragon and he was a dragon!

"So Deaglan must have taken over your bond with your sire thinking that was the only way to control you, since a sin eater wouldn't have been able to break a sire bond without killing himself." Prince Seireadan's expression turned grim. "He must have been seriously disappointed to find out you couldn't break spells for him."

That was an understatement.

I suppressed my shudder and kept my expression blank as the nightmare of those early days flashed through my mind. I hadn't thought I'd survive the pain and hunger and humiliation. But I'd been a newly made vampire. I hadn't realized just how much damage I could take or how psychological damage could be worse.

My hellfire snapped again, giving me away, and Prince Seireadan's eyes narrowed.

"So what were his favorite games? You're a vampire, you can heal a lot of serious injuries and pretty quickly." The prince pursed his lips. "I bet he got bored with that and started getting more creative. Sengoku period, hunh? With your skill, a ronin? Samurai? Pain *and* humiliation. How did he play you?"

My stomach roiled in anticipation, nausea churning into my hunger. That musing look always preceded pain. Pain through the hold he had on me, pain through my hunger, and the pain of my shame with his sadistic games and, when I was finally allowed to feed, the pain that I couldn't control myself.

"Did you lie when I asked you if Deaglan knows about my apartment?"

"No." That was the truth. Telling the truth hadn't worked for King Deaglan, he hadn't cared either way, but maybe it would work for Prince Seireadan. I had thought it would be better to be Prince Seireadan's prisoner than

King Deaglan's. Except with that look in his eyes, the implication that he was going to enjoy the same sick games, I wasn't so sure.

But the prince released a heavy breath and his expression returned to exhaustion, the musing wicked gleam in his eyes vanishing.

"Not a lie. We've bought ourselves some time until my mother finds us or the Winter Court calls Amiah back to Faerie." His eyes narrowed. "When was the last time Deaglan let you eat?"

Just asking about it made my hunger surge, but I kept my expression even.

I'd told the truth and he hadn't hurt me... which he could have done even thinking I was soul bonded with his wife. Hurting me wouldn't hurt her. Only killing me would.

"When?" the prince pressed.

"When His Majesty commanded me to bite your wife," I replied.

She'd barely had any magic left so all I could have safely taken was blood, and given her condition, I hadn't been able to take much. I hadn't wanted to take anything from her. I knew if I'd fed too deeply and she wasn't able to... *perform*, I'd have been punished.

Prince Seireadan's eyes narrowed again, probably because I'd just reminded him that I'd bitten his wife. "And before then?"

I'd been given a dribble of blood and magic before chasing after the dragon. But we'd failed to kill him and we'd all been punished. Before then... I couldn't remember.

"He's taking an awfully long time to answer you," Hawk said.

"Which either means he wants us to think he's weaker than he is or he doesn't want to confess how weak he actually is." The prince stood, looked down at me, and sighed. "Either way, I can't let you out until I know you won't hurt Amiah."

"Again," Hawk reminded, his hellfire flaring, revealing his anger. "Won't hurt Amiah *again*."

Except if I was branded, I wouldn't be able to hurt her without hurting myself.

Of course, if I was faced with an eternity of still being a slave with a bond that couldn't be broken no matter how powerful the magic, then the only way to end it would be to kill myself.

They left and my hellfire exploded, sending sparks spraying around me and hissing against the floor.

I couldn't remain a slave. I couldn't face more years of torture or shame for a royal's amusement.

They were wrong. They had to be wrong. She hadn't branded me. The only time she could have branded me was during the fight and the bond wouldn't have been strong enough to save her from my katana. And she hadn't branded me to take me away from Deaglan. It'd be safer for her to have not bound our souls and just have her bodyguards kill me. She had no reason to brand me.

I yanked up my tunic and shoved my pants off my left hip.

Delicate gold lines swirled over my hip, reaching up to my waist and around my back and down my thigh.

I was still a slave.

CHAPTER 5

HAWK

"We're putting him in hibernation," I said the second we were in Bane's study and the door was closed. "He's not getting anywhere near Amiah."

I didn't care that her profession of love to me hadn't been real and had been brought on by the shock of thinking Cassius was dead. She'd said she loved me and my soul had lit up with joy. Even when she was thinking straight and she realized she wasn't in love with me and took it back, I was going to hold onto that moment. She'd looked into my eyes and connected with me and said those three amazing words and I thought my heart was going to explode. Just three words.

Something the hybrid, Rin, had been short on. He'd barely said two dozen in our brief conversation, which didn't tell us anything about him other than he hadn't been with Deaglan of his own free will. We'd had to figure out for ourselves that he was half sin eater and we still didn't know if Deaglan had let him feed or not. And if he hadn't, his hunger could be deadly... which, from the way his strange black aura seethed around him, was what I'd bet on.

My gaze dropped to Cassius lying on the large carpet in the middle of the floor with no aura, not even a whisper of a spark, looking dead to my magical sight even though I knew he wasn't.

He looked even worse to my non-magical sight. We'd cleaned him up, taken off his bloody clothes, and wrapped a towel around his hips, but his complexion was gray, bloodless, from all the blood he'd lost, and he wasn't breathing. Blood welled in the ragged gash in his side and the horrific slice across his neck, frozen on the brink of pouring out of him, and would start gushing the moment Bane released his hibernation spell.

I didn't know if Cassius would even start breathing again when the spell was released, which terrified me. Amiah would need to work quickly to save him, and if she couldn't, she'd go through the horror of losing him all over again.

As it was, keeping his condition from her was cruel. It tore at my heart to see her grief when she shouldn't be grieving.

But Bane was right. She'd healed him before she'd healed herself. If she knew Cassius was alive, she'd give him everything she had. All her magic and probably everything in her soul if she could force it out of herself just to save him.

She loved him too. Loved him for real.

And he loved her. He certainly wouldn't want the hybrid getting anywhere near her even if they were soul bonded. He'd set the room on fire with his determination to protect her. And with bookcases crammed with books covering every inch of available wall space except the window and the fireplace, the room would ignite in the blink of an eye.

"Even if we're going to put him in hibernation," Bane said, "he and Amiah will still need to seal their bond. If they don't, she'll go crazy. Just as if he died."

Except sealing their bond meant sex.

God, could she even have sex with someone she didn't know? Could she have sex with someone who'd nearly killed her? She was opening up and accepting her desires, but her confidence was still fragile. She'd probably spent a lifetime being told how angels did and didn't have sex, and doing it with a demon, let alone a demon and someone else who weren't her soul mates, was probably frowned upon in the angelic world.

Being forced to have sex with Rin would be like the sex she and Bane had been forced to have in the Winter Court ballroom, except without any of the trust between them. There'd be nothing for her to hold on to that would quell her fears.

"You can't be okay with this," I said.

Sure, Bane had been emotionally closed off since Amiah had professed her love to him just before she'd passed out, but that didn't mean he no longer cared for her. Just that she'd shaken him. It had only been a few hours since her profession. Something that big took a man like Bane time to process, especially if he actually cared for her. And given that he'd sworn he'd never commit to anyone, closing himself off emotionally proved he had strong feelings for her.

"I'm not okay with any of this." He ran his hands through his hair and sagged onto the dark blue leather couch and stared at Cassius. He looked exhausted and the demonic magic trapped inside him, writhing and slicing into his magical channels, had now almost completely devoured his white high fae aura. "But we don't have a lot of options. He's her soul mate. There's got to be a reason for that."

"Yeah, because the universe is fucked up." Because if it hadn't been fucked up, I'd have been her soul mate.

I was impossibly in love with her. If she'd branded me, my love would have made sense. It wouldn't have been a mental disorder.

Of course, if she'd branded me and didn't brand any of the others, we'd still be faced with the original reason why incubi didn't fall in love. I'd starve or I'd drain her to death. And neither option was acceptable.

Except every time we made love she reached into my soul and connected with me. There'd even been a glimpse of that when she'd told me she loved me. I hadn't imagined it. Titus had said she needed us, but her soul bond with Rin was going to make her fall in love with him and only him.

And I had no idea what the hell that meant.

I knew I was going to eventually lose her, knew she was going to commit to someone and that would be the end of us. But I'd thought it would be Cassius not a complete stranger.

"She branded him and Deaglan had enslaved him. The hybrid— Rin. God, I should start using his name. Rin can't be a monster. Amiah's soul wouldn't pick a monster," Bane said, but it sounded like he was trying to convince himself of that. "From his reaction, Deaglan was torturing him. Making him think I'd do the same was the only way I managed to get enough of an emotional jolt for my intention glyph to register his intent."

"Just because he didn't lie about Deaglan knowing about your apartment, doesn't mean he's safe for Amiah. We saw more than enough of Michael's victims to know some people just don't come back from being tortured, and Deaglan had Rin for almost five hundred years."

Bane raised his gaze to meet mine and for a second I saw a ghost of the same horror that haunted me. It wasn't strong, in either of us any more. A lot of time had passed and we'd had the emotions of those memories taken away. But there were still times when I woke up hearing all those children screaming and crying and then the slow, terrible silence as they died.

Neither of us had come back from that the same and we'd only witnessed the torture. I couldn't imagine what hundreds of years of surviving it did to a person.

"She'd said the brand wasn't beautiful and sacred." The demonic magic inside Bane's aura flared, drawing a gasp, and his expression tightened with pain. "I hadn't really believed her, hadn't thought an angel would feel that way about the connection formed by a brand, especially after the brand had formed. I'd thought her determination to stay in control was what had driven her to have it removed—"

"She already had a brand?" How hadn't I noticed? I was a fucking Sensitive. Magic practically assaulted me everywhere I went, and I'd had sex with her. Numerous times. Surely I would have noticed a magical brand on her body being that intimate with her.

"It was only partially formed and you had to go looking for it to notice it," Bane said. "She asked me to remove it, but with this demonic shit inside me I wasn't strong enough, so we paid Karthick to do it."

Which explained the conversation they'd had in the cavern.

"I should have believed her. She'd said it was a nightmare." The muscles in Bane's jaw flexed and his grief turned to rage as the demonic magic spiked again. "*This* is a fucking nightmare. I don't ever want to see her on the ground bleeding to death, and I sure as hell don't want him touching her. If anyone should be branded it should be you and even that makes me angry. Fuck!" he yelled. "I want her brand." His eyes widened with shock as if he hadn't realized that was what he really wanted.

"Bane—"

"Fuck. No." He jerked to his feet and rushed to the bookcase behind his couch, gasping with another flare of demonic magic. "That isn't right. I don't really want her brand. It's got something to do with how we connect during sex. Something about what she is..."

"So you're just going to deny that you've fallen in love with her too?" Was he so afraid of a commitment that he wasn't going to acknowledge his feelings? I thought he already had.

"Of course I'm in love with her. We're all in love with her. I have no idea how, but we are." He yanked out a book and flipped through the pages. "Don't think I haven't thought about the three of us, hell, all five of us in something long term. But I can be in love with her without wanting my soul permanently and irrevocably bound to hers. I don't want her brand. And yet I do. There's something else going on. Something she needs from us."

Which was what Titus had said. There was something in her soul that needed the four of us. Could it be different from what her soul needed from Rin? Would she still want to be with us? And would I be happy sleeping with her to give her whatever she got out of our connection but not being the one she loved?

Bane shoved the book back onto the shelf and yanked out another, bigger one, but the demonic magic burst through his aura with sharp red spikes, stronger than before. He gasped and the book landed on the floor with a heavy thud.

"Shit." He bent down to pick it up, but just kept going, sagging forward on his knees, unable to stay upright against the fiery darkness consuming him.

"Just stop for a second," I said, hurrying to his side. Amiah had barely healed his burns and she wasn't able to do anything about his demonic infection.

"God damn fucking shit," he hissed, pressing his forehead against the floor. "And figuring out what she is isn't the priority. My mother will find us. She'll recast the spell tracking Amiah's connection to the Winter Court and come after us. Hell, for all I know, Deaglan could figure out how to track her too. He knows how to find the newly empowered keys without Titus." The demonic magic sliced and writhed. "I'm losing my fucking mind. I should be focusing on how to keep her safe, not why she makes a connection during sex."

"You need to sleep." We all needed sleep, even Titus, who was the only one who'd managed to get out of the fight unscathed.

"I need to get this demonic magic out of me. My connection to Faerie is almost completely blocked. I've got maybe a couple of days at most."

"At most?" I knew the infection was bad, but I hadn't thought it was that bad. I thought he had more time. If he couldn't connect with Faerie, he'd eventually die a very painful death. Being shut out for fae was worse than any other super being disconnected from their realm. Faerie's magic was woven into their very cells. They didn't just go insane. They couldn't live without its magic.

"There's a burner phone in my desk. Top drawer," he gasped. "I need to hope I haven't pissed off a really powerful demon and he only raises the price, not demands something else."

"Sargos?" I asked. There was only one demon in Union City who could pull the demonic magic out of Bane and he was a nasty piece of work.

"Yeah."

We were going to need more than hope if Bane had already pissed off that greater demon. The odds weren't good he'd just ask for more money and we had next to nothing to give him at the moment. Except Bane was almost out of time.

CHAPTER 6

AMIAH

I WOKE WITH MY CHEST STILL ON FIRE AND MY HEART AND
soul numb. I didn't know if the numbness was better than
the stabbing grief or not. Titus held me against his body,
and his breath, heavy with sleep, washed over the back of
my neck, while his wild life force taunted me, a constant
reminder that Cassius no longer had a life force and there
wasn't anything I could do about that.

Hawk lay in front of me again, higher than the last
time, letting me use his chest as a pillow—also asleep
and alive—and Sebastian lay behind him, his feet
tangled with mine. His face was scrunched tight with a
pain my magic couldn't touch even though he was unconscious and his breath was too fast and sharp. But he, too,
was alive, his cold bright life force struggling to stay lit
against the writhing darkness inside him.

They were all alive and Cassius's wasn't.

The puzzle in my soul was incomplete and now
always would be. Forever.

My throat tightened, my heartache burning through

the numbness and my fear twisting in my gut. All the courts in Faerie still wanted to control Titus or wanted him dead, Sebastian was barely hanging on against the demonic magic infecting him, and Hawk was so low on power he wouldn't be able to heal a papercut. People were coming for us. The Winter Queen and Deaglan were coming for us. I couldn't wallow. I had to heal myself, heal them, come up with a plan to ensure I didn't lose any of my other guys—

Which now also included the hybrid. The mate I didn't want.

That thought left a bitter taste in my mouth. I'd wanted to fall in love like everyone else, not be forced to love someone because of my mating brand. And I had. Somehow I'd fallen in love with four amazing guys, guys I'd never have thought I'd pick.

Well, if I really thought about it, Sebastian had been right all along. I'd always been in love with Cassius, I was just too naive and scare to admit it, even to myself. But I certainly wouldn't have thought I'd fall for Sebastian Bane or an incubus and now the idea of being without them made my soul ache.

Why did my brand have to pick someone else? Why not one of them. All of them. I didn't want to give up any of them.

And yet when my magic connected with the hybrid's strange life force and when I'd looked at him, truly looked at him, I hadn't seen a monster. I'd seen a man suffering. The agony I'd originally felt when I'd connected with him was gone, but he'd suffered for so long, the pain had been imprinted in his cells. I wasn't sure if he'd ever be able to be pain free, and I didn't know if I had the kind of power to heal that.

There was something more to the hybrid than just an assassin who killed for the King of the Shadow Court. But that didn't give my soul the right to take away my choices and permanently bind me to him. He wasn't the one I wanted.

Maybe there was still hope and the brand wasn't real, and Sebastian, once we'd figured out how to remove the infection, would be able to free me.

But that would only happen once all of Faerie wasn't trying to kidnap or kill us.

I drew in a shuddering breath, trying to draw on my professional persona to get through this.

Except the moment I thought that, I thought about Cassius and all the times he'd been at my side and watched me work. He'd been around a bit during the war and then at the hospital in the supers' quarter in Union City. And then he'd been around a lot—at first—in Operations when I took over as chief physician.

I'd healed him and his soldiers, and then him and his agents. I'd been in charge and in control and I'd known what I was doing and where I was going and what fate had in store for me.

And I'd been fooling myself.

I was only grateful I'd realized the truth before my soul permanently bound me to a stranger and I'd had a chance to be free, to be who I was supposed to be. It had only been for a few days, and they'd been far from ideal, but they'd been mine with no fate and no naive daydreams.

Tears burned my eyes. I didn't want to give that up, and damn it, I wasn't going to. Sebastian would figure out a way to break the bond between me and the hybrid, and if he couldn't—

If he couldn't—

My breath picked up. I wasn't going to give up what I had with them. I needed them. I knew that in the core of my being.

If he couldn't break the soul bond between me and the hybrid maybe there was a way to create a soul bond with them as well. I had no idea if any of them would want to permanently join the kind of messed up relationship that would be, but it was an option... it had to be.

And the only way for that to happen was for everyone—

A tear leaked from my eye, traced a path over the bridge of my nose and plopped onto Hawk's bare chest.

Everyone *left* to get through this mess with Faerie's Heart.

Meaning I couldn't afford to wallow. I had to shove my grief deep down, heal myself, then finish healing Sebastian and Hawk.

Another tear broke free and followed the path of the first one.

I wasn't going to be able to push my grief aside, no matter what I wanted. Everything I thought about reminded me of Cassius, or how I loved him and hadn't told him because I'd been afraid. He'd say I didn't have time to mourn and he'd be right. He'd say I had to carry on, be safe, survive.

I had to honor that wish. It was the only thing left that I could do for him.

I forced myself to focus on the power in my palms. I'd recovered about three quarters of my magic, but it was still dark outside—and I was pretty sure I hadn't slept through a whole day. I shouldn't have had this much power for the amount of time I'd been asleep.

And Cassius would say don't question it, just use it.

I pushed the power from my hands to the hole in my chest and slowly, agonizingly slowly, started to knit my flesh back together until the wound was partially healed and all the power left inside me was my constant small spark.

Exhausted and dizzy, even just lying there with my eyes closed, I trembled between my guys, my thoughts rushing back to Cassius, my will too weak to ignore them. I thought about his smile, his stern glare, his laugh that I hadn't heard in a long time, and all the time we'd spent together. How had I not known I was in love with my best friend?

More tears leaked from my lashes onto Hawk's chest, and I softly cried, not wanting to wake him or the others, until sleep tugged me back into blissful nothingness.

This time it was nothingness. I didn't dream of pain or cold or my horrible reality.

Except when I woke again, all my worries and fear and heartache rushed back in.

I bit back a sob but couldn't stop my tears. I was still sandwiched between Titus and Hawk, but Sebastian's life force wasn't nearby.

He was gone. Panic seized me before logic kicked in

and my senses reached out and connected with him. He was in the bathroom and still in pain. The demonic magic was so strong I could barely sense the cold radiance of his winter fae life force and his burns were still sensitive.

A trickle of power reached out to him and I yanked it, along with my magical senses, back into my body. He'd be furious if I healed him again while I was still bleeding. They all would—

Cassius most of all.

And I was still bleeding. My chest, however, wasn't nearly as painful as it had been before and my power was also back to half.

I cracked open an eye to check the light in the room and try to figure out how long I'd been asleep this time.

The room was dimly lit, but because I was facing away from the window, I couldn't tell if that was because it was early morning or because the heavy curtain on Sebastian's bedroom window was blocking out the sun. And really, it didn't matter. Both Titus and Hawk were asleep and I had the power to finish healing myself. I might even have some left over to help Sebastian.

I forced my power back into my wound, fighting to keep it turned inward when it wanted to go in any other direction but that.

It heaved against my control, jerked this way and that, straining to return to Sebastian, and I clenched down with everything I had and managed to seal my wounds shut. Barely. It was still tender and if I didn't push more power into it in the next few days I'd have a scar, but I was no longer bleeding.

Except the second I let go, the little bit of my remaining power jumped into Sebastian, determined to ease his pain.

Crap.

I wrenched it back under control. It was a waste to heal him from afar. It could just stay where it was until I could touch him.

The catch was getting out of bed without disturbing Hawk and Titus.

Except the moment I thought that, I knew it was going to be impossible. Hawk might be tired enough to sleep through me moving, but Titus's rapid healing had already healed the injuries he'd gotten during the fight. He was just sleeping with me to be with me, using his body to help steady my soul as if I was a shifter.

I tugged at his arm around my waist so I could turn in his grip and look at him.

His stunning golden eyes opened and met mine. They were filled with a deep, pure love that made my pulse stutter. He'd begged me to be his mate and I'd told him I wasn't in love with him.

Then I went and told all of them that I loved them.

And I'd meant it.

I wasn't sure how he was going to take that even though he'd said he would give me the connection I needed with him despite me still having sex with the others. But sex and love were two very different things.

"You're not allow to get out of bed until you've stopped bleeding," he whispered.

I inched down the towel still wrapped around me and showed him the healed, but still-sensitive wound.

His expression turned grim and my thoughts jumped to how I'd gotten it. My mate had stabbed me and Cassius had died.

My throat tightened and I fought my tears even though I knew I hadn't cried nearly enough. I doubt it had even been a full day. All I wanted was to cling to my guys and sob, but my magic wanted to heal Sebastian and that was something I could do. That was useful. That could distract me. That—

I pressed my lips to Titus's, cutting off my whirling thoughts, and letting him know with my mouth how much I cared for him and needed him. Life was too short, and I hadn't kissed Cassius nearly enough before I'd lost him.

I didn't care if they thought I was crazy or that it had happen too fast or that I'd fallen in love with all four of them. Essie had four mates. She was madly in love with all of them and without a doubt her soul bond with them was only a part of why she loved them. I could love four men. It was that simple.

Titus froze as if he hadn't expected me to kiss him, then huffed softly, a dragon-like sound of satisfaction, and kissed me back. It wasn't a deep kiss or a wild one like the ones we'd had before. It was gentle, just a touch of lips and tongue to steady our souls.

Except I needed more, needed a deeper connection, and I had no idea why. I needed to join with one of them and feel their life force inside me. Kissing Titus was good, but not enough to keep me steady and face my new reality.

The soft *shush* of the shower started, and my magic warmed my palms.

What I really needed was to heal Sebastian.

I eased back. "I've got a little extra left and Sebastian is still in pain."

Titus's gaze jumped to the bathroom door beyond the foot of the bed then back to me, and he gave me a soft sad smile as if he knew what I really needed from Sebastian. "I want you to stay and connect with me, but you're still weak and I..."

His pupils slitted, his beast starting to rise to the surface, and his erection dug into my thigh.

"You won't be able to fully control your beast our first time, will you?" He hadn't had sex in so long and his connection with his beast was still fragile. If his connection was too far gone, it would be best if I didn't have sex with Titus, the man, our first time. His beast would need to fully take over for his soul to mend, and I could only hope it would realize I wasn't as sturdy as a dragon. And yet... if I was at full power, I might be able to satisfy his beast's needs with no problem.

A shiver of anticipation rushed through me at the thought of the ferocious passion that awaited me, along with a hint of fear at his size. He'd given me a glimpse of what sex with him would be like with our first few kisses, and I didn't want him to be afraid to have it with me, but he was also a big man and properly proportioned and I was still very new to sex.

"Make him do all the work," Titus said, pulling me from my thoughts. "It's the least he can do for you."

His words didn't make sense. Sebastian had risked

dying to keep us safe during the fight with Deaglan. He'd channeled magic when he shouldn't have to keep the cavern lit so the shadow fae couldn't jump between shadows, and he'd given himself horrible burns for no doubt getting us back to the mortal realm.

I owed him for my life and the lives of my remaining guys.

My eyes burned at that thought and I blinked back my tears.

"Go," Titus whispered. He brushed his lips against my forehead then eased away and pulled down the comforter so I could get off the bed.

Careful not to wake Hawk, whose breath was still slow and deep with sleep—attesting to how low on power he still was—I climbed off the bed and tiptoed to the bathroom.

The door wasn't fully shut, and just like the last time I'd entered Sebastian's bathroom, it opened with a gentle push, letting a soft wash of moist warm air caress my skin.

Inside wasn't as steamy as before since he hadn't been in the shower for as long this time, and the mirror over the sink hadn't completely fogged up. It showed a too-pale woman, clinging to a bloody towel wrapped around her chest, with a wild mess of blond locks, red eyes from crying, and a weak angel glow.

"So Titus let you out of bed," Sebastian said, his smooth tenor drawing my attention from the mirror to the glassed-in shower stall at the end of the room.

And just like the last time, my pulse tripped at the

sight of him. I hadn't seen him fully naked since our first time having sex and he was breathtaking. Black tattoos swirled over his sleek sculpted body, the ones on his arms and some across his chest marred by the ugly burn scars, but the rest were perfect, a twisting, mesmerizing black pattern in his pale, luminescent skin. The ink encircled his neck, swept over his chest and washboard abs, wrapped around both thighs, and trailed down to his ankles.

I slid my gaze appreciatively down his body, a part of me stunned that I'd had sex with this man, that he'd want to have sex with a stuffy, uptight angel like me. He wasn't an incubus, but he was still sexy as hell and could have chosen to sleep with anyone—well, almost anyone since Essie had kept turning him down. When we'd first met, he'd proposition every woman he came across and, like an incubus, I doubted he'd ever gone without sex when he wanted it.

When this was done, he'd go back to that lifestyle.

Because he swore he'd never commit to anyone and as much as I'd fallen in love with him, I understood he couldn't love me back. Just like Hawk.

And given our circumstances, that would be the best outcome. As it was, either one or both of them could be killed the next time we faced Deaglan.

Like Cassius.

I needed to make the most of the time I had with him, and right now, my soul desperately needed to connect with his.

My gaze stopped at Sebastian's erection, full and thick and ready for me. I focused on my desire for him and how he always made me feel good and adored and perfect.

"So you just decided to walk into my bathroom?" he asked, repeating what he'd said the last time I'd walked in on him, except this time his voice was thick with desire, not shock at my intrusion.

"I've stopped bleeding." I dragged my attention back to his pale eyes and dropped my towel, giving him full view of my naked body, something I'd never have done the first time.

His gaze grew heated and he trailed it down to the towel at my feet then back up, pausing at my left hip... where my brand used to be— *was*. Where my brand now *was*.

Was he going to reject me because fate said I belonged to someone else? Like I was fate's property or something to be given away on its cruel whim?

A part of me wanted to follow his gaze and look. I'd only ever seen my brand as a barely-there ghostly swirl under my skin. Had it turned golden? And if it had, did that mean it was a real brand?

He jerked his attention up to my breasts, lingering on where I'd been stabbed then slowly lifted his eyes to capture my gaze, letting me see that he still desired me. I didn't know if he cared about my brand or not, or the fact I'd told him I'd fallen in love with him when I'd promised I wouldn't. Right now, in this moment, he desired me, and a small part of my soul relaxed with relief, while the rest of me tightened in anticipation.

CHAPTER 7

"I'VE STOPPED BLEEDING," I REPEATED, MY VOICE BREATHY.

"I can see that."

"I have a little extra left. Let me ease some more of your pain."

"Just my pain?" His lips quirked and for a second he was the Sebastian I'd first met, the one who'd relentlessly teased me and Cassius about sex.

My grief edged into my desire, but instead of diminishing it, my need for Sebastian, for our connection—and to just feel and not think for a little while—grew. God, it was so selfish. But I didn't want to fight it. I'd spent a lifetime fighting myself, denying who I was, and I was just too emotionally exhausted. I needed Sebastian right now. That was just the way it was.

"And my pain," I confessed, letting him look into my eyes and see me. All of me. The woman who was angry and frustrated and heartbroken and throbbing with need.

The desire in his eyes softened and he held out his hand. "Come here."

"Are you going to give me what I want?" I asked, afraid his softening desire meant we weren't going to have sex—even though the rest of him still clearly said he wanted me.

A hint of wickedness sparked back into the softness. "And what do you want, Miss Angel?"

"To connect with you."

"Really? Because I thought you wanted to fuck." He leaned back against the white tiles and put his hands behind his head. The shower spray sluiced down his body, drawing my attention to his stunning physique and his standing-proud erection—as he'd intended—making my breath pick up.

"You know that's what I meant."

"Then say it," he said with a sneer as if daring me to confess something dirty.

Well, fine then. Does he really think I'm still that embarrassed prim angel?

With my heart pounding—because I'd never done something like this before and I was still, just a little bit, that prim angel from a few days ago—I stepped to the shower's entrance and cupped my breasts, making his gaze dip to them. Then I slowly slid my hands down my belly, watching his gaze slide with me, and pushed my fingers into my curls, pointing him to where I wanted him.

"Sebastian," I breathed.

His eyes locked on the spot between my thighs.

"I want you to fuck me."

He swallowed hard. "Well, that backfired."

With a groan, he pushed off the wall and drew

close. His erection pressed against my belly, his pale gaze capturing mine and stealing my breath. "Any requests?"

Anything. Everything. Steady me. Make me feel something other than this heartache.

Except— "I'm not up for anything too strenuous. Or rather I won't be in a second, and neither are you."

He frowned, and I pressed my palm against his chest and released a soft stream of magic into him, healing his scars a little more, until all that remained inside me was my core spark of power again.

Exhaustion flooded me, and I leaned into him, laying my cheek against his collar bone and savoring the feel of his slick, naked flesh against mine.

"Oh, sweetheart," he murmured, wrapping his arms around me and helping me stand. "Stop draining yourself. You're going to give Hawk a mental breakdown."

"One more session and you'll be pain free. Scarred, but no longer in pain." I slid my hand over his pecs. He wasn't close to being as bulky as Titus or even as built as Cassius—

I'd run my hands over Cassius's chest like this, appreciating his well-developed musculature, before he— before we— my throat tightened. "Everything I do makes me think of him."

"I know," he said, his voice strange and husky.

"Make me forget, Sebastian." My gaze dipped to my hip and the shimmering gold lines swirling over my skin. "Make me forget everything."

He hooked a finger under my chin and lifted my gaze to his. He had the strangest expression, a mix of sadness and regret and frustration and anger and that same shocking love I'd seen in Titus's eyes.

Then he captured my lips in a tender kiss and I shoved all other thoughts aside. I focused on the feel of his mouth against mine, of his arm around my waist holding me against his wet body, and the straining weak pulse of his cool bright life force.

If we didn't deal with the demonic infection soon, I was going to lose him as well.

Except I couldn't extract foreign magic from someone and even if we could go to Operations, there wasn't anyone there who could do it either. We'd have to call in a specialist.

"Don't go there," he murmured against my lips as if he knew my thoughts had wandered. "You're supposed to be forgetting. You're supposed to be letting me make you feel good."

He turned us, so I could lean against the tiles, and kissed me with a surprising tenderness, exploring my mouth and letting me explore his. It reminded me of having sex with Cassius and how, unbeknownst to me, he was taking his time, memorizing the moment because he didn't think we'd ever have sex again.

He'd thought it was because his fire magic would come back and he wouldn't be able to touch me again. Neither of us had thought it would be because he was dead.

Tears slowly leaked from my eyes, mingling with the mist on my face from the shower's spray. I deepened our kiss, letting Sebastian feel my desire and heartache.

The barely-there wisp of magic left within me connected with him and his life force, adding to my ache.

He was struggling but still alive and fighting.

So was I.

We'd get through this together. All of us—

The *rest* of us.

He cupped my breasts like I had moments ago and kissed his way down to my nipples. I grasped his shoulders to keep my balance, tipped my head back, and closed my eyes. In this moment there was just the feel of his tongue rasping against the sensitive bud and then the gentle pull as he sucked me into his mouth, connecting my peaked nipple to the softly building desire in my core.

He slid his other hand down between my thighs, his fingers skimming the edge of my brand and sending a flicker of cold magic through the swirling lines. My pulse stuttered, but he teased my folds, just a whisper of a touch, and kept my focus on him and what I wanted before I could really think about the mate I didn't want.

His pace was languid, sensual, and exactly what I needed. He brought me to the edge of a gentle climax with his fingers, his mouth paying homage to my breasts, then returned to my lips and urged me to hook a leg behind his waist.

With a low masculine groan, he pushed into me with a delicious, slow, friction until he was fully sheathed.

His life force surged against my senses for a second, bright and cold like it was supposed to be, not barely lit and straining against the darkness. That thing in my soul that needed him, needed all my guys, clicked into place. I was stronger and steadier, and a hint of power, more than what I'd had before, warmed my palms, as if I'd been ever-so-slightly out of alignment and hadn't realized it, and now, with him inside me, I was properly connected to my magic.

Sebastian met my gaze, giving me a glimpse of that sparklingly powerful universe inside him that I'd noticed back in the Winter Court and the calm, powerful stillness newly awakened in my soul grew stronger.

He held my gaze as if he couldn't look away and started to move inside me, the desire in his eyes growing. I let those icy blue orbs hold me captive. My soul might be strong and still at the moment, but it was still fragile and even if I wasn't safe anywhere else, I was safe in those sparkling depths.

He built my need even higher, changing pace and rhythm and force to bring me to a beautiful high before letting me fall over. For a glorious moment there was just the bliss of my muscles contracting around him, the low groan of his own soft release, and whatever it was that aligned our souls. He was the lover I hadn't known I wanted, who lifted me body, mind, and soul. I could face what lay ahead with him, Hawk, and Titus, even mourning Cassius, even being soul bound to a stranger, even facing the Winter Queen and Deaglan.

My skin radiated a brilliant light, signifying my satisfaction, and so did his. This was the first time I'd seen him light up like that and his life force thrummed stronger, more powerful, pushing back some of the darkness inside him.

"You will never cease to amaze me," he murmured as I closed my eyes and gave in to the exhaustion of having drained all my power along with the heartache of losing Cassius and the eventuality that I'd lose Sebastian and Hawk as well.

Sebastian helped me dry off, wrapped me in a new clean towel, and brought me back to Titus and Hawk, snuggling under the covers with me—putting Titus on the outside of our foursome.

Hawk rolled over and gave me a long sensual kiss. It felt like he was saying he loved me, which I knew was impossible. Whatever that strange awe was that filled his expression every time we made love, it wasn't love. And it wouldn't last.

"Everything will be better when you wake up," he murmured. "I promise."

"Even if it isn't, I'll still love you," I mumbled back and once again let myself drift to the edge of a gentle darkness where my heartache and worry was blanketed by blissful nothingness.

"Your fae magic has gotten stronger," Hawk whispered.

His words flittered through me. I hadn't noticed if the foreign magic infused in my cells had gotten stronger or not, I'd been too distracted by everything else.

"And you're glowing just like she is," Hawk added. "I didn't think you were one of the fae who lit up with an orgasm."

"I'm not. Usually," Sebastian whispered back. "It was all her. When she came. It was like she was pushing her healing magic inside me, but instead of angelic magic, she gave me fae magic. I've never felt anything like it."

"Maybe you don't have to go to Sargos." Hawk

brushed a warm finger across my cheek and hooked a lock of hair behind my ear. "Maybe she can help you hold the infection at bay."

"That's not a real solution and we both know the second I start channeling magic the infection will grow again."

"But maybe it will be enough to buy us time to find someone else."

"Do you honestly think I won't have to use magic in the next couple of days? Hell, probably the next couple of hours, what with my mother and Deaglan looking for us." Sebastian pressed his cool lips to the back of my neck and his grip around me tightened. "I have no choice. I have to go to Sargos and pay whatever he wants. It's the only way to keep her safe."

His words made my heart tremble and my stomach churn. He was going to sacrifice something, pay a price he didn't want to pay to keep me safe, and I didn't want to be responsible for any more suffering. It was bad enough I selfishly wanted to keep all of them even though my mating brand was going to make me fall in love with the hybrid... if in fact my brand was real.

I drifted to sleep with the churning fear and hope that my brand wasn't real. If it wasn't, Sebastian, once he was well, could remove it, and I wouldn't have to give him up... not until he decided to move on.

I woke in Hawk's warm embrace, lying half on top of him, using his chest as a pillow, with the comforting crackle of his dark, demonic life force stronger than the last time I'd sensed it, sliding against my bright angelic essence. Both Sebastian and Titus were gone, their life forces beyond the bedroom, but still in the apartment, and I was overflowing with power.

The fae magic in my cells still radiated brilliant light as if I'd just orgasmed, and my healing magic heated my palms and rolled up my forearms.

Except this time I faced the window and could see bright slightly purple bands of light cutting around the curtain. Meaning even though the room was still dimly lit, it was clearly daytime. I couldn't have been out long enough to have regained so much power.

"Good morning, gorgeous," Hawk purred. "Or rather afternoon. I think."

"You're feeling stronger." I shifted so I could look him in the eyes.

His hellfire was banked, small red pinpricks in his unusual blue-gray eyes, but it pulsed in time with his slow, steady heartbeat, strong and sure. He wasn't at full power, but he was definitely better.

"You and Bane gave me a nice little boost," he said, making me think of having sex in the shower with Sebastian... which made me think of Cassius.

My throat tightened.

"Hey." Hawk brushed a strand of hair out of my eyes. "It'll be okay."

It wasn't ever going to be okay. Not completely. But I could give Hawk more power and ensure he survived this mess.

I pressed my lips against his and released my heartache and desire. He couldn't do anything with my grief, but my desire would make him stronger.

With a groan, he returned my kiss, but let me stay in

control. Even with just our lips connected, the sense of his life force grew stronger, teasing me with the promise of being fully connected and properly aligning my soul again.

I pushed the comforter back and straddled him, keeping our lips connected and rubbing myself along his hard erection. I wasn't completely ready for him, but I knew he'd easily get me there. He slid his hands down my body and captured my hips.

A crackle of heat swept through my brand and he froze.

"Please don't stop," I said against his lips. "I'm not his. It might not even be real."

"It's real," he replied, his voice husky. "You can't get rid of it. He's your soul mate."

It couldn't be real. I didn't love him. How could the hybrid be my soul mate when I *knew* I loved Hawk? When I needed him and Sebastian and Titus?

I drew back, an icy sliver of fear unfurling in my gut. "Are you ending this?"

"Never. I'm yours until your brand makes you fall in love with him," he said, his hellfire sparking. "But you should know everything before we continue. I've fallen in love with you."

My thoughts stuttered over his words. He couldn't be in love with me. Incubi didn't fall in love.

And yet I knew an incubus madly in love.

Except his bond with Essie made their love possible. With her other mates, he'd never kill her or starve and he wouldn't have to look elsewhere for sustenance.

"Are you sure?" Perhaps it was an infatuation. Incubi

didn't become infatuated or jealous either, but that seemed more likely than falling in love. Falling in love was just too dangerous for everyone involved.

"I'm positive." He cupped my cheeks in his warm palms. "That connection you need from us? I need it too, from you. And I'll take it for as long as I can."

Because it didn't matter how much I needed him or cared for him. Eventually there'd only be room in my heart for the hybrid.

Unless...

My pulse picked up with a mix of hope and fear. "Would you want this forever? With him?"

Hawk's hellfire sparked again, the smoldering embers turning into miniscule flames, and my heart pounded. I knew in my soul that I needed them, but they didn't need me and asking him to join an already complicated relationship was asking a hell of a lot.

"Sebastian might not be able to break the bond," I forced out, "but maybe he can add to it."

"I don't know if that's possible."

"Neither do I. But if it was, when this is over, would you want your soul permanently bound to mine?" *Please say yes. God, please.*

I couldn't believe trapping myself in a second soul bond was the best solution. I hadn't wanted any soul bonds, hadn't wanted the horror of feeling my mate in danger, of possibly being torn into two between my mate and my magic. But if it was that or losing Hawk, I'd take Hawk.

Except he stared at me, his expression strange, and I couldn't figure out what it meant.

Then he rolled us over, pinning me to the bed, and captured my mouth in a breathtaking kiss that made my whole body tingle with need. "I think you just asked me to marry you."

"I did?"

And I wasn't going to think about the possibility that my desperate need to keep Hawk came from my heartache over losing Cassius.

The idea of being permanently bound to Hawk didn't terrify me. Not like I thought it would, not like being permanently bound to the hybrid. My bond was real and I was about to be living in my worst nightmare. I wasn't ever going to be free. I was trapped—

Trapped trapped trapped.

But not with Hawk. I could do this if he was with me. I'd never have to doubt if my love for him was real. With him, I could get through this.

Oh, God.

I. Could. Do this.

"I think I just did." I ran my fingers into his jaw-length sandy-blond hair and teased them along the base of his horns, making him shudder and his eyes roll back in pleasure.

He flashed me a brilliant, heart-stopping smile. "This deserves a celebratory orgasm."

"I can't complain with that." If sex was how he celebrated, I was more than in.

"But a quick one. Bane is making lunch... or dinner... or whatever time it is." He dipped in and kissed me, releasing a soft, sensual curl of magic inside me.

I moaned as it swelled around my heart and slid

down to my core. He traced its path with his hand, plucking my left nipple then trailing his fingers down my belly and into my folds.

He expertly worked me up, teasing my clit, dipping a finger then two inside me, releasing more glorious magic, until I was panting and aching and on the verge of climax. I squirmed beneath him, my breath fast, my mind wonderfully empty.

Just like with Sebastian in the shower, I focused on just this moment, on the feel of Hawk's body pressed against mine and the amazing crackle of his life force.

And just like Sebastian, he slowly pushed inside me, releasing a little more magic allowing my body to relax and fully take him without pain. That thing inside me clicked again and that awe, that *was* love, filled Hawk's expression.

"I can't believe you always look at me like that when we join," he said.

"Look at you like what?"

"Like you see me. All of me. Not just my body or how I can make you feel."

"Because you're more than just that." I curled my hips up, taking him deeper inside me and savored the delicious surge of his life force. "You're strength and compassion and fire and need. You're incredible. Your soul is incredible."

"And so is yours." He slowly pulled out then pushed back in, igniting every sensitive nerve in my channel.

Oh, God, yes.

I locked gazes with him, letting him see how much I loved and needed him, and we started a rhythm that quickly picked up speed. I couldn't deny that I did also love his body and how he made me feel—and the feeling was incredible. My high fae glow undulated with our movement, its waves growing, sweeping higher and faster through my skin as Hawk twisted my need tighter and tighter, until every muscle in me contracted, my eyes rolled back, and glorious sensation exploded within me.

My glow burst into a brilliant light and my connection with Hawk surged into my soul. I cried his name and he tensed with his own release, sending another powerful orgasm crashing through me.

"Oh, Hawk," I gasped, clinging to him, feeling his life force and his erection throb inside me. "Oh, wow."

I was never going to get tired of that, and if Sebastian could figure out how to add to my unwanted soul bond, I'd never have to give him up.

CHAPTER 8

I PASSED OUT OF COURSE, BUT HAWK WOKE ME, AND WE had a sensual—and unfortunately quick—shower, and changed into clothes Sebastian had set out for us. For Hawk, a set of Sebastian's loose workout clothes, and for me the scrubs Chris had brought over from Operations when this mess had first started.

Everyone in the apartment had to have heard me call out Hawk's name and known I'd orgasmed, and I didn't care. Life was too short and I was done hiding the fact that I wanted sex. That, and I wouldn't have been able to hide it anyway with my new fae glow. And now that I'd recovered all of my magic—and much to my surprise every last drop—I was ready to connect with Titus.

A shiver of desire swept through me and Hawk chuckled.

"You're insatiable."

"Don't tell me you're complaining," I said, reaching to open the door, but he pressed his hand against it, leaned close, and gave me a quick, passionate kiss.

"Nope. And I've got something that's going to make you really happy."

"Pretty sure you just gave me something that made me really happy." Or as happy as I could be still knowing Cassius was dead.

My thoughts must have shown on my face because Hawk's expression softened.

"I told you it'll be okay, and it will be." He interlaced his fingers with mine and tugged me out of the bedroom. "We're going to your office," he called out.

Sebastian rushed into the archway between his living room and kitchen, wiping his hands on a dishcloth. He looked more like himself than he had since we'd been abducted into Faerie even though the glamour that I'd originally thought was his real appearance was still down. He was still the stunning Winter Court prince, a full high fae and not the not-quite-as-handsome faekin glyph witch everyone thought he was. But he wore a pale blue button-down, the sleeves rolled up to his elbows showing off the heartbreaking mix of black tattoos and scars, and loose beige slacks, and for some reason that made me feel like I was seeing the real him. Not Prince Seireadan and not Sebastian Bane semi-illegal magical items dealer. Just Sebastian. "It she—?"

"She's got more power than I've ever seen her have," Hawk replied before Sebastian could finish.

"Oh, thank God." He tossed the cloth onto the counter beside him and hurried to meet us as Hawk opened the door and led me into the office.

I knew the room had floor-to-ceiling bookcases stuffed with old, rare, and magical books, and that Sebastian had a large sturdy desk at the back by the window, a dark blue leather couch, and a wood-burning fireplace, but the only thing I could focus on was Cassius's body.

My heart leaped into my throat and tears burned my eyes.

The guys had cleaned him up, stripped him, and wrapped his hips in a towel. His complexion was pale and the laceration across his neck was shockingly deep, but somehow it still only looked like he was just asleep.

A tear rolled down my cheek.

That was just what I wanted to see. I'd lost my connection with his life force and couldn't sense it now.

I dropped to my knees beside his head and pressed my palms against cheeks that should have been room temperature but weren't. They were warmer. More like his natural body temperature as if he were still alive.

My pulse stalled and I jerked my attention from his face to his neck. It looked like blood welled in the wound ready to spill free but wasn't. Same with the wound at his ribs.

"I managed to get him into hibernation just before he died," Sebastian said, crouching beside me.

Hawk crouched on my other side. "He's not dead. You can still save him."

He wasn't dead?

He wasn't dead!

My breath turned sharp with a whirling mix of relief and joy and anger. "You let me think he was dead."

They'd held me while I'd cried.

We'd made love and they'd known Cassius had been alive all this time and hadn't told me!

My heart had broken. Even with this revelation it still hurt. I'd thought he'd died without knowing I loved him, thought there was always going to be an empty spot in my soul that would never be filled.

I'd lost my best friend and they'd known all along I hadn't.

"You let me think he was dead! You *all* let me think he was dead." How could they!

"It was my call," Sebastian said. "Don't blame Hawk or Titus."

"Hawk and Titus could have said something." I turned my glare to Hawk and he met my gaze head on. The awe— no love that I saw in his eyes was edged with fear.

"You were barely alive," he said. "You couldn't even save yourself."

"You've proven time and again that you have no sense of self preservation," Sebastian added. "I wasn't prepared to lose you."

"Right. Because I'm the healer. Everyone else is expendable." God, I hated that they all thought that, that all I was good for was keeping them alive. But it was true and that hurt even more. I couldn't defend myself in a fight and I kept getting hurt and putting them in danger. I'd become that person who drove me crazy and I had no idea how it had happened.

"You know that's not true." Hawk pressed his hand against my back giving me space by not holding me, but comfort with his touch.

"Because there was no reason for you to sacrifice yourself. Cassius will keep. If my spell isn't removed, he'll keep forever," Sebastian said. "Don't tell me you wouldn't have drained yourself to death trying to save him,"

I opened my mouth to disagree. I'd already been drained, my magic wouldn't have locked onto Cassius, but my compulsion to save him would have been overwhelming. And it was Cassius. I would have given everything to save him. I'd already stained my soul by killing people, I would have given what was left to keep him alive.

"Yeah, thought so," Sebastian said, taking my lack of response as an admission of guilt.

"Bane knows I can't lose you like that," Hawk added.

"Neither can I," Titus said from the doorway, his shaggy red hair wet and dripping onto his bulky, muscular—and completely bare—shoulders and chest, his hips wrapped in a towel.

I wanted to yell at all of them, scream all of my frustration and anger and fear, but if the situation was reversed, I'd have done the same thing.

God, I hated the part of myself that saw reason. They'd lied. They'd hurt me.

And I knew in my heart I'd lie to them, let them believe the most horrible things, make them hate me if it kept them alive. I'd do whatever it took.

"Don't make us give you up before we have to," Sebastian said, shocking me, his voice strange and soft and making my heart ache.

I knew there was something between us. He wouldn't have kept having sex with me if there wasn't. But I didn't think it was so deep that he'd want to hold onto what we had for as long as possible.

I opened my mouth again but didn't know what to say. I wanted to be mad. I *was* mad. But I was also in love with them and a century of striving to be practical made me understand why they hadn't said anything.

"Now what are the odds I can convince you to eat something before you save Sparky?" Sebastian asked.

Just the thought of walking away without healing Cassius made my insides churn.

Sebastian sighed. My thoughts must have been clear in my expression yet again. "Didn't think so."

Hawk leaned closer and this time did draw me into an embrace. "What do you need?"

And just like that, he had my back. Like he'd had it from the very beginning of all this... which was the whole reason he'd lied to me about Cassius. He'd support and protect me. Even if that meant protecting me from myself and my magic that compelled me to sacrifice everything to save lives.

I shoved those thoughts aside and focused on the medical problem. "Lots of towels. I don't know how much blood he's lost, but the moment the hibernation spell is gone, he's going to start bleeding out again. I'll also have to heal him quickly, which will be painful and might set off his fire." I glanced at all the flammable books surrounding us and so did Sebastian.

"We should move him into the clean room," Sebastian said. "The protections on that room are strong enough his fire won't get out. If we put him in the corner there'll be enough space to keep Rin locked up while Amiah works."

Rin?

Right.

That was what Deaglan had called the hybrid.

Which meant the guys had already had a conversation with my unwanted mate and learned his name—

And there'd be time to ask about that later. Right now, I could get Cassius back. That was what I needed to focus on.

"Do we think it's wise?" Hawk asked. "If Deaglan actually did starve him for a long time, any amount of blood might send him into a feeding frenzy."

"I'd rather have Rin lose his shit behind a barrier than have Cassius burn down the building." Sebastian's gaze slid to me and just like his tone before, his expression was strange. "Better to find out now that he'll be unable to control his hunger than let him out and Amiah get a papercut."

"He's not getting out," Titus growled. "Ever."

"Really? And how's that going to work?" Sebastian jerked his attention to Titus, frustration sweeping through his expression. "He's her fucking mate."

Titus's canines extended and he snarled at Sebastian.

A new horrible realization flooded me.

I'd branded him.

I was going to have to seal our bond or both of us would go crazy.

Oh, God. I was going to have to sleep with him whether I wanted to or not.

Hawk's embrace tightened.

"Hey." He shot a dark look at Titus and then Sebastian. "Not what we should be talking about right now." He turned his attention back to me. "We need towels and we need to move him. Anything else?"

I was going to have to have sex with the hybrid. I'd seen what happened when an angel tried to ignore the bond and it hadn't been pretty. How could I have possibly thought being made to fall in love with him was the worse part about the brand?

"Amiah." Hawk hooked a finger under my chin and lifted my gaze to his. "Let's get Cassius back. We can deal with everything else later."

Because everything else was inevitable. This was my fate and I had no say in the matter. The only things I did have control over was how I faced my new mate and saving my best friend.

So I'd do that. I'd save Cassius, tell him that I loved him, and then have sex with the hybrid before I went insane.

I'd steeled myself to have sex with Sebastian with everyone watching. I could steel myself to have sex with the hybrid.

I sucked in a sharp breath.

Focus on saving Cassius.

"He'll be in shock from both the injury and the rapid healing." I made myself meet Sebastian's gaze and face the pity in his eyes. I wouldn't be ashamed of what I had to do. "Do you think you have enough magic to use your sleep glyph?"

"I do, but it would be best if you used it," Sebastian replied. "We've bought ourselves some time by coming here, but eventually my mother will recast the tracking spell, and she and Deaglan will figure out we left Faerie and catch up to us. Better if I save what I've got left for that."

"And I can still use it?" I'd used his glyph on him after we'd escaped the Winter Court, but it hadn't occurred to me that I could do it again, let alone in the mortal realm or on someone else.

"You still glow, so you're still high fae," Sebastian replied. "You just need to press one hand on the glyph and the other over Cassius's heart, think about pushing power into the glyph, and say ignite."

"Okay then." Hawk stood. "I'll get the towels."

He hurried out of the room, and Titus entered, picked up Cassius, and slung him over his shoulder. The towel dropped to the floor, but Sebastian grabbed it before I could.

"You're eating after this," he said. "I don't care what else happens, you haven't eaten in over a day."

"I'll eat. But on the roof." A shudder swept through me at the memory of being attacked on the roof by Balwyrdan, and I shoved it aside. We were limited in where we could go and I'd recover my magic faster if I could see the open sky. I'd just have to deal with the memory. Sebastian had been right. We could be in a fight again soon. I had to get my magic back as fast as possible. In the very least, I had to get enough back so I wasn't exhausted and dizzy and a liability.

"Sweetheart, I don't care where you do it, so long as you do it. And I will shove it down your throat if I have to."

"I'll hold you down while he does it," Titus said heading down the hall toward the clean room.

Jeez. Overprotective much? Just like my safety back in the aerie, it looked like they all agreed on me eating, too. "That won't be necessary. You may have to keep shaking me to keep me awake, but you won't have to force me."

And they wouldn't have to force me to have sex with the hybrid. I couldn't run away from that reality, so I'd face it head on.

I would.

Really.

Titus opened the clean room door and strode in. I followed, but my attention jumped to the hybrid kneeling in the middle of the enspelled circle.

My mouth went dry with fear even as something inside me warmed at the sight of him and drew me a step closer to the edge of the barrier. I was going to have to sleep with him.

The thought was horrifying. And it was even more horrifying that the warmth inside me sank low and started to softly throb.

God. This was a nightmare. I didn't think I'd feel the pull of the brand so soon, and not only was my life not my own any more, neither, it seemed, was my body.

Had he realized he was going to have to sleep with me as well? Did the brand make his body desire mine like mine desired his even though the rest of me was furious at the thought? Was this situation just as terrible for him?

His hellfire smoldered, red pinpricks in black eyes that were locked on me, and the expression on his sharp, sculpted face was flat, no indication about how he felt about me or his situation. Just like it had been when I'd staggered in earlier.

Would he look less intimidating if he let any kind of emotion through? If he smiled, he might almost be as handsome as Cassius. Funny how I could notice something like that now that he wasn't trying to kill me.

Or was that just my brand making me find him attractive?

His long black hair had been pulled back into a ponytail, but a few shorter locks had escaped framing his face, drawing my attention to the white scar across his neck. He'd had his throat slit before he'd been turned. Most likely he'd been killed, not just drained, before his sire had performed the ritual to turn him into a vampire, suggesting he hadn't become a vampire willingly. His strange life force seethed against my senses, hot and cold, alive and dead, and always with the pain that had been permanently imprinted in his cells.

Now that I was fully conscious, it was clear to my magical senses that he was starving. He hadn't properly eaten in a long time and I could only assume that was Deaglan's doing. Just like the pain permanently imprinted in his cells. Bringing Cassius in here and letting him bleed even into a handful of towels was cruel, but we didn't have any other options.

The hybrid—

No. Rin.

Rin didn't say anything and didn't move, only followed us with his eyes, as Titus set Cassius on the floor in the corner where there was enough space for all of us to gather.

"How fast can you get bagged blood up here?" I asked Sebastian as he wrapped the towel back around Cassius's hips, giving him the modesty he wouldn't know he had but would undoubtedly appreciate. Which was silly, since everyone now, including the hybrid, had seen him naked.

"He needs more than just blood," Sebastian said. "He's half sin eater."

Well that would explain why Deaglan would have wanted him... although it didn't explain why he was still behind the barrier. There wasn't a spell a sin eater couldn't consume. It was why Michael had slaughtered every last one of them—or so everyone had thought—fearing that they'd be able to destroy his magically created army.

Of course he was only half sin eater. He might not have inherited all of his sin eater parent's abilities.

And that didn't address the problem of him needing to feed on magical energy to survive. That wasn't something that could be easily bagged like blood, and I doubted Sebastian would want to sacrifice one of his rare, magical books to feed the hybrid.

We were going to have to figure out something else that kept everyone safe, and the first, easier, step was dealing with his vampiric hunger. Right now all of him was starving and he was certain to go into a feeding frenzy the second he smelled blood. It was a miracle he hadn't lost it when I'd staggered in earlier still bleeding. Perhaps if one of his hungers was satiated, he might be able to control his other hunger enough to not kill someone while he fed on their magic.

"Blood will still help," I said as Hawk hurried into the room with a pile of white towels—I was pretty sure

Sebastian only had white towels—and set them by Cassius's head.

"I've ordered some blood along with clothes for everyone, since the only changes of clothes Titus and Cassius had are still in the trunk of my car where we left it when we—" Sebastian snapped his mouth shut.

But I knew what he was going to say. *When they rescued me from Balwyrdan.*

I shuddered, the memory of that horrible night rising to the forefront of my mind, and I shoved it back down. I wasn't going to think about what Balwyrdan had done to me. Not ever again if I could help it. "When will the blood and clothes arrive?"

"We agreed putting in a rush order would draw attention. It won't get here until at least the morning," Sebastian finished.

I glanced at Cassius. Could I resist my need to get him back until the morning? "What about getting blood from the club downstairs?"

Sebastian's apartment was above the most popular vampire nightclub in town. There was blood aplenty just three floors down.

"I don't want to risk my landlord finding out I bought blood from her club. Victoria and I might have come to an arrangement since the last time I had angel visitors, but I trust her even less than I trusted Mavis."

And Mavis had sold us out to Balwyrdan.

Not going to think about it.

"Okay, then we wait."

But the moment I said that, the compulsion to heal Cassius twisted in my chest and my magic swelled into my palms. I hadn't locked onto him, but I was one step away from that even though he felt dead to all my magical senses.

"I'm not sure it's wise to let Cassius stay down. Even until just the morning," Hawk said. "We keep having our asses handed to us *with* Cassius in the fight. We're going to get squashed if Deaglan finds us and he's still down."

"Except Deaglan can take Cassius's fire." And the last time that had happened, Cassius had almost died.

"And that's one of the many items at the top of my things to deal with list," Sebastian replied. "Just as soon as I deal with this." He jerked his thumb to his chest, indicating the demonic magic trapped inside him.

Titus huffed. "Even without his fire, it's better if he's awake and defending himself than one of us having to protect him or carry him around."

Which was something I couldn't argue with.

But jeez, I didn't want to be cruel to Rin. He might have almost killed me, and I didn't want to be soul bound to him—and I most certainly didn't want to desire him—but I wasn't Deaglan. I didn't purposefully try to hurt people. And without a doubt, the pain imprinted in his cells was because Deaglan had hurt him. With him trapped behind a barrier and starving, healing Cassius was going to be torture.

Not to mention, Sebastian was right. At some point we were going to have to let Rin out and taunting him with blood was no way to build trust. And I doubted we had the time to wait for the brand to make him love me. That could happen in a few days or a few months. It was different for every brand.

Except with his current state of hunger, it wasn't safe to let him out. Even if the brand made his body want me like it was making me want him, that didn't mean he trusted us or wasn't going to hurt us.

I crouched at the edge of the barrier, my pulse pounding. With my rushing blood and my magic heating my palms, just being in the room was probably taunting him.

But he gave no indication he was hungry or angry or feeling the same frustrating attraction I was. He didn't move, didn't breathe—he didn't have to because he was already dead—and he gave no indication about what he was thinking. Not even a flicker of hellfire to show he had any kind of emotion at all.

He just watched me.

His lifeless essence oozed across my senses before his unusual life force overwhelmed it. He was just so strange. He wasn't alive and my magic couldn't fix that. His undead nature made my magic shrink away from him.

But the part of me that sensed life forces didn't care that he was dead, which meant that power was a different, separate ability from my healing. He had a life force and I could connect with it. Just like I'd been able to connect with Deaglan's and his men's.

"You heard our conversation," I said. "We have blood coming for you, but I need to heal Cassius and that's going to involve blood."

His expression didn't change. He didn't even blink.

"I know you're hungry and I wouldn't do this here if we weren't afraid Cassius's fire would burn down the building."

Still nothing.

I glanced at Sebastian. "Is there a sound block on the barrier? Can he even hear me?"

"He can. Do you understand what Amiah is saying?" Sebastian asked him.

"I do, your highness," Rin replied in his barely-there soft voice as he bowed his head.

Except I wasn't sure he understood that I didn't mean to be cruel, and he'd looked down awfully fast when Sebastian spoke... although I didn't get the sense he was being completely submissive to Sebastian. More like he was going through the motions he thought Sebastian wanted to see.

But I had no idea why I thought that. His expression hadn't changed. There hadn't been fear or anger or anything else in his eyes.

Maybe he couldn't have emotions. Unlike Cassius, who struggled to keep his contained so he could control his fire, maybe Rin didn't have any at all.

Would that make it easier to have sex with him? Would I be able to just satisfy the brand's needs and go through the motions like he was now if there wasn't any emotion involved?

Would the brand even be able to make him love me?

The thought broke my heart, because I could have emotions and the brand would make me love him. I'd spend the rest of my life with an unrequited love that I hadn't wanted in the first place.

And there wasn't anything I could do about it.

CHAPTER 9

AMIAH

I COULD, HOWEVER, GET MY BEST FRIEND BACK, SO I TURNED away from Rin to focus on saving Cassius. I'd need to work fast. For once, I wouldn't have to hold my magic back. The faster I could get it into him, the better. Except if he was too close to death, it wouldn't matter how fast my power rushed in.

Which was something I wasn't going to think about. This was my second chance to save him and I wouldn't fail.

I knelt beside him, grabbed one of the towels, and pressed it against the laceration in his side.

"Titus, can you hold this?"

"Sure." Titus nudged Sebastian out of the way and knelt beside me.

I handed him a couple more towels just in case as Hawk sat on my other side, and without being told, pressed a towel against Cassius's neck.

I turned to Sebastian. "Can you release the hibernation spell without touching him?" Out of all of the guys, he was the least able to handle Cassius's fire. Titus was immune and Hawk could rapidly heal serious injuries.

"I can," Sebastian replied. "You want me on the other side of the room?"

"No, I want you behind me. I want to use your sleep glyph the second he's healed. Hopefully that will contain most of his fire. But the fastest way to do that is to heal him while having one hand on him and one hand on your glyph."

"Will touching both of them affect your magic?" Hawk asked.

"Cassius has the more serious injuries so my magic will heal him first, but," I gave Sebastian an apologetic grimace, "if I try to control my power, I might not be able to save him."

"Which means any extra is going to go into my scars and it'll be painful." He unbuttoned his shirt and tossed it on the floor by the door, making Hawk raise his eyebrows in question. "Hey, I like the shirt. I don't want it to go up in flames."

"Yeah, and that little gleam in her eyes just now when she saw all your bad boy tattoos had nothing to do with it," Hawk said.

Sebastian flashed Hawk a lopsided grin. "Well, maybe there's a bit of that, too." He crouched behind me, grabbed the back of my scrubs, and twisted the fabric around his fist. "I'll try to pull you away after you cast the sleep spell, but if your magic is too strong, I can't make any guarantees."

"I've got both of you," Titus said.

I adjusted my position so I could place one hand over Cassius's heart, his bare skin strangely warm even with my power heating my palm, and the other on Sebastian's small, swirling sleep glyph on his shoulder.

"Don't pull me away until I say I'm done or you sense the glyph has been activated. No matter what. I don't know if I have enough power to save Cassius without touching him." Not without killing more people, since healing from afar required a lot more magic than healing while in contact with someone. God, I hoped I never felt I had to take someone's life to save a life again.

"I'm not losing him."

"You won't," Hawk said, and Titus grunted.

"Remember to push power into the glyph and say ignite." Sebastian tensed, ready to jerk me away. "You just say when and I'll release the hibernation spell."

I drew in a deep breath and focused on my palm pressed against Cassius's bare chest. It rested over a heart that wasn't beating which made my heart twist with grief, even though I knew he was in hibernation and not actually dead.

Please don't be dead. Please let Sebastian be right about freezing him before he passed.

The power in my hand flared to life, creating a brilliant white nimbus, brighter than my unnatural fae glow. It burned under my skin, racing up my forearms and past my elbows, eager to be released.

I could do this. I had more than enough power to heal the cut in his side and neck and restore his blood... but only if he still had a life force.

"Okay."

Sebastian hissed a soft sibilant word and the pain in his life force surged against my senses.

But so did a small, flicker of fiery life force.

It whispered inside me then went out, making my soul stutter. Cassius. My whole essence snapped to a pinpoint focus on him, jerking away from the pain in Sebastian that I couldn't heal. There was only Cassius and my magic's desire to save him. Now. If I didn't do something now, I'd lose him.

Save him. Save him. Now.

My pulse leaped into a rapid tattoo and my magic exploded out of me before I even thought to release it. It slammed into Cassius, surging into the lacerations now gushing blood and filling up the towels, as well as seizing onto the last bit of his life force and clinging to it, forcing it to stay lit—something my magic had never done before.

In the blink of an eye, my power tore into the cells of his damaged flesh, wrenching them back to the way they'd been before his injury, and reignited the spark of life in the core of his being.

Every muscle in my body contracted as my power roared out of me in a violent rush, and then every muscle in Cassius's body seized as well.

His eyes snapped open, his angel glow so bright I couldn't see his pupils, and he released a great, heart-wrenching howl.

My connection with him shattered with a sharp, painful *snap*, all of his injuries fully healed, and my power slammed into Sebastian. He screamed as well, and then Cassius's fire exploded from his body and I was in the middle of an inferno.

Sweat burst over my skin with the sudden ferocious heat, and my healing magic stuttered and went out, completely spent in the blink of an eye. The towels Hawk and Titus held and the one around Cassius's hips burst into flames because Cassius was in shock and wasn't conscious enough to control his magic.

Flames raced through Hawk's pantleg and he scrambled back as Titus reached for me and Sebastian.

Fire scorched my hand pressed against Cassius's heart with an agonizing pain, turning my skin red when his remained perfect, and the flames caught in my scrubs.

Crap. I thought I'd at least have a second.

I mentally yanked at the fae magic in my body and shoved whatever I could into Sebastian's glyph.

"Ignite," I screamed, hoping the force of my word would ensure I properly powered the spell.

Cassius's eyes rolled back and his flames went out. Titus yanked off his burning towel, ripped the fiery end off with a quick jerk, and Sebastian shoved me to the floor so Titus could smother the flames in my scrubs.

"Fuck, now I know why Cassius is always on the verge of a mental breakdown," Hawk groaned. Both of his pantlegs were scorched—one burned all the way up to his knee—but his flesh underneath, while bloody, was back to normal.

Unlike mine. Titus had managed to put out the fire in my clothes so I hadn't been burned there, but my hand that had been over Cassius's heart was bleeding, and the pain was almost as bad as when I'd taken too much of Hawk's power. Much to my surprise, the damage was mostly first degree burns with a little bit of second— which was why it hurt so much.

"Do you have anything left?" Sebastian asked, gathering me in his arms, careful not to touch my burned hand and forearm.

His life force thrummed against my senses and so did the pain of his demonic infection. It wasn't as bad as it had been before we'd had sex in the shower, but he wasn't getting a complete reprieve from it either.

Titus's life force joined Sebastian's, drawing my attention to him. His pupils were slitted and his canines extended, his dragon on the verge of taking over. He growled low in his throat and brushed aside a strand of hair that was pasted to the side of my face with my sweat then cupped my cheek with his large palm.

The ferocity of his life force surged with the contact, wild and primal and furious.

I was wrong. His dragon was the one in control right now and was barely holding it together.

Hawk crouched beside me and grabbed my good hand, clinging to it as if he were afraid to let go. His eyes were too wide and filled with fear, and his life force crackled with desperate fiery darkness, matching his rapid pulse.

My magical senses added him to the mix with Sebastian and Titus then reached out and connected with Cassius's strong, sure blazing life force, and Rin's strange alive yet dead force.

I let their swirling mix of life, hot and cold, bright and

dark, fiery, ferocious, and wild, whirl inside me. They were *all* alive—or in Rin's case, undead—and Cassius was perfectly healed. So, too, were Sebastian's burns. My magical senses told me there wasn't a hint of physical damage left in either man's body.

Thank God, they're all alive.

And all I'd had to pay was the exhaustion of having drained myself and some excruciating pain. But I didn't have a life-threatening injury or any broken bones, which meant that in a few hours, I might have enough power to turn the burns into sensitive scars.

And strangely enough, I did have a little bit of magic left.

Hunh.

I'd thought I'd spent it all. Just a few seconds ago, it had felt like I had.

I pushed my remaining power into my burns, easing some of the pain, and the exhaustion of really having spent all of my magic this time swept through me... again?

My lids drifted shut and I savored the feel of the guys' life forces pulsing against my senses. It almost felt as if they pulsed inside me, like when we joined during sex. Except the sensation wasn't nearly as powerful as what I felt during sex.

And now all I could think about was having sex.

With my guys.

All of my guys... including Rin.

No. Not Rin. I didn't love him. Only my body wanted Rin because of the brand, not my heart or soul.

"Wake up, Amiah." That was Sebastian, and his

words tugged my thoughts back to where I actually was. In his clean room, exhausted and in pain.

"Maybe we should just let her sleep," Titus growled.

"She hasn't eaten in over a day," Hawk replied. "She'll recover her magic faster if she eats something before passing out."

I forced my eyes open. "I'm okay. I just need a minute and then I can eat."

The exhaustion and dizziness would pass. Slowly, but it would pass enough for me to move around a bit, certainly eat something.

The hellfire in Hawk's eyes flared. "Don't you ever do that again."

God, I wish I could say I wouldn't. "Like I tell Cassius, I make no promises."

"This being in love thing sucks." He rubbed his face, smearing blood down his cheek but didn't seem to notice.

Behind him, Rin still knelt in the middle of the circle, his expression tight with pain. His hellfire writhed in his eyes and his fangs had fully extended, and he stared at me with a desperate hunger. I had no idea how he was still kneeling. His force of will was extraordinary, but it was clear his hunger was starting to overwhelm him and if it did, there was a chance he wouldn't be able to get it back under control until he'd fed.

"We have to feed Rin," I said.

The desire that I didn't want and couldn't do anything about because I was exhausted swelled, along with my need to heal even though all of my magic was gone. Which was ironic since I couldn't *heal* him. And yet it still urged me to go to him, release him from the circle, let him feed, and ease his suffering, something I'd never felt before for a vampire. If I pressed my palm against the wide thick glyph at the top of the circle, the barrier would come down.

I started to sit up before I fully registered what I was doing, but Sebastian held me tight. "Don't you dare. It's too dangerous."

I knew that, and yet the pressure of my healing compulsion mixed with my unwanted desire for Rin only grew stronger. And God, if we kept him in there starving, we were probably just as cruel as Deaglan. "We can't treat him like Deaglan did."

"We aren't and he knows that," Hawk said. "Blood is coming. He'll be okay, but I'm not willing to bet your life by assuming your brand will stop him from killing you while in a frenzy."

He was right. But it took everything I had to ignore my need to help him and focus on what I needed to do next.

I turned my attention to Cassius, beautiful, completely naked, and outlined with the charred remains of his inferno. The white floor, walls, and ceiling around him had been scorched black, and he was surrounded by burned and bloody towels and a lot of ash.

"In the very least, we should clean up this blood and get him into a bed," I said.

"Will his fire go off again when he wakes?" Titus asked.

"No, he's fine now." I'd never healed Cassius from so

serious an injury, but he wasn't in shock or pain any more. When he woke, he'd have full control of his power like normal... or as full control as he could get with it tied to his emotions—which was something else we were going to need to deal with on top of everything else.

"Okay," Sebastian said. "Who's getting Amiah food and taking her to the roof and who's cleaning up and moving Sparky."

"Not me," Titus huffed, smoke curling from his still-human nostrils. "My beast is getting tired of waiting. I'm not sure how much longer I can control it before it doesn't care if it hurts you when we mate."

"As soon as I get some power back," I promised.

Hawk glared at me. "And you've healed this burn."

"All right. Hawk, take Amiah. We'll meet you on the roof so we can talk about what were going to do about—" Sebastian ran a hand over his spikey white and silver hair. "Fuck, about everything. We seriously need a plan."

Hawk gathered me in his arms, even though I insisted I could walk. My pace would have been slow and I would have needed his help to balance, but I could have walked, except he wouldn't listen.

I kept my gaze off of Rin and prayed that eventually my need to heal his suffering would go away. He'd get blood in the morning. He'd be okay until then.

He would.

Really.

Hawk carried me to the kitchen where Sebastian had plates of penne primavera with generous amounts of freshly grated parmesan on top already doled out. After a quick reheat in the microwave—where I almost fell asleep while we waited despite the agony in my hand—we headed out of Sebastian's apartment, Hawk with a blanket slung over his shoulder and still carrying me, and me balancing my plate of pasta on my stomach and holding it with my good hand.

Outside, the hall was just as opulent and white as Sebastian's apartment with a marble floor and gilded frescoes on the ceiling. A part of me still couldn't believe the excess even though I now knew he was a Faerie prince. It just seemed so unnecessary, and the theme carried into his private stairs that led all the way down to the ground floor without entrances to any of the other floors, and up to the roof.

The last time I'd climbed these stairs, I'd just had sex with Sebastian, and then Hawk had made me come again with his fingers. I'd been so confused, had thought I'd just made a horrible mistake, and yet I'd loved it, craved more of it. Having sex with Sebastian had been amazing and it still was, even in comparison to Hawk—who was mind blowing, like an incubus was supposed to be.

Sex with all of my guys so far had been special, and I had no doubt Titus would be just as amazing. Even if he didn't have the experience Hawk and Sebastian did, our connection made it special and always would.

Would I feel that way about Rin? We supposedly had a deeper connection, our souls were now permanently bound together. We were supposed to be fated for each other.

Except I didn't love him.

I loved Cassius and Hawk and Sebastian and Titus.

Which, if I really thought about it was crazy. The only one who I'd spent any real time with was Cassius. But it didn't matter. I'd fallen in love with them, like a real person, not forced to love them by a magical bond. I didn't want to love Rin. And I certainly didn't want my body to desire him like it currently did.

We stepped out onto the roof and were instantly enveloped in late-afternoon heat. The air was thick with humidity and filled with the familiar rumble of vehicles on the streets down below. In front of us, the UV-blocking canopy that protected Union's vampire citizens from the sun for this one section in the Quarter, connected with the edge of the building, blocking us in, and only rose seven feet overhead before stretching to the building across the street. But it was enough to ease the pressure from around my heart because everywhere I looked I could see sky, the Supernatural Quarter's beautiful skyline, and the beginnings of a brilliant summer sunset.

Hawk set me on my feet by the security door so I could lean against its sun-warmed concrete blocks while he laid out the blanket on the roof's rough surface. Then he helped me settle with his legs on either side of me, letting me lean against him to keep upright so I could eat.

The memory of Balwyrdan finding me up here, confused and even more sexually frustrated than before, shivered inside me, and I shoved it back down. Again.

I couldn't leave. I needed to see the sky and I needed to be with my guys and let their life forces thrum against my senses. And I knew the tension in my body would only ease more once Sebastian and Titus came up.

Already I felt lighter, more powerful—although the power was just in my mind. I couldn't have regained any amount of magic in the short time it had taken us to get up there.

Hawk held my plate so I didn't have to lean too far forward to eat, and I obediently ate while trying to not fall asleep. And the moment I took my first mouthful, I realized I *was* starving. Too much had happened— was *still* happening, and I'd somehow managed to ignore the fact that I hadn't eaten much of anything in far too long.

That was probably why I thought the pasta was the most incredible thing I'd ever eaten. Sebastian might be a good cook, but I doubted he was that good.

We sat in silence for a long time while I tried to stay awake and eat even with Hawk's raised demonic body temperature making me far too warm with the summer's heat to properly relax. But I didn't care about being too hot. I needed his arms around me more than I needed to be comfortable—

Which made me think of the Winter Court. I hadn't felt its chill since we'd returned to the mortal realm, and I suspected that was because of something Sebastian had done and not because I was no longer in Faerie... except hadn't Sebastian said he couldn't form a portal?

"How did we get out of Faerie?" I asked, taking another bite of pasta, even as my lids drifted shut.

"Bane summoned this short guy and said he owed you," Hawk replied. "Said you paid him to remove your brand."

And just the mention of my brand made my body ache for Rin.

I gritted my teeth, fighting the desire swelling within me. I didn't want him.

But my brand didn't care. Fate said we were meant to be and I had no say in the matter.

Hawk pressed his lips against the top of my head. "You're already feeling the pull of the bond, aren't you?"

There was no point in denying it. Hawk could sense sexual desire. He knew exactly what my body wanted even if my heart and mind were screaming in defiance.

"It's just my body. It's so frustrating. I don't love him. I don't want him. And yet the minute I look at him or think about him, all I want to do is have sex with him."

And while yes, I'd desired my guys almost as quickly as I desired Rin, this was different. With them I'd had a choice. I could have resisted my desire, slept with only one of them, done any number of things.

But with Rin, if I resisted for too long, I'd lose my mind or die just like if someone killed him.

It wasn't fair that my body wanted sex before my brand had made me fall in love with him.

"I don't know how I'm going to get through it," I said, my voice frustratingly small even though I'd told myself that I'd face my situation head on. "I don't know how I can have sex with him if the brand hasn't forced me to love him."

Hawk tightened his embrace. "I can be there with you and use my magic to help you through it. You don't have to do it alone, do you?"

No. I didn't. There wasn't anything that said a bond had to be sealed with just the branded mates doing the act. Except I wasn't sure how Rin would react to that.

Hawk was up for anything, but Rin might not be and he was just as stuck in this mess as I was. Was that really the right way to start our relationship? And did it really matter if having Hawk join us was the only way I could get through it? Our bond had to be sealed. There were no ands, ifs, or buts about it.

CHAPTER 10

AMIAH

"WE'LL WORK SOMETHING OUT AFTER HE'S PROPERLY FED," I said to Hawk, even as the fear of having sex with Rin and my need to ease his suffering surged, battling inside me.

He'll feed soon and I don't have to do it alone. He only needs to last a few more hours and then Hawk will help me seal my bond. And then...

I had no idea what would happen after that, and I was just too tired to try to figure it out.

"Work what out?" Sebastian asked as he stepped onto the roof with Titus—who had a new towel around his hips—both men carrying a plate of pasta.

"Sealing my bond with Rin."

"That's not something you have to worry about right now. You've got at least a few weeks." Sebastian sat beside me and dug into his pasta.

"I don't." Which made me want to scream with frustration. "The brand isn't making me love him, but it is making me desire him. I don't know how long I can resist."

Sebastian shot Hawk a surprised look. "Already?"

"Yeah," Hawk said. "I can help her through it, but whoever said an angelic mating brand was a beautiful thing was fucked up. No one should have to have sex if they don't want to."

"We should put him in hibernation," Titus said, sitting on my other side, his plate piled high, easily double Sebastian's serving.

"Already had this discussion with lover boy," Sebastian said, pointing his fork at Hawk. "Amiah and Rin still have to seal the bond."

"If the bond hasn't made her love him, then it hasn't made *him* love *her*." Titus's pupils slitted. "We all know how vampires have sex. He's going to bite her and there's nothing stopping him from hurting her even if he isn't in a feeding frenzy."

"Which is why I'm going to be there," Hawk said.

"We should all be there," Titus growled back.

The idea sent a shiver of desire racing through me, although I was pretty sure Titus hadn't really meant for us to all have sex together.

"God, I love you," Hawk said.

Titus frowned, Sebastian snorted, and then Titus realized what he'd said and his eyes went wide.

"You know what I meant," Titus said, his voice gruff.

"I did," I said, my lids drifting closed again.

"We all did," Sebastian chuckled, bumping my shoulder with his and waking me up. "Eat."

I speared a piece of penne and made myself eat it, but the weight of having spent all my magic—again and again and again—was stronger than the strengthening thrum of the guys' life forces or even the pain burning through my hand, and I wasn't going to stay awake much longer. Except if I passed out, they were going to go ahead and make a plan without me. Again.

"So what's the plan?" I asked.

"We can't do much of anything until you've gotten the demonic magic out of you," Hawk said to Sebastian.

"Yeah, but I haven't been able to get ahold of Sargos," Sebastian replied.

Titus huffed. "How long have we got until your mother can recast the spell tracking Amiah's connection with the Winter Court?"

"Karthick blocked Amiah's connection to the Winter Court and we've left Faerie." Sebastian frowned at me and I realized I'd been pushing a piece of penne around the plate without actually spearing it. "If we're lucky, that will buy us a few more days. But even if I can get to Sargos before then, my mother is still going to come after us."

"And she and Deaglan are cozy," I said, giving up on eating and leaning back into Hawk's embrace. "How much do you want to bet he's offered to help find us?"

"It wouldn't surprise me if she lets him and his team come after us instead of risking more of her harem and her constructs," Sebastian replied. "And really the only thing I can do is keep breaking her spell after she's found us and then move us to a new location."

"That isn't really a solution," Hawk said.

"No shit." Sebastian rolled his eyes at him. "As long as the Winter Court has such a strong claim on Amiah and my mother remains Queen, she'll always be able to find us. No concealment spell will be able to hide her, not like it hid me." Sebastian set his plate on the rooftop and stared through the purple glass canopy at the Quarter's skyline. "I can't believe I'm saying this, but Cassius was right from the beginning. There's nowhere we can go. Getting the Heart is the only solution. We'll be more powerful than anyone else and we could use it to get the Winter Court to relinquish its claim on Amiah."

"But we don't know when the final key will be empowered," Titus said. "And Deaglan has the other keys."

"Which is why I need to get rid of this infection." The muscles in Sebastian's jaw flexed, the only indication of the now-constant pain he was in. "If I'm at full power, I can prevent Deaglan from taking Cassius's fire *and* get his keys. Deaglan thinks I'm weak and has no clue how powerful I've become in the three hundred years since he tried to kill me. We'll use that to our advantage."

"So we what? Hope you can get to Sargos before your mother and Deaglan find us?" Hawk asked. "That's a terrible plan."

"I'm not going to stop looking for a better option, but even if I find a way to hide us or break the Winter Court's claim on Amiah, I'm still going to need to get my power back." Sebastian sighed. "Which means I should get back to my books to find our option B."

Something he shouldn't have to do alone. "I'll help," I said, struggling to sit up.

Sebastian leaned in and gave me a tender kiss, using it to push me back against Hawk's chest.

"You're going to fall asleep before you've finished reading a single sentence. We still have time, probably a few days before my mother finds us. For God's sake, rest," he said, worry flashing in his eyes and not saying what I knew he wanted to. Rest so I had all my magic back, because we were going to need it.

Sebastian stood and Titus took his place, capturing my mouth in a hard kiss that stole my breath and left me reeling, before jerking back. His body trembled, need darkening his eyes, and his erection tented his towel, but he managed to stand and step away.

"I'll help you," Titus said, his voice gruff.

Sebastian and Titus left, and I drifted into a half sleep in Hawk's embrace unable to keep my eyes open any longer.

The sun slowly sank below the Quarter's skyline, the sky darkened, and the streetlights turned on. Below, the *thump thump thump* of loud music pounded from the club beneath us in a primal, rhythmic beat, and more activity sounded from the street below as most of the vampire section's residents started their day even though the area was protected from the sun.

Hawk didn't say anything and didn't ask to change positions. He just held me as his heat and life force sank through my skin, into my veins, and swelled around my heart. Somehow, it connected with the core of my power there even though I always felt the source of my power in my palms.

But this wasn't my healing magic he was connecting with. It was whatever was inside me that connected with someone's life force. And whatever power it was, it loved the feel of Hawk. It yearned for him, strained to be wrapped in his life force, was strengthened by it without taking anything from him, not like how I'd used my magic to steal the life forces of Deaglan's men to power my healing.

I let it sink into my soul and savored the feel of it, fiery and dark, caressing my light. Somehow our life forces aligned. I didn't know how Rin was my soul mate and Hawk wasn't when we fit together so perfectly. But it was just more proof about how wrong everyone was about the angelic mating brand. Everything about it was a lie. Rin wasn't my soul mate, he was just the soul I ended up bound to when my brand finally awoke.

And I was going to have to figure out how to make the best of this horrible situation.

Everything in my soul said he wasn't a monster. Except I had no idea if that was the brand making me think that or not—

No, I'd felt his pain and, if I concentrated, could feel it now. Someone, most likely Deaglan, had hurt him for a long time, and he'd spoken up when he knew biting me would hurt me. I had proof that Rin wasn't a monster.

But that didn't mean he was my soul mate or that without the brand I would have naturally fallen in love with him. And while my body was drawn to him, I didn't feel that tug inside me that said he had what I needed like the tug I felt for Hawk, Sebastian, Titus, and Cassius.

We were trapped. Both of us.

God, there had to be a way out of this.

Except a bond once formed couldn't be broken... or could it?

Faerie's Heart was so powerful it could do anything. If we had the Heart, both Rin and I could be free.

I jerked awake with a gasp.

"You okay?" Hawk asked.

"I can get free," I said. "The Heart can do anything. I don't have to be trapped."

"It might not be able to break the bond."

"But out of everything, it's got the best chance." I grabbed my plate that sat by the edge of the blanket—where Hawk must have put it after I'd fallen asleep—and hurried for the door. I had to ask Sebastian if he thought it was possible.

"Amiah, wait a second. You might still be dizzy. You haven't been asleep for that long."

I turned back to Hawk and his eyes widened, and that's when I realized I had power and it must have been brightening the angel glow in my eyes. It wasn't a lot of power, but like the last time I'd woken, it was more than I should have had for only being out for a few hours. That, and my hand didn't hurt like it had before, as if I'd somehow healed my burns to a low throbbing ache while I'd been asleep. Which should have been impossible. I needed to concentrate to heal anyone, including myself, I couldn't do it while unconscious.

Except I was imbued with fae magic and had one of the keys to unlocking the Heart. I could use Sebastian's glyphs when I shouldn't have been able to power them at all.

"It's the key," I said, "or the Winter Court's claim. It must be affecting how fast I can get my magic back."

"We should tell Bane." Hawk grabbed the blanket and

we hurried into the stairwell. "He might know for certain."

"And hopefully he'll know if the Heart can break my soul bond."

I could be free. For real this time.

God, free!

We rushed back to Sebastian's apartment and were halfway across the living room when Hawk glanced behind us and swore.

The air between us and the front door burst into a shimmering liquid mirror that rapidly swelled into a portal big enough to let at least two of the Winter Queen's guards to step through at the same time.

"Bane, a portal," Hawk yelled as two large ice guards indeed stepped through.

Hawk turned to face them and I scrambled to get out of the way. As much as I could rip out someone's life force, that was a last resort... although given our situation, we might already be at our last resort.

I focused on my magical senses, connecting with Hawk's dark, fiery life force, Sebastian's cold, barely-bright straining life force, Titus's wild ferocity, Cassius's fire, and even Rin's dead-not-dead life force. But I felt nothing from the ice guards—

Because—*crap*—they were constructs, made of ice and magic. They weren't alive and didn't have life forces.

Sebastian rushed out of his office with Titus close behind. "Fuck. Already?"

One of the guards swung its large ice spear, knocking aside Sebastian's couch and flipping over his coffee table, sending the marbles that had been in the bowl on top of the table bouncing and rolling across the floor in all directions.

The other guard lunged toward me, but Hawk shoved Sebastian's grand piano in its way. The construct batted it into the wall. One of its front legs broke and that side crashed down with a dissonant boom.

With a roar, Titus barreled past me—losing his towel and not seeming to care he was naked. He tackled the guard and they crashed into the piano, shattering it.

"Hawk, get Amiah out the door," Sebastian said. "I'll grab Cassius."

But another guard stepped through the portal, along with two shadow fae. Behind them were Deaglan's nightmare and female werebear, the Winter Queen's werepanther, and Sebastian's sister, Padraigin.

"Jeez, overkill much?" Hawk said.

"You murdered Her Majesty's most powerful sorcerer, and the Winter Queen wants my brother, the dragon, and his murderous wife alive." Padraigin's hard gaze landed on me, filled with a rage so cold it sent a shiver racing down my spine. "She's not going to take any chances."

"Most powerful sorcerer?" I asked.

"Noaldar," Padraigin spat. "You murdered Noaldar, you bitch."

Except we hadn't killed him. Deaglan had.

But with Deaglan's nightmare and werebear beside her and two shadow fae crouched in front of her, my guess that Deaglan had *graciously* offered to help the Winter Queen apprehend us had to be correct.

"So please, don't come peacefully," the werepanther snarled as he flexed his hands and extended his claws from his fingertips. "The only one we really need alive is the dragon."

Titus smashed his fist into the ice guard's head, shattering it, and the rest of its body collapsed, a puppet with its strings cut. "I won't be Deaglan's prisoner again. I won't be anyone's."

Two of the guards lunged for him as everyone else—except Padraigin—rushed toward the rest of us.

Sebastian grabbed my wrist and frozen magic exploded inside me. The pain in his life force flared, his full-body glow dimmed, and he groaned in pain. "I've broken the tracking spell. Get to the circle."

Right. We couldn't leave without Rin. Even if I didn't trust him, we were soul bonded and he'd eventually be able to find me through the bond—and with my luck, that would be sooner rather than later.

"Hawk, get Cassius." Sebastian grabbed his left forearm and hissed a sibilant word. His glow dimmed again for longer this time, his complexion terrifyingly gray. A force-wave slammed into the group in front of us, sending them, the furniture, and the dozens of marbles tumbling to the far side of the living room.

He sagged to his knees, gasping for breath, his expression tight with an agony that made my heart and soul scream. I had to help him and yet there wasn't anything I could do.

I reached for him on instinct and he slapped my hand away, but the contact sent a frozen spark slicing from my hand to his and his glow flickered a little stronger for a second.

Somehow I'd given him fae magic like I had when we'd had sex.

His eyes widened.

"I can give you more."

"No." He jerked back to his feet. "Later. There's no point if they kill you. Get to the circle. I can get us out of here using the circle. Everyone to the circle. Titus and I will cover you."

Deaglan's assassins, Padraigin, and the werepanther scrambled to stand, and Titus tossed one of the ice guards into them, knocking the shadow fae and the were-bear back down again.

Padraigin leaped out of the way and raised her hands. A thick stream of water shot out of the kitchen—from the sink?—across the living room, and swept around Titus, encasing his head. But Sebastian sent a gust of wind and blew it apart before Titus could suffocate, spraying water in a fine mist across the floor and making the marble slick.

Both of the shadow fae—a man and a woman with shadows undulating under their pale skin—melted into the wildly shifting shadows around them created by Sebastian's swinging crystal chandelier, and lunged out of the shadows beside Sebastian.

"Behind you," I yelled and my senses snapped to their life forces ready to yank it out of them. But my power slammed against a wall like the wall Deaglan had made during our fight in the cavern and I couldn't grab hold.

Sebastian shot a force-wave at them, throwing them back. They crashed through the window and Sebastian snatched the shattered purple-tinted glass from the broken window in a wind gust and shot them at the shifters and the nightmare. But his glow stuttered again, the little bit of magic I'd given him already consumed by the demonic infection, and I could sense heat building under his skin. He wasn't just using his glyphs, he was channeling extra magic to weave spells on the fly with his sorcerer's ability.

He wasn't going to last long and there was no way we could win. Not even if he sacrificed himself. Which wasn't an acceptable option. We had to get out of there. Now. Except Sebastian wouldn't leave until I did.

I wrenched my attention away from him just as Hawk grabbed for my wrist, ready to pull me away.

"I'm okay. I'll meet you in the clean room." I couldn't help Hawk carry Cassius, and if I couldn't wrench out someone's life force, I couldn't fight back. Best to stay out of the way and not distract anyone. No matter how much that frustrated me.

I bolted to the end of the hall and rushed into the clean room.

Rin's gaze instantly leaped to mine and everything within me stalled at the sight of him, my mind, breath, and soul. The aching need that I didn't want roared into an insistent throb, urging me to go to him, embrace him, join with him, and complete the bond.

No. No no no no.

I wanted Hawk and Sebastian and Cassius and Titus. *They* were who I wanted, not Rin. And when we got the Heart, I'd break my bond with Rin and be free.

And I still had no idea if he was fighting the same compulsion. His expression and body language didn't change. Nothing about him changed. He still knelt in the middle of the circle. His hellfire was back to smoldering red pinpricks in his black eyes and he'd retracted his fangs. Just looking at him, I wouldn't have known that he was starving and on the verge of succumbing to a feeding frenzy or anything else.

Outside in the living room, Titus roared and something crashed, the *boom* so powerful it reverberated around me. Rin's gaze jumped past my shoulder and his hellfire snapped. It was just a flicker, but it was a change, a reaction.

Except at what?

I jerked around and came face to face with the nightmare. The icy fear of the nightmare's power seized me, darkness surrounded me, and Balwyrdan's fist smashed into my face sending me reeling.

CHAPTER 11

AMIAH

My knees hit a cold floor and the nightmare's face materialized out of the darkness. His hellfire hair hissed and snapped, writhing over his head and between his tall thick horns as if caught in a wild storm, and the hellfire in his eyes blazed bright.

He grabbed the front of my scrub top and jerked me close. "Since you're still alive, His Majesty of the Shadow Court has changed his mind, Ms. *Healing* Angel," he said. "You're going to give him your key and serve him in every way he desires." The nightmare sneered at me. "But I'm allowed to try to break you first. Want to join in, Rin?"

I glanced back at Rin, who hadn't moved and still wasn't showing any kind of emotion. A small spark *popped* from the hellfire in his eyes, but the darkness swept around me again before I could figure out what that meant and Balwyrdan punched me again.

This time my nose broke with agonizing pain and a sickening crunch. Stars burst across my vision and fear clenched frozen around my heart. Tears streamed down my cheeks and I fought to breathe past the agony of my broken ribs.

Please, no. I never wanted to think about this again, let alone relive it. I had to break free of the nightmare's magic.

I searched my mind for his sour, nauseating darkness, but Balwyrdan grabbed my hair and wrenched my head back up.

I tried to bite back my cry of pain, but it still escaped as a pathetic mewling whimper. God, I needed to be strong. I could survive this if my guys came for me—

Except they had.

I mentally heaved against the nightmare's magic. I couldn't feel it, but I knew it was there.

A crack of light cut through the darkness.

"You know you want this sweet ass with her sweet blood and magic," the nightmare mocked. "You think you're so perfect. King Deaglan's favorite. Well not any more."

The nightmare yanked me up and slammed me face-first against the barrier, its invisible magic biting my skin and as hard as any wall.

Rin remained kneeling, which made the nightmare snarl, yank me back, and slam me against the barrier again, this time breaking my nose for real with a blinding flash of agony and a sharp *crack*.

Blood gushed over my lips and dripped off my chin, and the nightmare jerked my head around, smearing my blood on the barrier.

Rin's gaze locked on it and his hellfire grew from smoldering pinpricks to miniature flames.

"I'm going to fuck her and make her bleed and watch you lose your precious control, you high and mighty asshole."

The darkness swept through my vision again and my pulse pounded. I wouldn't be able to fight back if I was trapped by the nightmare's magic. I had to get free, had to at least call out for help.

But Balwyrdan punched me in the chest, cracking my ribs, sending agony screaming through me and scattering my thoughts. A massive weight crushed around my heart and the air around me vanished.

I gasped, unable to help myself, knowing it was useless, that I wouldn't be able to breathe through the activated leash spell, but unable to stop my body's reaction.

My lungs burned and somehow the already dark world darkened even more and started spinning despite not being able to see anything.

I knew I was in an abandoned reception hall—

No. I was in Sebastian's clean room and the nightmare had me. Not Balwyrdan.

My air returned with another *crack* of Balwyrdan's fist in my face, this one sending agony exploding through my cheek.

I hit the floor again—

Except I knew I was still standing.

Balwyrdan grabbed the front of my dress, lifting me up, and my neck strap broke, the metal catch slicing my neck. Cold air rushed over my skin and I fell back to the floor, everything spinning. I couldn't breathe, couldn't think. *Please stop. God, stop.*

Balwyrdan yanked me back up by my hair again and howled with pleasure... or was that the nightmare? Balwyrdan had enjoyed beating me, knew exactly how to extract the most pain while keeping me alive, but I didn't remember the howling laughter.

He pounded his fist into my face again and shoved his hand down my pants... but I'd been wearing a dress... and Balwyrdan had gotten off on my pain, nothing else.

This wasn't real. It was the nightmare.

It. Was. The. Nightmare.

I mentally shoved with everything I had.

Get out.

Get out get out. "Get out."

The darkness exploded and I was back in the all white clean room, my face painfully pressed against the barrier and blood oozing from my nose. It also flowed from a deep cut in my neck, soaking into my scrub top, and had Rin's avid attention. He still hadn't moved, but now his hellfire raged and his fangs had extended. The nightmare had one hand on the back of my head pinning me to the barrier and was unlacing his fly with the other.

No. No no no.

Fear clenched my chest and my magic pounded and clawed at the wall surrounding his life force, desperate to find a crack, anything that would let it in and save me.

"Hawk! Sebastian!" I bucked against the nightmare's grasp and he pressed harder against my head.

"That's it, little angel, fight me," he said with a dark chuckle.

No. No!

I scratched deeper rents in the wall surrounding his life force.

Nothing. No way in.

God, there had to be a way in, a way to save myself. I had to do something.

"Titus—" I twisted and tried to scratch the nightmare's face, but he rammed his free hand into my ribs, cutting off my cry and shooting agony screaming through my chest as if my ribs were broken even though my magic told me they weren't—which was one of the horrifying powers of a nightmare so he could better feed on his victim's fear.

Out in the hall, the screams and yells and crashes of the fight were still happening. It had felt like an eternity trapped in the nightmare's magic, but I doubted it had been more than a few minutes.

"Sebas—"

The nightmare slammed my face back into the barrier making the room spin.

This wasn't happening. It couldn't be happening.

I renewed my mental clawing at the wall protecting his life force. I had to get in. Please. God. Let me in.

"You're supposed to be screaming my name. I want you begging, little angel. Beg me not to hurt you."

But I wasn't stupid enough to think begging would stop him.

"Come on. Beg," the nightmare said.

My magic ripped a hairline fissure in the wall and a trickle connected with the nightmare's fiery sour life force, but it wasn't enough to take hold and rip it out of him.

"Please, Nezener, make me bleed," he said in a mocking singsong, rubbing his now-freed erection against my rear, sending terror—no matter how hard I tried to fight it—rushing through me and feeding him, giving him strength.

I heaved at the fissure, desperate to make it bigger, to shove my power past the wall, but the nightmare slammed my face against the barrier again, shattering my concentration and making the room spin.

"Make me scream and bleed. Fuck me, Nezener."

My magic wasn't going to save me.

"Go fuck yourself," I spat.

The nightmare, Nezener, froze.

Yeah, didn't expect an angel to swear like that.

Which was exactly what I'd hope for. He'd stopped for just a second, but it was more than enough time.

I jerked in his grip, grabbed his erection, and wrenched on it with all my might.

He howled in agony, his erection instantly going flaccid, and his pain exploded across my senses. My healing magic snapped into him, somehow not deterred by the wall protecting his life force, and connected with the membrane in his penis that I'd purposefully torn. But he backhanded me and my connection disconnected from him for a second.

My not-broken cheek hit the barrier, shooting pain through my face as if it were broken, and I crumpled to the floor... right beside the glyph that let the barrier down.

Rin's gaze was still locked on the blood leaking down my neck, and his hellfire now licked across his cheeks.

The emotionless expression from before was gone, replaced with a ferocious, desperate hunger.

If I let him out, would he kill me even though we were soul bonded?

Did he even know we were bonded?

"You fucking bitch," Nezener screamed. He grabbed my face and smashed the back of my head against the barrier again.

The room darkened and spun. Real agony screamed through my skull and my magic stuttered, connecting and disconnecting with him—since his injury couldn't be fixed without surgery and my magic had decided it was more serious than the cut in my neck, my concussion, or my broken nose.

"You God damn fucking bitch." He smashed my head again and the room went dark.

One more and I'd be unconscious. He was no longer able to get an erection, but that didn't mean he couldn't hurt or permanently maim me.

He jerked my head forward to smash it a third time and I slapped my hand against the glyph and released the barrier.

I fell back onto the floor, Nezener lurching forward with me, and Rin launched himself at us. One second he was kneeling, the next he was a wild, frenzied monster coming at us.

Nezener scrambled off me and shoved me toward Rin, but Rin kept going. He tackled Nezener, flipped him, and smashed his face on the floor, stunning him.

With an animalistic snarl, Rin ripped open the side of Nezener's neck, sending arterial blood spraying across his face and clothes, and over the white walls and floor. He latched his lips over Nezener's carotid artery and started feeding with the desperation of a starving man.

My magic instantly locked with Nezener and surged, heating my hands and making them glow. The urge to go to him and save him squeezed inside my chest.

Save him. Save him.

No way in hell.

I crossed my arms, shoved my hands into my armpits, and tried to make my power turn inward to heal my broken nose and the cut in my neck. But I couldn't get it to leave my hands. I *had* to use it to save Nezener, and if I didn't go to him—*now now now*—it was going to heal him from a distance.

Nezener moaned and thrashed, his fiery sour life force straining, desperate to stay lit. The agony in his neck blaze through me, consuming all my other pain, and I could feel his heart pounding, desperate, gushing his blood into Rin's mouth and onto the floor.

Save him.

No. I won't. I can't.

It wasn't even a matter of not wanting to, although I really didn't want to save him. It was a waste of power. Rin was going to kill him. Using my magic would just prolong Nezener's suffering and waste my magic when any one of my guys could be hurt and need me.

Except the need to heal twisted tighter, wrenching me forward onto my hands and knees to crawl closer, even as my magic surged through the connection it had already made with Nezener.

No. Absolutely not.

I heaved my magic back, fighting the burn and pressure, and the promise of an excruciating backlash.

Save him.

No.

Nezener's life force and heartbeat stuttered.

Save. Him.

Another stutter, and the pressure of my power howled inside me.

"No."

With a whoosh, Nezener's sour life force vanished and my magic slammed into me, the backlash stealing my breath and igniting every cell in my body with a pain so powerful I prayed I'd just pass out.

Except I couldn't pass out. The guys might need me. Even if I couldn't access my magic until my backlash subsided, I still had non-magical medical knowledge.

That, and I was still in the room with a man who'd tried to kill me more than once and was in the throes of a feeding frenzy.

I tried to drag my attention to the door to look for help as Rin jerked his head up, his gaze zeroing in on me. Blood splattered his forehead and upper cheeks, and fully covered the lower half of his face. His hellfire was a wild ferocious fire with sparks snapping free and hissing when they hit the floor, and his lips were curled back in a vicious snarl. Nothing about him looked human. Even Titus when his beast took over looked more human than Rin did right now.

He lunged at me.

I tried to scramble back but my muscles seized with the sudden movement and I collapsed to the floor instead of getting away. Not that there was anywhere to go. He was between me and the door.

Rin straddled me, pinning me with his body, grabbed my jaw, and jerked my head to the side, giving him better access to the cut in my neck.

"If you kill me, you kill yourself," I gasped, the agony of my backlash screaming through me even as my body thrilled at his touch.

God, this was such a mess.

I was in excruciating pain and I *still* wanted him to unlace his pants and take me. My body didn't care that he was going to kill me. I needed him inside me, needed to seal our bond.

I grabbed his wrist, trying to move his hand enough to turn my head and properly meet his gaze, but I couldn't make him budge. "We're soul bonded. I die, you die."

"Maybe I'm done being someone's slave," he snarled, his voice still barely above a whisper and filled with menace. He trembled, every muscle in his body tight, his hunger only partially satiated from killing Nezener. "You're worse than King Deaglan, making me desire not just your blood and magic, but your body, too. I'm not dumb. You're going to make me watch you sleep with your husband while your magic twists up my insides, that's how you're going to make me obey you. Be a good boy and you won't have to watch. You just have to live with this... this need."

Oh, God. Did he think I'd branded him to torture him like Deaglan?

"King Deaglan denied me, made me watch when I

disobeyed, but he never went so far as to make me *need* someone like I need you." His grip on my chin tightened, his sharp small vampire claws digging into my cheeks, and some of the wildness bled out of his expression, turning into a hard darkness. "Your chains are worse than King Deaglan's, and this is the only time I'm going to get to touch you, isn't it?"

My pulse stuttered with fear even as my body screamed with the agonizing burn of backlash mixed with throbbing insistent desire.

"I'm just as trapped as you are," I said, fighting my hips from rocking forward and telling him what my body wanted. Tears of pain and frustration burned my eyes. I didn't want any of this. For either of us.

Just knowing that he thought this was done on purpose to torture him broke my heart.

And while I might not trust him, I didn't think he trusted anyone. He'd been a slave, tortured physically and psychologically, and I was sure being starved and denied sex was just the tip of the iceberg.

"The bond makes me want you too, and I have no control over it," I continued. "All I can hope is that we can get Faerie's Heart and it'll be able to break it."

He glared at me and I prayed that he'd somehow be able to know I was telling the truth.

"You didn't do this on purpose?" His grip on my face eased enough so I could look him straight in the eyes. His hellfire had shrunk to small flames, but he still trembled. "Why do I want to believe you?"

"Because it's the truth. Angels can't control when or with whom their mating brands bond them with. And if I had a choice, I wouldn't have picked you. If we don't find a way to break the bond, it's going to make me fall in love with you and I'm going to fall out of love with them." My desire and backlashed surged, making me groan half in pain and half in pleasure and my eyes roll back. "I don't know what your history is or what Deaglan did to you, but no one deserves to be tortured or forced to desire someone. You're not my slave or Sebastian's or anyone's any more. And I'll be damned if we're both slaves to this stupid brand."

Please believe me. We couldn't keep him locked up and if the next key didn't become empowered soon, I'd have no choice but to sleep with him.

And I couldn't have sex with someone who I feared was going to kill me, even if Hawk was with me to help me through it.

Rin opened his mouth to say something when Titus —still naked—barreled into the room, wrenched him off me, and slammed him face-first into the floor.

"Get off her," the dragon snarled.

Sebastian staggered into the room, his fae glow completely gone, and Hawk rushed in behind him with a naked Cassius slung over his shoulder.

"God, Amiah." Hawk hurried to my side and I curled into a ball unable to stop myself.

"I'm okay," I gasped, as Hawk set Cassius down and reached for me.

"Never touch her again." Titus wrenched Rin up and slammed him back down, not even drawing a grunt of pain from the hybrid.

Was he going to take the beating without saying

anything or crying out? Was that what he'd learned from Deaglan?

"Titus, I'm okay. I swear."

Titus snarled. Yeah, given how I looked with my nose broken, blood oozing from my neck, and curled up in pain, I wouldn't have believed me either.

"Rin didn't do anything. He saved me from Deaglan's nightmare," I said, and Titus's gaze jumped to Nezener's corpse, his blood painting the all-white wall and floor around him.

"Get your beast under control. You can't kill him and we can't stay here," Sebastian gasped. "Now everyone get in the fucking circle."

He sagged to the floor beside me and pulled me into his arms and pressed my hand against his inner left thigh over his pants. "Amiah, push power into the glyph under your hand and say ignite. It'll activate the teleportation spell I have embedded in the circle."

Titus jerked Rin up to his feet so all of him was inside the circle and Hawk pulled Cassius closer even though he didn't have to.

My magic connected with all of them. Sebastian had a deep laceration in his side that needed healing that I couldn't give him with my magic raging out of control inside me, and Hawk was low on magic. Titus had broken ribs—that, with his rapid healing, were already knitting back together—and Cassius was still out, his body feeling like he'd been given a strong sedative even though I knew he hadn't. And Rin was still hungry.

Footsteps clattered down the hall and the werepanther rushed into the doorway. Behind him were more shadow fae.

"Amiah, please," Sebastian gasped.

I wrenched my thoughts from my guys and imagined shoving as much of my fae magic through Sebastian's pants and into the glyph under my hand. "Ignite."

Sebastian cried out in pain and blinding white light blazed around us. The light shot into my body, the pain of the spell overwhelming everything else inside me including the agony of my backlash, and it ripped my cells apart in a way I'd hoped never to experience again.

CHAPTER 12

HAWK

Agony screamed through me as Bane's teleportation spell ripped me apart then put me back together again. My hellfire flared out of my eyes and I completely lost my hold on my magic. At the same time, something heavy crunched, shattering glass and making metal squeal, and a white-feathered wing slapped me in the face.

Everyone moaned with desire, and I yanked my magic back under control as quickly as I could. I'd never been teleported before and I hoped to God I never would again. I was only grateful Bane had the spell already preset on his circle, because in his condition he wouldn't have been able to teleport just himself let alone all six of us. He'd have just burned himself to a crisp and we wouldn't have gone anywhere.

And he still, even with Amiah powering his glyph, looked like shit.

He lay on his back on the cool damp concrete of his underground garage in a growing pool of blood, his expression stunned, and only a hint of white aura flickered through the writhing black darkness and angry red spikes inside him.

Amiah had heaved forward, her wings fully extended. Her unnatural fae glow blazed bright as her aura, now flecked with gold—likely from the mating brand because the gold hadn't been there before—snapped and churned inside her. Every time it flared, she tensed and her expression pinched tighter with pain, as if her power had been released without focus, was raging inside her, and couldn't escape from her body.

Cassius lay beside me—the reason a wing had slapped me in the face—his aura burning bright again with his fire magic, while Rin with his strange seething black aura, had dropped to his knees. His hellfire roared from his eyes like mine had and his fangs were fully extended.

Titus, in his massive dragon form, sat fifteen feet away from us. He was half on a flattened blue sedan as well as the flattened front of a brown pickup, and crammed between a concrete pillar, and a minivan that had been squished against a second concrete pillar.

His gold-red aura heaved with his beast's rage and I couldn't blame him. Everything within me had frozen in horror when we'd run into the clean room and seen Rin straddling Amiah, her nose broken and bleeding and a bleeding gash in her neck. And worse, I'd felt a desperate, painful desire radiating from both of them.

They were fighting it. Both of them. Neither of them wanted to feel what they were feeling, and yet they couldn't help themselves. The ache was almost as strong as the overwhelming need I'd felt from Amiah when she'd first entered my tent. It was filled with power and too much pain.

She was going to fall in love with him and hate herself for it.

And all I could do was be by her side, help her through it, and pray the Heart could free her... or add me to their bond.

Except to do that, we needed to get as far away from Bane's apartment as possible.

Even if Padraigin wasn't a sorcerer and hadn't brought one along, she was going to figure out that in Bane's condition we wouldn't have been able to teleport very far.

Titus huffed smoke from his nostrils and smacked his head on the low ceiling then, with a grunt, shifted back into his human form—not seeming to care that he now stood barefoot on the shattered glass from the vehicles.

"Get me to the SUV," Bane gasped, pointing to a full-sized expensive black SUV that was lit up like the sun with all the spells on it—one of which being a lock spell that kept the vehicle locked until the owner deactivated it. "I need to touch it to unlock the protection spell on it."

"Does it need a key?" I helped him stand and stagger to the SUV.

He pressed his palm against the door, his touch releasing the lock spell with a flash of magic that only I could see, then passed out, going completely limp in my hands.

Fuck.

He was the one with the better contacts... and the money... and hell, given that he'd had a teleport spell already in place—not to mention a spell on his library that sent his entire office into an interdimensional space only he could get to—this was clearly his escape plan. He probably already had a safehouse set up. If he was unconscious, he couldn't tell us where to go. And my place was a terrible alternative. I lived in my tent in Left of Lincoln. Even if it hadn't been sliced open, Lincoln wasn't a safe place to hide.

"Come on, man. Wake up." I gave him a shake, but he didn't even groan.

"He's drained himself too deeply and he's losing too much blood," Amiah said. "Even if I give him my fae magic, he'll still be exhausted and won't wake for a while."

"How long is a while?" Titus asked.

"More than a few minutes," she gasped, her power slicing deep inside her. "We need to get him some place where I can stitch him up."

Titus stalked the fifteen feet back to us. "But you have power."

"I can't access it." Another slice made her squeeze her eyes shut and hug herself.

God, she looked just like Bane with his demonic infection.

"My power locked onto Deaglan's nightmare and I refused to heal him," she said. "My power turns in on me when I don't release it. I won't be able to connect with my magic until the backlash passes."

"Which will be when?" Titus growled.

"It's bad," she said, biting back a groan. "Could be a couple of days."

A couple of days?

Fuck.

God damn fucking hell.

And there wasn't a damned thing I could do about it.

Fine.

The first order of business was to get everyone out of here and given that Amiah was in pain, Cassius unconscious, and Titus and Rin knew next to nothing about Union—not to mention, I didn't even know if we could trust Rin—that left me in charge.

How the hell did I end up in charge?

I yanked open the SUV's door, put Bane in the closest seat, and buckled him in.

The SUV was luxurious, spacious, fully loaded, and smelled like it was new. The back seats were down—which was perfect for Cassius and his wings—and a large duffle bag, glowing with spells only I could see, had been shoved half under the driver's seat.

This was definitely Bane's escape plan.

"Everyone in the car."

Titus jerked toward Amiah, his expression filled with his need to hold her, but he grabbed Cassius instead without me having to ask him. Which was good, because with Titus's greater strength it'd just be easier for him to get the angel with his released wings into the SUV.

"The last row of seats is down, you can put him in there," I said, then bent to pick up Amiah.

But she pulled her wings in and, with a strength of will that made my heart ache, stood before I could lift her.

I grabbed her before she fell and slid a thread of what little magic I had left into her to help ease her pain.

She clung to my shoulders, panting and trembling, and turned to Rin.

"You can go," she said. "You're not our slave or prisoner. But until our bond is broken, it'll keep drawing us back together no matter what we want."

Rin stared at her.

I couldn't read his expression and had no idea what he was thinking. I could only hope feeding on Deaglan's nightmare had satiated some of his hunger. He'd regained control of his hellfire and retracted his fangs, but still looked ferocious with blood covering most of his face while still radiating his unwanted, painful desire.

"It's your choice," she added.

A spark popped from his right eye.

"I swear."

Except it wasn't his choice. Not really. Fate had already taken away their choices and if they separated now and Rin was recaptured by Deaglan, or worse, went back to him willingly, Amiah would get hurt.

He continued to stare at her.

For fuck's sake!

"We don't have time for this." I helped Amiah climb into the SUV then glared at Rin. "Get in the fucking car."

His gaze jerked to me and another spark popped from his eye.

Jeez, this man had a crazy amount of control. I'd never seen any demon able to control his hellfire like that.

"If Deaglan gets his hands on you, that's going to hurt Amiah." My hellfire flared with my fear and anger and frustration, licking across my cheeks, and I didn't bother to control it. I *wanted* him to know I was serious. Deadly serious. "I won't let you hurt her."

He was getting in the SUV whether he wanted to or not. Except I had no idea how I was going to force him in. I was decent in a fight, but he was stronger than me and had claws. His vampire claws were small, not like a shifter's, but he still had natural weapons and I didn't. The only chance I had of overpowering him was if he were into guys, then I could use my magic on him, but I wasn't going to bet Amiah's life on that. Especially since I already knew he was into women, which lessened the odds that I'd be able to seduce him.

He dipped his gaze, the only indication that he accepted my order, and climbed into the SUV following Amiah, who knelt between the seats and had started unbuttoning Bane's shirt.

I hurried around to the driver's seat, Titus got into the front passenger seat, and Rin settled in the seat behind me with the duffle bag at his feet.

The SUV's key, one of those fobs that you didn't have to put into an ignition sat in the cup holder. Thank God. I pressed the button to start the car and drove to the ramp on the far side of the garage.

Once on the street, it took everything I had not to speed away, but I knew speeding would draw more attention than anything else. No one knew we were in an SUV and everyone's concealment charms were still active—including Titus's, much to my surprise, since he'd broken the glamour hiding his identity and the two spells had been tied together. Even if Padraigin had someone who could track us by the blood Titus, Bane, and I had lost during the fight, the charms would keep us hidden—

Except Rin didn't have a concealment charm, and he'd been Deaglan's slave.

Crap.

"Rin, can they track you?"

The light ahead turned red and I turned right so I could keep moving away from Bane's apartment. I didn't have a goal in mind, I just wanted to get us as far away as possible.

"No," he replied, surprising me with his quick response. Of course, he didn't elaborate, but I supposed I didn't need to know anything else.

If he couldn't be tracked, that meant they could only track Amiah through her connection to the Winter Court, and Bane had already broken the tracking spell when they'd first arrived. They were going to have to return to Faerie to get the Winter Queen to recast it and that meant we had a little bit of time. Not much, certainly not as much as we'd expected, but still some.

Titus squirmed in his seat, his dragon's head superimposed over his human one, a sign his beast was starting to regain control.

"Move faster," he growled.

"I don't want to draw attention." I stopped at a red light, my insides churning, everything within me screaming to move, go, escape. But we were barely out of the vampire's section of the Quarter and the streets were busy with vehicles as well as pedestrians. That was a lot of people who'd notice if a black SUV started driving erratically. I also didn't want to take another right. That would take us back toward Bane's apartment. Which meant as much as it made my pulse pound, I *had* to stop. "But we do need to figure out where we're going. We can't drive around forever."

I caught Amiah's gaze in the rearview mirror, my heart clenching at her appearance. Blood trickled down her neck and seeped into her scrub top and leaked from her broken nose, and bright red bruises had formed under her eyes and were starting to swell. Her expression was tight with pain and worry, her gaze slightly out of focus—probably from a concussion—but there was also determination in her eyes. She was going to get us all out alive if it killed her, and I'd be damned if I let her sacrifice herself.

"As much as I want to go to Operations, Cassius would say no," she said, bunching up Bane's shirt and pressing it against the deep gash in his side.

"I agree." The light turned green and I calmly—so fucking calmly it was driving me crazy—continued down the street then took the next left away from the Joined Parliament Operations Building. "If Deaglan or Padraigin know anything about the mortal realm, they're going to know every angel in town lives in Operations. That's the first place they'll look for us."

And while there were people and weapons at the Joined Parliament Operations Building, we didn't know how many people Deaglan and the Winter Queen would send after us the next time.

Three ice guards, two shifters, a handful of shadow fae, the nightmare, *and* Padraigin had already been overkill. Sure, we'd managed to get away, but barely. And while I'd heard that Union City's primary JP team was powerful—especially since they added the world's only archnephilim, a being who was half powerful archangel and half powerful hellfire queen to the team—there were also a lot of civilians living in the Operations Building, it being a significant JP research center.

Which was likely one of the reasons Cassius hadn't wanted to take the fight to Operations when this whole mess had started.

And that left us with what?

Fuck. I had no idea.

Amiah couldn't heal Bane and we couldn't just take him to a hospital. Wherever we went, we were going to get noticed. Amiah was clearly an angel and yet clearly had a fae glow. Bane even without his glow was still obviously high fae with his sharp facial features, strange white and silver hair, and delicately pointed ears. Titus was huge. And naked. And Rin, just as a demon-vampire hybrid without anyone knowing he was half sin eater, was almost as rare as an archnephilim.

Even Cassius was naked, something an angel would never do in public, and while we could probably find him clothes, angels also didn't spend a lot of time with demons. Just being in our odd group would draw attention to him.

Which meant somehow me, with my non-demon-like blue eyes and my magic that made most women and a good handful of men look my way, was the one who stuck out the least.

"Do you know of a vet's office? Ideally not in the Quarter?" I asked. There was probably at least one vet in the Quarter, and dozens in the city proper, but I'd never had a pet, so I didn't know where to go. "Will your angel nature let you break in so we can stitch him up?"

"We're still going to need some place to go so he can rest," she replied.

"*You* need to rest," Titus growled.

I turned onto a less-busy narrow side street and realized I was headed toward Squatters' Row, an area of the Quarter that had yet to be redeveloped. And while it had a lot of abandoned buildings where we might be able to find a place to hide, there were still too many people illegally living there who could notice us.

"There's a duffle bag under my seat by Rin's feet," I said, glancing in the rearview mirror confirming that we weren't being followed then pulling to stop at the curb. "Maybe Bane left an address to his safehouse in there."

I doubted it. He wasn't that stupid. Even though a magical lock was hard to pick, it could still be picked. But hey, I could hope.

Rin tugged the bag free and Amiah unzipped it. Inside was a magical book, a change of clothes, and two packets of hundred dollar bills.

Amiah's eyes widened. "Is that—?"

"Twenty thousand dollars?" I said. "Yeah. That'll buy us some discretion."

"If we can get there without being noticed," Titus added.

"And it still doesn't solve our medical needs." The magic in her aura snapped and she drew in a sharp breath. "We have to go to Voth's. He has a clinic in the back of his hotel."

"Are you sure?" Voth was a greater demon who was known to not like angels. Yeah, he'd fought in the war for the Angelic Defense, and had accepted an angel medic as part of his team when they'd started getting the worst of the worst assignments, but that didn't mean he *liked* angels. "And how do you know he has a clinic?"

"Long story." Another snap, and her hands, still keeping pressure on Bane's wound, started to tremble. Her swollen eyelids fluttered closed for a second before she wrenched them open and the muscles in her jaw tightened.

She wasn't going to last, although because of her concussion we had to keep her awake for—

Hell, I had no idea how long we were supposed to keep her awake, just that we had to.

However long it needed to be, it would be better if she was only fighting to stay conscious and not also trying to take care of Bane at the same time.

"Offer Voth the money," she said. "And if that's not enough, tell him he can meet another bonded couple."

I wanted to ask why that might be the currency that got us into his clinic, but another snap of her magic had me putting the SUV back into gear and heading toward Voth's hotel on the outskirts of the Quarter.

It didn't matter what got us someplace safe, so long as she was safe.

God, nothing else mattered.

Why couldn't she have branded me? I was already hers, heart and soul, and if we couldn't free her or add me to her bond with Rin, I was forever going to be on the outside looking in.

CHAPTER 13

AMIAH

H<small>AWK DROVE THROUGH</small> S<small>QUATTERS</small>' R<small>OW TO</small> V<small>OTH'S</small>
luxury hotel on the far side of the Quarter. The greater
demon had been a barely controlled deadly powerhouse
during the war, and the Angelic Defense commanders
had basically pointed him and his team at a target and let
him go at it, which had ended up giving him the moniker
Angel of Death. After the war, his team had been instru-
mental in hunting down and killing most of Michael's
magically made monstrous army, but for some reason
that I couldn't figure out, he'd stopped hunting nephilim,
bought the 19th century hotel, restored it, and settled
down.

Or at least I'd thought he'd settled down until a few
months ago when Essie and her guys, along with me,
Cassius, and Sebastian, had fled Operations seeking
protection from the Director the Joined Parliament
Bureau of Supernatural Law Enforcement, and we'd
ended up in the small, fully stocked clinic at the back of
Voth's hotel.

During that time, I'd had almost no interaction with Voth and I doubted he'd remember me well enough to just help me if I asked for it. Which is why I'd suggested money and the information about a bonded couple. I'd kept to myself, had probably looked like an angel who'd wanted nothing to do with her demon host while I'd helped Marcus through yet another horrible shifter transition and had my heart shattered. It had been Essie, not me, who'd gotten him through his transition from werewolf to hellhound, his beast responding to her and not me and confirming without a doubt that even though she hadn't branded him like she had the others, she was his mate.

That had been the final nail in the coffin of my dream. There hadn't even been a glimmer of hope left. The man I'd been so certain was my mate, that I'd secretly fallen in love with and had patiently waited for him to do the same with me, wasn't mine, had never been mine, and never would be.

Add the horrible realization that the mating brand wasn't the wonderful beautiful thing I'd been led to believe, and everything I thought I knew about myself and my destiny had been shattered.

Essie had branded Marcus shortly after that. I'd finished healing Sebastian, who'd been critically wounded during that whole mess, and quietly left Voth's hotel, returning to Operations a broken and lost angel.

Except going to Voth was our only option. I could only hope that the money would be enough for Voth to let us use his clinic, no questions asked. I didn't want to deal with the potential pity, or worse the congratulations

I'd get for being one of those rare angels with an angelic mating brand. And I didn't know how Voth would respond. He'd demanded to see Essie and Gideon, the newly mated couple, as a non-negotiable part of the payment for a rare magical item that they'd needed. Had it been morbid curiosity since mating brands were so rare? Or was the Angel of Death secretly a romantic?

Regardless, if the only way we could get to his clinic was to show my brand, I'd do it. Whatever it took to save Sebastian and give us a moment to figure out what we were going to do.

Voth's large hotel sat sprawled on top of a gently sloping hill with a long circular driveway leading to a grand front entrance that was fully lit against the evening's darkness so everyone could clearly see its grandeur.

I'd never been through the front doors, but I knew— everyone knew—that Voth had beautifully restored the yellow-brick, ten-story building, sparing no expense on the lavish details.

It was still early evening and lights were on in many of the rooms, the glow warm on the top five floors, and slightly purple on the bottom five from the UV-blocking glass. The light was welcoming, and also a reminder that there were a lot of people awake and moving around the hotel who could notice us.

"Front door?" Hawk asked, pausing on the road instead of heading down the driveway.

"No, go around to the side. There's a parking lot and another way in," I said. That was how we'd arrived the last time.

Cassius had marched through the almost-as-grand side door, somehow convinced Voth to help us, and we'd been directed around back to the loading bay.

The parking lot was only half full, which hopefully meant Voth didn't have anything big going on in his theater at the moment and we'd be able to sneak into his clinic without anyone but Voth noticing us.

Hawk parked as far back in the lot as he could while still having a few cars around us so the SUV didn't draw attention. Then he quickly stripped out of his bloody and burned clothes and changed into the clothes that had been in the duffle bag.

"Titus, take over holding Bane's shirt," Hawk said, hopping out of the SUV. His gaze shifted to me. "I don't like the idea of you driving with what I'm sure is a concussion and barely able to see, but I'm pretty sure Titus and Rin don't know how to drive."

I didn't like the idea of driving in my condition, either, and while Titus had spent the last five hundred years in Faerie as Deaglan's prisoner and probably had no clue how to drive, Rin had been Deaglan's assassin. He might have had an opportunity to visit the mortal realm and learn.

I glanced at him and he gave a slight shake of his head. No.

Great.

"If the money doesn't work, telling him he can meet a bonded couple will," I said. It had to work. We had nowhere else to go and Sebastian was losing too much blood.

Hawk headed across the parking lot and entered the

hotel while Titus climbed into the back and took over keeping pressure against Sebastian's side.

I slid into the drivers' seat, gritting my teeth against my magic writhing inside me. I just had to stay focused enough to stitch up Sebastian and then awake long enough to ensure my concussion wasn't going to be a problem. Then I could collapse.

Sebastian moaned, making my heart squeeze, and I glanced back at him. He was still unconscious, and even without access to my magic, I could tell by the tightness in his expression and body that he was still suffering a pain deeper than just the laceration in his side.

God, we just needed to get through this. I just needed all of them to survive this.

Was that what Essie had been thinking when we'd driven, bleeding and broken, to this very spot?

No. The fear and desperation induced by her brands had to have made it worse. I was only bonded with Rin who was, more or less, fine. She'd been branded to three of her four men and they'd all just barely escaped with their lives.

I couldn't imagine what it would be like to be soul bonded to all of them. My soul was already furious and terrified for Sebastian, and still broken over Cassius even though I *knew* he was alive. I didn't want to be the one lying on the floor screaming in terror. And yet even without the bonds, a part of me felt I already was. At least if I was bonded, I'd not just get the detriments, but the benefits as well. Bonded angels' abilities were stronger, some developed new powers, and they could share life forces with their mates and possibly save them from dying.

God, I couldn't believe I was actually hoping for more bonds.

Although with my luck, I'd be one of those angels who didn't have anything enhanced no matter how many mates I claimed.

And yet, in the very least, I had to find a way to brand Hawk. If he was part of my bond, he wouldn't go crazy or starve ... and I wasn't going to think about how not giving Rin a say in the matter would be unfair to him.

We were just going to have to get Faerie's Heart. That solved everything. I bet it could even cure Sebastian's demonic infection.

My thoughts ping ponged between hope and fear and desire while my magic sliced into me, muting my sense of the guys' life forces. Blood still oozed from my neck and my whole head hurt, but I was determined. I was going to get Faerie's Heart. I'd do whatever it took—

Except as soon as I thought that, I realized I wouldn't do whatever it took. No matter how much I wanted the Heart, I wouldn't sacrifice any of my guys to get it, and I could only pray it wouldn't come down to that.

Movement by the hotel door caught my attention and I dragged my gaze from the steering wheel to look out the window and saw Hawk running toward us.

"We've got a deal," Hawk said, opening the driver's door. "I got him to give us full access to his clinic and his private suite with its private elevator, along with complete discretion, but..." His expression turned grim.

"But he wants to see the bonded couple." At least

Hawk had gotten us a lot for the deal. I hadn't even known Voth had a private suite.

"Yeah," Hawk said as I moved over into the passenger seat and Hawk started the SUV. "You knew that would seal the deal. Do you know what he'll do about that?"

"No." No one on the primary JP team had talked about what had happened with Voth when they'd first visited him, and I hadn't asked.

Hawk drove down the sloping parking lot to the big modern addition at the back of the hotel where Voth had his massive stadium style theater. The loading bay door was already open and the bay empty, and we parked near the concrete steps at the back that led into the hotel.

"The clinic is the second door on the left," I said, trying to focus on what needed to be done before I passed out. Stitches for Sebastian and a little more blood for Rin would be ideal. "Titus, you get Cassius. Hawk, take Sebastian." He was going to get blood on his clothes, but I suspected it would be easier for Titus to manhandle Cassius's limp form with his wings out than Hawk.

I pushed open the door and climbed out of the SUV. The loading bay darkened and lurched, and I sucked in deep breaths, trying to stay focused.

All I needed to do was get to the clinic, stitch up Sebastian, and then Hawk could take over and get us into that suite.

With that held firmly in my mind, I staggered to the steps, but before I could climb them, Rin swept me into his arms and cradled me against his chest.

Everything within me froze with fear... *and* with desperate need.

His strange life force snapped across my senses, the physical contact allowing my magic to sense him past the backlash firestorm blazing inside me, and all of me strained for more. More of his life force, more of him.

His black gaze caught mine and my brain stalled again. Then he jerked his attention away, giving me no indication why he'd decided to help or if he was barely holding himself together against the same aching yearning or really anything. Had he decided he was safe with us? Or was it the brand forcing him to help me? Because the brand would do that. It would twist up a mate's insides until they couldn't do anything but help.

A spark of hellfire popped from his eye and he hurried us inside.

"The clinic's there," I said, pointing at the door.

He strode into the small room that was barely big enough to hold all the medical equipment Voth had packed in there along with the two gurneys. Rin set me by the first gurney, hesitated as if he wanted to stay close —and God, I wanted him to stay close—then moved as far away from me as the small room would allow. I guess he'd come to the same conclusion I had. The need to be close was the bond. It wasn't really how we were feeling.

"There's blood in the fridge," I said to him, pointing to the small fridge under the counter, thankfully close to him. "I can't do anything about feeding your magic right now, but we can end your hunger for blood."

Another spark popped from his eye, and I turned my attention to the sink, not waiting to see if he'd get the blood or not. I had other things to worry about. Like stitching up Sebastian before I passed out.

I scrubbed my hands clean as Titus and Hawk entered and set Cassius and Sebastian on the gurneys. Both men drew close to me, but gave me space to work, as if they wanted to be near me like Rin did but also didn't want to get in my way.

From the last time I'd been here, I knew the suture kits were in the cupboard over the counter to my left, and I pulled one out and set it on the counter by Sebastian's gurney. Then I turned to the cupboard on the other side of the sink where Voth kept his drugs. Sebastian didn't need a sedative, but it would still be good to numb the area around the laceration, or better yet, give him a strong analgesic that might help with *all* of his other pain until the shock and exhaustion of having used all of his magic had passed.

Except I was having trouble focusing on the small text on the vials.

Hawk inched closer to me so he could place a warm hand on my back while still holding Sebastian's bunched up shirt against his wound.

The fiery darkness of his life force slid across my senses and I leaned into his touch. It wasn't enough to completely steady me, but it helped.

"What do you need?" he asked.

"An analgesic, like morphine or—" My magic snapped inside me, stealing my breath and making me clutch the edge of the counter.

Oh, jeez. I needed more of my guys touching me, adding their life forces to Hawk, if I was going to get steady. And even then, given the backlash raging inside me, I wasn't sure it would help.

"Maybe you should talk me through stitching him up," Hawk said, moving my hand to Sebastian shirt to take over applying pressure and grabbing a vial from the shelf.

Yeah, maybe I should. "Wash your hands first. There are syringes in the drawer below the drug cupboard, and saline in that one." I pointed to the next cupboard over. "And you'll need gauze, and—"

Hawk's attention jerked up to the doorway. "What the hell?"

My thoughts stuttered, but I didn't have to look to see who'd arrived. Even with the backlash muting my ability to sense life forces, I could feel Voth's massive dark, burning force the moment Hawk had spoken, and I was pretty sure if my magic hadn't been slicing through me and my head pounding in agony, I would have felt the greater demon from all the way down the hall.

Except with him, just at the edge of my senses, was also a warm, bright life force that I didn't recognize... and likely the cause of Hawk's reaction.

I dragged my attention up to the doorway, the room around me twisting out of focus with the movement. We'd been promised discretion and a second person wasn't discrete.

Voth, an enormous man—as tall and broad as Titus —stormed through the doorway, radiating darkness and danger, and with him was my fellow healing angel Priam, a warm-natured, boy-next-door kind of guy, and the source of the other life force.

"Amiah!" Priam's eyes widened and his angel glow

flared. He grabbed a stool on wheels by the door and rushed to my side, urging me to sit. "You're glowing."

"Priam?" My sluggish thoughts lurched. He couldn't get involved in this. And why was he here? Not enough time had passed for Voth to call Operations and for Priam to get here... had it?

And that wasn't the point. Only Voth was supposed to know about us. Everyone else was in danger. That, and in that moment, I realized I hadn't wanted anyone to know I'd been branded. I'd hoped the Heart would get rid of it and no one but my guys—and Voth—would need to know the truth.

Priam's gaze flickered to Hawk, then he cupped my cheeks between his palms, forcing me to look him in the eyes, and a trickle of his healing magic slipped into me. But my magic lashed out at it, making him jerk his power back.

"What happened? I've never seen your backlash this bad or you hurt like this." He swept an appraising gaze over the rest of my guys, looking for anyone else who was injured like a good triage doctor, and I couldn't begin to imagine what he thought of us.

Titus was completely naked, but at least he gave off a shifter's essence, so his nudity could be explained—since a shifter's magic destroyed his clothing when he shifted —but Cassius's nudity couldn't be. While Rin's face was crusted with blood and Hawk still had a hand on me— something that, as an angel, was supposed to make me uncomfortable.

"Is Mr. Bane—?" Priam frowned.

Guess he'd finally looked past the tattoos covering

Sebastian's chest and arms and realized that he didn't look like himself, or rather, he didn't look like the glamour he'd used to hide his identity while in the mortal realm.

"Sebastian is worse than I am and Cassius is just unconscious from a sleep spell."

"And you promised discretion," Hawk said to Voth.

Priam's gaze slipped to Hawk again before he nudged my hand away from Sebastian's side and looked at the fae's wound.

"You promised a bonded couple," Voth shot back, his voice low and gravelly like far-off thunder, and I couldn't tell if he was angry at thinking we'd lied to him or not.

God, would he throw us out?

Priam might solve our healing problem—because he wouldn't abandon us if Voth kicked us out—but we still needed a safe place to rest and hide.

I tried to meet the demon's gaze through my swollen lids. Right now, he looked human, with the exception of his size and his all black eyes with their simmering hellfire. That was one of the things that made a greater demon a greater demon. They, like angels, could keep their wings—and in Voth's case his fangs and horns— inside their bodies and release them at will. But no one would ever mistake him for a human. Even if he hadn't been huge, he still radiated a ferocious heat from his increased demonic body temperature, revealing just how magically powerful he was. And right now, he looked more intimidating than I'd ever seen him.

"I don't like being lied to," Voth growled to Hawk. "You should have just said it was for the doctor."

My thoughts stuttered at that. "You remember me? But would you have helped us even though I'm not here with Essie?" I didn't know why Voth liked Essie, but he did and had gone out of his way to help and support her even though she was a nephilim—a being that up until a few weeks ago had been enemy number one to the whole world. I'd just been the angel who'd come along and patched everyone up. I was the angel who'd tried to stand between Essie and Marcus, and hadn't been very nice about it.

At the time, I'd thought I was protecting him, thought that she was going to shatter him because she'd branded the others and not him and she was being selfish for stringing him along. I'd thought he was my mate.

I'd thought a lot of foolish things.

"Of course I remember you," Voth said, leaning against the doorframe. "I'd know you even if you hadn't shown up with Essie. Priam hasn't stop talking about you for twenty-five years."

"What?" That didn't make sense.

I dragged my gaze to Priam. His eyes were closed and his hands pressed against Sebastian's laceration, blood oozing between his fingers and light radiating from his palms.

"I talk about other things than just Amiah," Priam said, releasing his magic.

"You talk about—?" I tried to focus my whirling thoughts. My good-natured friend talked to Voth? How did he even know the greater demon and— "What are you doing here?"

"It's poker night," Priam said, turning to the sink to wash Sebastian's blood from his hands.

"You play poker?" Voth's hotel had a casino, but I didn't know any angels who gambled. In fact, I wasn't sure any angels ever visited Voth's hotel. It just wasn't our style.

"He doesn't play poker. He *loses* poker," Voth said, rolling his eyes at my friend. "He's so bad we've stopped asking him to buy in and just give him chips."

I frowned. None of that made sense.

"Remember when I took that medic position close to the end of the war?" Priam said, cupping my cheeks again, and making both Hawk and Titus inch protectively closer to me. "I was Voth's medic. Those of us from the squad who are still alive get together once a month and play poker."

How had I not known Priam had been Voth's medic? We'd spent a lot of time working together during and after the war.

He shot a spike of healing magic through my neck sealing the laceration shut, making me gasp before I could clench my jaw and hold it in. Fast painful bursts were the only way he could heal me with my backlash raging inside me, and my concussion and nose were going to hurt worse than that. I just needed to grin and bear it until it was done.

But another spike, this one exploding in the back of my head, made me whimper, and Hawk stiffened and Titus growled.

"It's okay," I gasped. "It's the only way he can heal me with my backlash."

Titus huffed and Hawk didn't relax, and Voth straightened, his hellfire flaring.

"Well that's interesting," the greater demon said. "Maybe you didn't lie about a bonded couple. Or is it a bonded trio?"

"We've all just been through a lot," I said. God, I didn't want to confess anything about my bond in front of Priam. He'd never understand.

"It's more than that," Voth replied. "Both the incubus and the shifter had a rise in power at your pain. They wouldn't have had that reaction if you were just a normal angel to them."

Priam sent another spike of healing magic snapping through my head.

"I don't want to talk about it," I ground out, as Titus and Hawk drew closer, their bodies tenser.

"Amiah, if you're branded, that's amazing," Priam replied, his eyes wide with an awe that made my stomach churn. "First Essie, and now you—"

"I said, I don't want to talk about it."

"But that was the deal." The hellfire in Voth's eyes flared.

God, was he really going to attack us because I didn't want to tell him I was bonded? "The deal was I talk to you and *only* you."

"So you're ashamed to be bonded to a demon." The danger radiating from Voth grew as if the idea of me not wanting to be bonded to Hawk was a personal slight.

"That's not it."

"Then you're ashamed he's an incubus." More fire

sparked from his eyes. "He should be the one who's upset, fated to a lifetime of boring angel sex."

"Hey." Priam sent another painful spike into my head, this one wrenching my broken nose back into place, making me cry out in pain and my eyes water.

"Prove it isn't true," Voth said to Priam. "Prove angels are more adventurous than the rumors say. Show me."

Priam rolled his eyes at Voth not seeming to care about the danger radiating from the demon. "I'm not letting you watch me have sex, and I doubt Amiah will let you watch, either."

"My point exactly," Voth replied.

"I'm not ashamed to be bonded to an incubus. I wish I was bonded with Hawk."

Voth's eyebrows raised at that. "Then who are you bonded with?"

"Does it matter?" Hawk asked.

"I'm just surprised an angel doesn't want to tell everyone how special she is," Voth said, his gaze locking on me and his eyes narrowing.

God, he wasn't going to give up, and I had no idea why.

And in the end it didn't really matter. We needed his help. "Because I'm in love with someone else."

Hawk added his other hand to my back, adding another point of contact even though it was through my scrub top, and his life force swelled against my senses, steadying me a bit, as Voth's expression turned sad.

"You might love him now," Voth said, "but I've seen the truth of the soul bond. You're meant to be with your mate. You always have been."

Except I didn't want to accept that. It couldn't be true. I *knew* I needed Hawk, Sebastian, Titus, *and* Cassius. I didn't feel that way about Rin... at least I didn't think I did.

No. I didn't. It was just the soul bond messing with my emotions.

Priam sent another painful snap of magic into me and the agony in my face vanished. I still had the pain of my backlash, but there wasn't anything he could do about that.

"Okay," Priam said, turning to the sink and washing his hands again. "You're good to go."

Hawk grabbed Priam's arm. "She's still in pain."

Priam blinked, as if his thoughts had stalled, then gave his head a sharp shake and jerked his attention away from Hawk as if he couldn't look at the incubus and speak at the same time. "I can't heal her backlash. Just like I can't get rid of whatever is causing Mr. Bane's pain. It's magical, not physical."

"It's okay." I turned my attention to Voth, who was still looking at me with pity.

It felt like he knew the hurt caused when an angelic brand formed but not between the people who were in love. Except I wasn't sure exactly how I knew that.

"Is there any way our deal could involve clothes as well as the place to stay the night?" I asked.

Although given that I hadn't told him who I was mated with, I wasn't sure if we still had a place to stay.

"I'll have clothes sent up to the suite," Voth said.

Guess not knowing everything was okay with him. Thank God.

"It doesn't have to be a suite," I quickly added. "It can be the same rooms as last time."

Those had been the plain rooms at the back of the hotel that he gave to his visiting performers. And while I'd have liked to have kept everyone together, beggars couldn't be choosers.

"I have a show moving in later tonight. You can have those rooms, but you'll get noticed, and the incubus made it clear you wanted discretion."

"The less people who see us, the safer everyone is," Hawk said, and Titus huffed his agreement.

Voth heaved a heavy sigh. "It must be something serious if you're not going to Operations."

"It is." I turned back to Priam. "Do Cassius and I even have jobs any more?"

We probably didn't, given that we were on probation from the last time we'd run to Voth's hotel and had abandoned our jobs again.

"Chris has kept your disappearance a secret from head office, but he doesn't know how much longer he can do that," Priam said.

My throat tightened. Neither Priam nor Chris were obligated to protect us. In fact, if head office found out they'd been withholding information, they could lose their jobs, too.

"If head office presses, tell them the truth. Don't lose your jobs over this."

"It won't come to that," Priam said.

God, I hoped not. I'd miss working for the JP, but I could handle having to work—and possibly live—somewhere else. Cassius's whole world had been the JP since the war had ended, and I had no idea how he'd handle losing his job.

Of course, if we didn't survive what was coming, or if I couldn't get the Winter Court to release its hold on me, it wouldn't matter if I had a job or a home to return to.

CHAPTER 14

AMIAH

Voth sent a quick text then led us—with Titus carrying Cassius, Hawk carrying Sebastian, and Priam supporting me—down the hall deeper into the hotel to a plain door marked EMPLOYEES ONLY.

Inside was a narrow gray cinderblock and concrete hall that led to a small vestibule with a metal security door that presumably led outside, and an elevator door that was locked by a card reader.

Voth pulled two cards from his pocket. "Both of these will open all the doors, the suite's door, the elevator, and the outside door in case you need to leave and come back." He used one to open the elevator then handed both of them to me. "Your clothes will be sent up in the dumb-waiter in the kitchen. And that's how your room service will arrive. Try to order the most expensive things on the menu. That will draw the least amount of attention."

"How much will that cost us?" Hawk asked.

The door started to close and Voth pressed his big

hand against it, holding it open. "Nothing more than you've already paid. I'm taking a loss, but you're Priam's friend and someday I might need your help."

"You know if you asked, I'd help you regardless," I said.

"Not all angels would." His hellfire flared. "You helped Essie and her mates even after you knew what she was, even after the Director had proclaimed her a criminal, and even when it was clear you were unhappy. I've met angels with healing who aren't so generous. Your kind doesn't make the same vows as human doctors and I had real trouble finding one to join an all demon squad during the war."

Which was how he'd ended up with Priam. Because Priam had almost as hard a time saying no to someone in need as I did. I'd met a few of those angels who were selective in who and how they healed, but they didn't have the same compulsion that I did that forced them to heal whether they wanted to or not. Of course, they also weren't as powerful as me. Priam had a bit of the compulsion, but not to the same degree, and his power was somewhere in between them and me. But Priam was also a good man. He understood that any demon who'd decided to join the Angelic Defense was just as good as any shifter or human or angel—and because of Michael, I couldn't understand how any angel could still claim to hold the moral high ground just because they were angels.

"The steak with the truffle sauce is amazing," Priam added, helping me shuffle into the elevator.

Hawk snorted, following us. "You might regret that offer. Titus could probably eat a horse."

Titus rolled his eyes at him. "Two if I shift."

"How does that work?" Hawk asked as Rin stepped in, again moving as far away from me as he could in the small space. "Your human stomach isn't big enough to hold a horse, let alone two."

Titus shrugged, making Cassius's wings brush against the back of the elevator. "It's a shifter thing. We lose our clothes, but we don't have to worry about overeating in our beast form."

Voth rolled his eyes at my guys. "The suite doesn't have a booking until late next week."

"And you can call me if you need anything." Priam leaned me against the elevator wall and joined Voth back in the vestibule. "Get rest. All of you."

The greater demon let the elevator door close and, without us pressing a button, it took us up to the suite's small but lavish vestibule. Not that we could have pressed a button. There weren't any in the elevator.

The vestibule had a gold and crystal chandelier that brightly lit cream-colored walls and reflected in the black marble floor. Both the suite's door and the elevator's door were black, and the black, cream, and gold theme carried into a suite that was the size of Sebastian's apartment.

Actually, it was probably bigger. The suite had a formal entrance with a coat closet. To the right was a full kitchen and a formal dining room with a table that sat eight, and ahead and to the left stretched a luxurious living room with a large bank of floor-to-ceiling windows taking up the far wall. Beyond, lay a large patio with potted trees and shrubs and an amazing view of the city's Supernatural Quarter, while stairs at the back of the living room led up to three bedrooms—presumably all with en suites—and an office.

Warm soft light emanated from all of the bedroom doorways, and when I glanced into the closest one, I confirmed that the bedside light had been turned on and the crisp white sheets and black comforter on the king bed had been folded back, ready and waiting. And God, I just wanted to fall into one of them and pass out.

Except I was in burned and bloody clothing. The only one of us who wasn't filthy was Cassius.

"Let's get Cassius and Sebastian in bed," I said. I'd managed to make it up the stairs by clinging to the railing with Titus behind me to stop me if I fell, but I was running out of strength. Sure, with my concussion gone, I was no longer dizzy, but my backlash was still slicing through me, and I was exhausted.

"You need to get in bed, too," Hawk said, setting Sebastian on the black comforter of the closest bedroom and pulling it over him instead of tucking him in while he was still filthy.

"I will. I just want to clean up and then be with Cassius when he wakes." We'd been in Faerie the last time he'd been fully conscious, and I didn't want him to wake alone and naked in a strange place.

That, and I wanted to tell him about Rin before he saw Rin to avoid burning down the hotel.

"Titus, if you and Rin are hungry, order something from room service." I didn't doubt given that Voth catered to every known super, that he'd have food as well as blood. Voth probably had a license to house blood bunnies for those vampires who wanted to drink straight from the vein.

I dragged my gaze back to Hawk. "I won't be able to help you for a bit." And really, I needed to have sex with Titus before I had sex again with Hawk. It was a miracle Titus was still managing to control his beast, and I needed to help him mend that connection even if I wasn't at full strength. He wasn't going to last much longer, especially if I kept sleeping with the others and not him.

Hawk dipped in and brushed his lips against mine with a whisper of a kiss that sent soft heat unfurling within me. It wasn't strong enough to set off my desire— or rather make my desperate need for Rin any stronger— but it did help ease a bit of my pain.

"I'm fine," he said. "You take care of you for once."

He wasn't fine. His life force wasn't as strong as it should have been, but none of my guys were fine, and neither was Rin.

"The first time Bane broke the Winter Queen's tracking spell it was a little more than twenty-four hours before Padraigin showed up in his apartment," Hawk said. "We have a day. We have time to catch our breaths." His gaze slid to Rin and went slightly out of focus, a sign he was using his magical sensitivity to check for something, probably spells. "It's easier for me to restore my magic than the others, so when Amiah gets me back up, I'll let you feed on me."

Which meant Rin was going to have to wait to satisfy his sin eater's hunger. The question was, did he trust Hawk to keep his word?

Except there wasn't anything I could do about it if he didn't. I could only hope he wasn't going to attack us while we were down since there was no place to lock him up. That, and I didn't really want to lock him up. He'd had a chance to kill me and he hadn't. He might not be a perfect match for me, but a part of me, the part that even now with my magic raging inside me could still sense that whisper of pain forever trapped in his cells, wanted to believe he wasn't evil like Deaglan.

My magic sliced deep, making me gasp, and all of their gazes leaped to me. Hawk with heartbreaking worry, Titus with worry and need, and Rin with... nothing. But he *had* looked and I couldn't help thinking that just looking meant something.

Titus put Cassius in bed, on his back with his wings spread out behind him and the black comforter pulled up to the middle of his chest, then went back down stairs.

The tension in his body twisted at my heart even though there was nothing I could do about it right now. He needed me. Out of all of them, he was the one who needed me the most, and I was too weak to help him. I could only hope whatever rest I got while I waited for Cassius to wake up would be enough to make me look strong enough for Titus to think it was safe for us to have sex.

I went into the en suite of Cassius's bedroom to clean up, turned on the shower, and stared at myself in the mirror while I waited for the water to warm up.

Priam, as usual, had healed everything. My nose was back to normal, my eyes no longer swollen, and I knew once I cleaned away the blood on my neck, there wouldn't even be a scar where the cut had been. He'd even finished healing my burned hand. I still, however, looked like a mess. Blood crusted my lips and chin, my right cheek, and down my neck, and had soaked into my burned scrub top.

Groaning, I peeled off my top and stepped out of my pants, leaving them in a heap on the floor that I'd deal with later, and stepped into the shower.

As much as I wanted to just stand there and soak, Cassius could wake at anytime. It was actually a little surprising he'd slept through the fight. Although given that I'd pumped too much magic into Sebastian's sleep glyph the last time I'd used it, and had been in a panic when casting it on Cassius, it wouldn't have surprised me if I'd used too much magic on him too.

I quickly showered, my backlash surging and snapping through me, dried off, and wrapped myself in one of the thick plush robes hanging on the back of the bathroom door, then dragged a heavy chair from the corner of the room to the bed.

My soul ached at just sitting there. I wanted to crawl under the covers with Cassius, but we'd only had sex once and hadn't had time to figure out our relationship, not to mention the last time we'd woken up together, he'd nearly lost control of his magic, something I really wanted to avoid.

That, and once he learned I was soul bonded with Rin, we wouldn't have a relationship.

The thought made my heart ache. I loved Cassius. I wanted a relationship with him and all my guys. But he, like everyone else, knew that the mating brand would make me fall in love with Rin and fall out of love with him. And while I desperately wanted to have as much as I could with Cassius for as long as I could, he wouldn't want that, not knowing I belonged with someone else.

And while I could try to keep Rin a secret from him, that would only make things worse. Even if I could somehow hide my brand from Cassius, the others knew the truth and it wouldn't be fair to them to ask them to hide it.

No matter how much it hurt, Cassius had to know, and it was best if he heard it from me.

I curled up in the chair, letting Cassius's strong fiery life force thrum against my senses, thrilled and sad that he was alive but no longer mine, and closed my eyes.

Despite the backlash, I dreamed of cold and darkness, and of being trapped, unable to move, and forgotten. No one was coming to save me. No one knew I existed. But I did exist. I *wanted* to exist. I didn't understand how they couldn't remember me. They needed me just like I needed them, but the darkness was too thick, my cage too strong, no one could hear my screaming, my begging, and I was never going to be free.

And then the cold deepened, crackling like a fast-moving frost through my essence. The Winter Court. Yet another prison. It called to me, had forced itself into my soul, and was never going to let go. I couldn't hide from it forever. It would find me. It would possess me. I'd be imprisoned in its icy essence.

That was the deal I'd made to save my guys.

I belonged to it, and my soul bond with Rin was

nothing compared to the chain the Winter Court had wrapped inside me.

A blast of ice sliced through me, stealing my breath and jerking me awake.

Except it hadn't been ice. It had been my backlash.

"Amiah?" a groggy tenor asked, making my heart soar.

I'd heard that voice for over a hundred years, loved that voice, and I loved the man it belonged to.

I raised my gaze to meet Cassius's. His blue eyes—so like mine—were filled with life and light and love and desire. He was alive and well and he was at full power. He sat up, pulling in his wings with a flash of white angelic magic and giving me a perfect view of his beautifully muscled chest and arms. The memory of him naked, his stunning physique moving on top of me, rushed through my mind's eye and sent a tremor of desire racing to my core.

He'd be furious to know we'd thrown him into the back of the SUV without any clothes and mortified at being naked in Voth's clinic. Having spent most of that face-down didn't make it any better... only gave me really good memories of his tight glutes and how much I wanted to clutch those glutes when we—

"Hey," I said, suddenly feeling awkward. And while yes, I wanted to have sex with him again, what I really wanted in this moment was to wrap my arms around him, never let him go, and tell him how much I loved him. But that wasn't fair to him, not until he knew the truth.

His angel glow dimmed with worry and his expression darkened. "Who did we lose?"

"Lose?"

"I can see it in your eyes." A hint of smoke curled around him and the muscles in his jaw flexed. "You're upset. Who didn't survive the fight with Deaglan?"

"Everyone is alive. You were the worse and—" My throat tightened and another snap of backlash sliced through me.

More smoke curled from his skin and he clenched his hands. "God, I want to hold you, but..."

But he couldn't control his magic if he held me. Before he'd been injured, he'd barely been able to control it just being near me.

In fact, I needed to make this as emotionless as possible for his sake.

I drew in a sharp breath and tried to draw on my professional persona, but too much had happened. That Amiah was gone. I was never going to be her again. Everything I'd thought and believed had been wrong. I could never have enough control over my life or be careful enough to guarantee I'd be safe. I'd been taken again and hurt worse than the first time. I belonged to the Winter Court and without a doubt it was looking for me, determined to take me back to Faerie.

And really, I didn't want to be that cold, desperate-to-be-in-control woman any more. She'd only hurt me, made me ignore a part of myself that I hadn't realized I needed.

Except who I needed were Cassius and my other guys, something I didn't know how to keep while I was soul bonded with Rin.

"Whatever it is, we can get through it," he said.

"I don't know if we can. My mating brand formed."

Another burst of smoke swept around him. "I thought you got rid of it."

"I thought I had."

"Oh God, Amiah. I'm so sorry." The light in his eyes flared. "Maybe it won't be the prison you're afraid of. Just because you're bonded doesn't mean you're trapped. You were already feeling a connection with us—" His eyes widened and realization flashed across his expression. "It's just with one of us, isn't it? And it isn't with me." His voice turned hard and his expression icy. But I knew now that wasn't because he was angry. It was because he was trying to control his emotions and not let his fire escape his body. "Who is it? I hate that it isn't me, but all of them have proven that they're worthy of you."

"The demon-vampire hybrid," I forced out.

"Deaglan's hybrid?" Flames burst around Cassius's hands, lighting the comforter on fire. "Shit."

He clenched his jaw and the flames swept back under his skin, but now he was so tense, he trembled.

I jerked forward to help him—which was stupid because there wasn't anything I could do to help—and managed to force myself to sit back before touching him and making the situation worse. Going to him would just make everything more difficult. "You still think this is okay?"

"There's got to be a reason you branded him."

"Because fate is cruel and the brand is a lie. Everything about the mating brand has been a lie." I bit back a bitter laugh. "How is being soul bonded with someone I don't love beautiful? Fate had four guys to choose from. Four guys who I *know* I love."

His eyes widened at that.

"Yes. I love you. I thought you'd died and it killed me knowing I'd been too afraid to tell you the truth because I also love Sebastian and Hawk and Titus. And even though you said you'd wait, that still meant you were going to ask me to give them up. Now I have to give all of you up." Tears of frustration burned my eyes. It wasn't fair. And while I knew life wasn't fair, it just made me so angry that I'd finally figured a part of myself out and was finally starting to accept who I was, and now fate had taken that away. "I know in my soul I need all of you and I refuse to let the mating brand change how I feel."

"So how do we fix this?" he asked.

My thoughts stuttered at that, but only for a second and then my heart soared. God, I loved him. He hadn't said it couldn't be fixed, even though everything we'd been taught said it couldn't be. This was the man who'd had my back from the moment he'd rescued me from that faith healer's tent... well, from the moment he decided I wasn't going to emotionally fall apart and had stopped looking at me like I was weak and pathetic. This was my best friend. This was the man who'd been missing since the war, the one I'd been desperate to get back.

Who I was *going* to get back.

"I'm hoping Faerie's Heart will be able to break the bond."

"Then we'll get Faerie's Heart," he said.

My backlash surged, slicing deep, and I gasped, making him frown.

"Backlash?" he asked.

"Yeah."

His frown deepened, but he didn't ask me what happened. He knew if I'd fought my magic and refused to heal someone I'd had a good reason. "You'll get rid of it faster if you sleep."

"I know, but I wanted to tell you about Rin—"

"Rin?"

"The hybrid. His name is Rin. He's here with us. The others dragged him into the mortal realm with us when we fled Faerie," I said, realizing I still had a lot of explaining to do. Cassius might not have known that we were back in the mortal realm until I'd just off-handedly mention it. "You needed to know about him and I wanted you to hear it from me."

"Do we trust him?"

"I want to, but I don't know if that's the brand making me feel that way or not," I said. "I haven't had a chance to really talk with him, but I know he was Deaglan's slave, was tortured, and is angry about that."

"Which will either make him more dangerous, or an ally." Cassius drew in a deep breath and reached to push the comforter and sheets back but paused, probably realizing he was naked. His expression grew pained and more fire sparked over his hands, but he managed to suck it back before lighting the comforter on fire again. "It'd be best if you left. Give me a few minutes to get into the bathroom, then you can have the bed."

"Right." I stood.

His gaze dipped to my breasts and I realized the robe had slipped open a bit. Not enough to be indecent, but enough to show an enticing amount of cleavage.

I tugged the fabric closed. "There are other rooms. You can keep this one. No one will make you share."

"But you'll share," he said, his voice suddenly low and dangerous, smoke curling from his arms. "How many more beds are there?"

"Two others." Which meant I was most likely going to share with more than just one of the guys. "Does that upset you?"

I wasn't sure I wanted the answer, but a part of me needed to know. I'd really liked falling asleep with all of my guys, but I only had two sides. Not everyone would get to sleep beside me and while Hawk didn't care who he slept with, and Sebastian didn't seem to mind either so long as I was present, I still wasn't sure about Titus or Cassius.

"Only if they don't give you what you need," he replied, and I realized his tone wasn't anger, but desire.

Another flame licked up his forearm and the comforter caught on fire again.

"Fuck." He wrenched his gaze away from me and the flames vanished. "You need to leave before I accidentally hurt you, and I need to get someplace less flammable."

God, I wanted to stay. We'd only just begun to explore our desire for each other, but he was right. Until he could get his magic under control, I needed to keep my distance.

I hurried into the dimly lit hall, closed the door behind me, and stood there, not sure what to do. Yes, I needed to go to bed, but a part of me didn't want to go to bed alone.

Somewhere down stairs, I heard Titus say something, but his voice was just a little too quiet for me to make out his words. Given that the light in the living room was on, he was most likely talking with someone, and since Sebastian was probably still unconscious, Cassius was in the room behind me, and Rin practically mute, Titus had to be talking with Hawk. And while it wouldn't be fair to Titus to ask him to just sleep with me and not have sex, I could ask Hawk.

I turned to head downstairs but stopped at the sight of Rin kneeling on the office floor with his eyes closed.

The only light in the room came from the weak illumination in the hall, but with my night vision it was clear he'd washed the blood from his face. He still wore the same calf-length wrap tunic and leather pants as before, and while I couldn't see the blood on his black clothes, I had no doubt it was still there. A part of me wanted to believe that made him a monster. That would make it easier to hate him and resist our bond. He'd tried to kill me. He'd killed that man in Left of Lincoln without any emotion. But that silvery scar across his neck and the pain imprinted in his cells said he'd only done whatever it had taken to survive captivity at the hands of a real monster.

My desire for him swelled, overwhelming the pain of my backlash for a second, and I gritted my teeth against my aching need. That was just because of my brand. And yet, my body still took a tentative step toward him before I realized what I was doing.

CHAPTER 15

AMIAH

Rin opened his eyes. He must have heard me step closer. Heck, with his vampire-enhanced hearing, he'd probably heard my pulse pick up with my yearning.

Be mine. Seal our bond.

Tears burned my eyes.

I didn't want him. I wanted them. Why couldn't fate have bound me with them?

"You love all of them? Not just your husband?" he asked, surprising me. Not because his voice had changed —he'd still spoken in that intense whisper—but because he'd spoken first and more than a single word.

And then my thoughts stuttered on that. "My husband?"

He'd said that before when we'd been in Sebastian's clean room, but there'd been more important things to talk about.

"Prince Seireadan," he said.

Oh. He thought—

But of course he did. He didn't know we'd lied to the

Winter Queen so Sebastian wouldn't have to marry a stranger on the spot, and everyone thought because the Winter Court's wind responded to me that I was Sebastian's wife.

A part of me wondered if maybe that was true, if somehow we *were* married. Except even if it was, Sebastian would never accept that. He'd sworn he'd never be bound to anyone like that and as much as the idea of letting him go hurt, I wouldn't keep him when he said he wanted to end whatever it was between us. Besides, if I couldn't resist my bond with Rin, none of that would matter.

"He's not my husband." I said against the lump in my throat.

Jeez. Couldn't I just be strong for a minute? But grieving over the loss of someone wasn't a weakness. Not doing anything when there were things I could do, was.

And I hadn't given up. I was going to get the Heart and keep my men... those who wanted to stay with me.

A spark snapped from Rin's eye. "But you love him."

And I was going to free Rin from this mess as well.

"I do." I didn't know how. With the exception of Cassius, I barely knew the men I'd fallen in love with, but I loved them and knew I needed them. "I love all of them, and I promise, I'll find a way to remove our bond."

I took another step toward him, my unwanted desire throbbing between my thighs even as my backlash sliced through my body.

Rin's hellfire swelled into miniature flames and a hint of hunger bled into his expression before quickly vanishing.

"Did you get more blood?" I asked.

"Do all vampires in the mortal realm drink blood in a bag?"

If he was asking that, it meant he hadn't had much experience with this realm. Although maybe he just hadn't had mundane experiences. He'd been Deaglan's assassin and had probably spent most of his time hiding in the shadows—even though I was sure his demonic nature made him immune to sunlight, unlike most vampires.

"No," I said. The memory of him biting me and his seductive magic swelling inside me rushed through me, making my voice breathy.

I swallowed a moan and struggled to stay where I was. I did *not* want him. I didn't. "Most vampires don't drink bagged blood, but you need consent."

"And that's hard to get?"

"No." God, I needed him.

I took another step toward him, but my backlash surged, thankfully cutting through my need, and I forced myself back to the doorway.

If I was smart, I'd just leave him until I could get myself under control, but I also wanted to earn his trust. Everything would be easier if we weren't watching our backs or chasing after him.

"There are people who look for vampires to feed on them and people who've made that their profession," I said. "They're called blood bunnies."

"Are there magic bunnies?"

"No. There aren't any sin eaters left in the mortal

realm." I hadn't thought there were any sin eaters left in any of the realms.

His hellfire sparked then shrank back to smoldering red pinpricks.

"But don't worry," I added, praying that him shutting down what little emotion he'd shown wasn't because he thought we were going to let him starve like Deaglan had. "Hawk said he'd let you feed on his magic just as soon as I can restore it for him."

My magic surged with a painful burst, tearing at my insides and drawing a pained gasp before I could stop it. "I just need to get through this backlash."

Another spark snapped from his eye. The smoldering red ember drifted to the floor and hissed when it hit the marble before going out.

"I'm sorry, but that'll probably be a few days," I added.

Except we didn't have a few days, not before the Winter Queen recast her tracking spell on me and we had to run again.

He continued to stare at me, no indication he understood what I'd said or that he'd done the same math and knew that he wouldn't be able to satiate his sin eater's hunger until after we'd run for our lives again, something we needed to figure out how to stop doing.

But we'd been reeling since this whole mess had started and every time we seemed to figure something out, something else threw everything into chaos.

My backlash snapped again, this one so sharp it made me whimper.

And if I couldn't get my magic to calm down and

regain control of it, I wouldn't be able to save any of my guys if we ended up in a fight again.

"I need to get something to eat and some rest."

With Rin.

My desire for him surged again, and I gritted my teeth and forced myself to stay where I was.

No. I needed to do it with Titus or Hawk or both of them.

No. I needed to go to bed. Alone. At least until my backlash was gone.

"Rest will help with the backlash," I said. "With luck it'll pass within the day."

Except my luck lately had been terrible.

"I can ease your backlash," he said, with still no indication of an emotion in his expression. "If I take some of your magic, the storm inside you will dissipate."

"And by take you mean feed on me."

"Yes."

My pulse picked up with a horrifying mix of fear and desire. Feeding meant he'd have to come close. And God, I *wanted* him close.

No. I want the others. It's just the brand. It isn't real.

"I can't afford to lose too much magic," I said, my voice back to frustratingly breathy. If I could access my magic, I could save my guys, but only if I had enough left.

Was it worth the risk?

Did I really have much of a choice?

No.

If letting Rin feed on me meant I'd never have to go through thinking one of them was dead again, I'd do it.

"Can you control your hunger?" I asked.

"Yes."

"Can you control your desire?" Could I control mine?

His hellfire swelled into miniature flames for a second before returning to smoldering pinpricks. "Yes."

"Okay."

He stood and my pulse throbbed. My whole body throbbed. God, I needed him, needed to connect with him, seal our bond—

I gripped the doorframe as if that would help me stay where I was as he drew closer. For a second his hold on his essence slipped—I hadn't even realized he'd been holding it back—and I saw who he really was, felt the full intensity of his demon-vampire nature, alive yet dead, dark, and completely dangerous.

But then my magical senses connected with his life force and I felt his pain. Yes, he was a predator, a creature of the night who fed on blood and magic, but he was also a man who'd suffered greatly. That, and he couldn't do anything about his nature. He was who he was and the sense from his essence wasn't a sense of *who* he was, only *what* he was.

Then he pulled his essence back and returned to the dark, silent man who'd been kneeling alone in the office.

"I'll have more control if we connect with our lips," he said.

"You mean kiss." The idea sent a shudder of desire racing through me that sunk hot and sultry into my core.

"Yes." His gaze dipped to my lips.

A small part of me screamed that I should get one of the other guys, have them chaperone this... feeding, but the rest of me was possessed by the brand, and it was all I could do to not throw myself at him.

"Make it quick." I didn't know how long I'd be able to hold my desire at bay.

"Yes, your highness," he breathed, using the title I'd have had if I really were Sebastian's wife.

I opened my mouth to argue, tell him I wasn't a highness, or princess, or whatever I was, but he slid a cool hand over my cheek, tangling his fingers into my hair, and pressed his lips against mine.

Any words or thoughts I might have had vanished. His strange life force surged against my senses, and my need for him twisted in my core, an insistent throbbing, urging me to complete the bond. I tried to swallow my moan of desire, but a soft, breathy sound still escaped my mouth.

His grip tightened and he deepened the kiss, turning it into something more than just touching our lips, and yet it was still soft and sensual, a strange contrast with his life force and essence.

I wasn't sure what I'd expected. But it hadn't been tenderness. It made my unwanted desire billow, drawing another moan and making my knees weak.

Then a crackling thread of magic shot into my mouth, down my throat, and wrapped around my heart. It sliced into my backlash, even as my desire for him grew.

I gasped at the sudden pain and Rin cupped my other cheek, fully capturing my head. His magic grabbed something inside me, deep in my heart, and started pulling it up my throat and into his mouth.

Panic seized me and I tried to wrench away from him—

Or was I trying to get closer?

No, get away. *Get away!*

But he held tight, his lips still capturing mine, making it impossible to call for help. I could feel my magic pouring out of me, warm and viscous like how it felt when I pushed it out of my palms. Except this was rushing up my throat, making me gag.

My backlash sliced and heaved, still a wild storm raging inside me, but the core of it was weakening, sucked up by Rin, and was being replaced with my desperate, burning need for him.

I clutched the front of his tunic, caught between wanting to get away from him and wanting to get closer, and my breath turned ragged.

Then Rin's crackling magic snapped free and shot out of my mouth back into him and my backlash suddenly shattered, my desire surging to fill the void.

With a low soft groan, he shoved me against the door-frame, pinning me there. He slid his tongue into my mouth, returning our lip lock to a kiss that was anything but soft. It was hard and desperate and made the brand on my hip blaze bright with a golden heat that shone through the bathrobe.

Everything within me cheered. *Oh, yes. Yes!* This was what I wanted.

But it wasn't. God, why was that so hard to remember?

I. Didn't. Want. This.

"No," I gasped, tensing at the same time Rin tensed, and he pulled his lips away as if he too had remembered his desire for me wasn't real.

Gasping, he pressed his forehead against mine. "I'm not feeding on you again."

"Not until the brand is gone," I said, trembling with need and fear and frustration at the brand's control over my body.

"You'd let me feed on you after we're separated?"

"If you're still caught up in this mess. Yes," I said. "I'm not going to let you starve."

"What will your lovers think?"

"It's my body. My choice." Although I was pretty sure that was going to be a huge argument with all of them. But it didn't matter what any of them wanted. No one deserved to be starving, and the pain imprinted in Rin's cells made my healing compulsion twist in my gut. I might not be able to do anything about it, but I could deal with his current suffering.

Except a part of me screamed that I only felt that way because of the brand. I didn't know him. Yes, Deaglan had treated him badly, but that didn't mean he wasn't also a bad person. For all I knew, he enjoyed killing people.

"It'd be better if I didn't," he said, as movement in the hall caught our attention.

We both looked up as Titus, dressed in a pair of beige shorts and nothing else, snarled and lunged at Rin.

Rin jerked away from me, sidestepped Titus's punch, and used the big man's forward momentum to toss him face-first to the office floor.

Titus hit with a hard thud, crashing into the heavy dark-wood desk at the back of the room, but leaped to his feet and curled his lips back, flashing his extended canines at Rin. He flexed his hands and claws grew from his fingers, while his pupils slitted and his life force writhed in a wild, ferocious frenzy. His beast was taking control.

Oh, crap. I'd put off having sex with him for too long.

"I said you're never touching her again," he growled, his muscles bunching, ready to attack.

"Stop." I jumped between him and Rin before he could strike, and raised my hands to him. My pulse roared in my ears, a mix of fear and frustrating desire, and I prayed Titus still had enough control over his beast that he'd listen to me. "I said he could. He's calmed some of my backlash."

Footsteps pounded from down the hall as well as up the stairs and Cassius—in a robe—hurried into the study, smoke billowing around him. Hawk—in a light blue T-shirt and beige shorts—was right behind him, his hellfire blazing.

"It's okay." God, this could get out of hand quickly. "I'm okay."

Red-gold scales rippled up Titus's neck and along his jaw, and his trembling increased. He was trying to fight his beast's instinct to protect me, but he'd spent too long in Deaglan's captivity without being able to shift or having the flesh-to-flesh contact that his shifter's soul needed.

"Titus." I took a step toward him and held out my hand in invitation for him to take it. My soul ached for his pain even as my desire for Rin still throbbed inside me.

No, I wanted Titus.

Except I wanted both Titus and Rin. If I was being honest with myself, I wanted all of them.

"Let me help you. Let's heal your two halves." That

would go a long way to helping him think straight. Logically he *knew* he couldn't kill Rin, but his beast wasn't logical. It was wild primal emotion, and I didn't know if right now it was thinking beyond believing that I was in danger.

"Amiah, please," Cassius begged. "Wait until your backlash has passed."

"Her backlash is a fraction of what it was before," Hawk said. "You're magically weaker, but not drained."

"Not helping," Cassius snapped. "At least let Titus regain control of his beast."

Titus snorted and smoke curled from his nostrils. His life force grew stronger as his human nature battled with his beast's, neither able to accept each other or properly reform their connection.

And it was worse than before. There'd been a time in the Winter Court where I'd thought he was on the mend, that just flesh-to-flesh contact and being able to shift might be enough, but now it was clear he needed more, and I could only pray I'd be enough.

"He's not going to be able to regain control without help. We've waited too long." I took another step toward him. One more and I'd be able to press my palms against his bare chest. Hopefully, even though I wasn't a dragon or his mate, I'd be able to help him. God, everything within me yearned to help him.

Except he needed so much more than just steadying now. He needed to re-find that balance between the two halves of his soul, he needed to trust his beast.

"I can get control," he said through gritted teeth. The scales melted back into his skin, but his chest heaved with rapid breaths and his expression was tight with pain.

"You don't have to do it alone." I took the final step and pressed both of my palms to his broad muscular chest and a part of me thrilled at the contact even as my need for Rin throbbed stronger.

Titus stiffened instead of relaxing like I'd hoped and the scales swept back up his neck, but his frenzied life force whirled into a more cohesive storm, both parts of him sharing a desire for me.

Yes. Complete our connection. Make me forget about Rin, just for a little while.

He wrenched his attention past me to the others. "Get out."

"No." Cassius jerked forward a step, fire curling up his forearms.

Titus wrapped an arm around me and yanked me tight against his body, sending desire rushing to my core as my gaze flickered to Rin.

No. I heaved my attention back to Titus who bared his teeth and snarled, his beast fully taking control. "Get. Out."

"Not until I know she's safe," Cassius said, surprising me. He wasn't saying no to me being with Titus like I— and probably everyone else—expected, he was saying I could when Titus got his beast under control.

Except Titus wasn't going to get his beast fully under control until I helped him, and to do that, I needed to trust and accept him. All of him.

And even then it was a longshot to healing his soul. Yes, we had a connection, but given how broken his connection was with his beast, it might not be enough... or it might confirm what he believed, that I was his mate, since connecting with a mate's soul was the most powerful and steadying connection a shifter could make.

Which excited and terrified me at the same time. I needed him. I needed all of them. But if I was his soul mate and I couldn't break my bond with Rin or add to it, Titus, along with Hawk and Cassius, was going to get hurt.

"Titus, let her go," Cassius repeated. "At least until you've gotten your beast under control."

"No," Titus— or rather his beast growled.

"Cassius. I'm safe." I reached up and urged Titus to press his forehead against mine, adding another point of contact and drawing his focus away from Cassius and back to me. "Your beast isn't going to hurt me."

I need you. I don't need Rin.

Titus shuddered and closed his eyes, his whole body tense and trembling. "I don't know that he isn't."

"I do," I said. God, the others had to get out of there so I could take off my robe and press more of my flesh against his... to have him inside me and complete the circuit that I knew we shared just like I shared with the others. "We have a connection. I know it in my soul, in the core of my being, and branding Rin isn't going to change that." *Please, God, don't let it change that.* "You know that, and so does your beast. He's not going to hurt me."

"But you're not a dragon. I'm too strong. I need to be careful."

"And your beast knows that as well." I wasn't interested in mixing pain into my sexual experiences, but that didn't mean the guys had to treat me like I was glass. I could handle a bit of roughness. In fact, the idea made me ache for it, for a repeat of my first time with Sebastian or my first kiss with Hawk where both men had completely taken control, overwhelmed me, and sent me reeling in the most amazing way.

I turned to Cassius and Hawk in the doorway, but my gaze slid past them to Rin, standing in the corner, his expression revealing nothing about how he felt.

My desire for him churned stronger and I struggled to force it into my desire for Titus. What I felt for Rin wasn't real. My need for Titus was.

"I'm helping Titus heal his soul," I said, dragging my attention back to Cassius and Hawk. *I'm helping me forget about Rin.*

Cassius's eyes narrowed and fire rippled past his elbows, but Hawk gave me a tight nod.

"You want me to help?" he asked, his gaze dipping to Titus's crotch, reminding me that I was still inexperienced and Titus was a big man. If he didn't get me worked up enough and take it slow—which I doubted he'd do either—this first time was going to be painful.

"This mating is mine," his beast snarled.

A whisper of fear cut into my desire, but my eyes found Rin again and my need swelled.

God, this was such a mess.

Hawk raised his hands in defense. "Hey man, if you're worried about hurting her, maybe having someone there is a good idea."

"Mine." He curled his lips back and growled.

He wasn't going to say yes. It had to be difficult

enough for Titus to share me with the others, asking him to open up his bed was clearly too much.

"It's okay," I said, leaning my cheek against Titus's bare chest, giving him more flesh, savoring the feel of his hard muscle and concentrating on my desire. To hell if it was for Rin. "Titus needs this."

And I could deal with a little pain to help him and to make me forget, just for a moment, that I wanted Rin. I wanted to feel our completed connection more. If I focused past my desire and the remnants of my backlash, my soul begged to connect with Titus's life force. God, it hadn't even been a day since I'd connected with Sebastian and Hawk, and my soul needed to feel that completed circuit again.

"Okay." Hawk ran a hand through his jaw-length sandy blond hair, not looking happy about agreeing. "The moment it's anything other than desire, I'm coming up and stopping it."

"Agreed." Cassius yanked his fire back under his skin.

"Now get out," Titus growled.

Hawk rolled his eyes at him. "How about taking her to a bedroom, big guy."

Titus blinked as if he didn't understand Hawk, then his dragon huffed. "Right. Yes."

He swept me into his arms and shoved past Cassius and Hawk, and I pushed aside everything but the core of my desire. I wanted this, I ached for this, I needed this.

CHAPTER 16

AMIAH

Titus carried me to the empty bedroom at the end of the hall, used his heel to knock the door closed with a heavy thump, and sat me on the edge of the bed.

My thoughts slipped to Rin, and I wrenched them back to Titus and the throbbing between my thighs.

"The moment you think I'm going too far, stop me. Don't wait for Hawk," he said, kneeling on the floor in front of me, his golden gaze capturing mine, his body trembling with the effort to control the wild desire he'd had in the office, making my heart ache.

The warm light from the bedside lamp caught in his eyes and reflected back like cat's eyes, but it didn't hide the turmoil that I could see there. A battle between man and beast raged inside him, and it made my soul weep.

God, he'd been so close to just letting it out. A quick walk down the hall and he was back to fighting himself.

I cupped his cheek with my hand and the sense of his life force swelled, a wild, ferocious, desperate storm. This wasn't the way it was supposed to be. He was powerful and amazing and his beast was a majestic creature. He hadn't deserved what Deaglan had done to him—

Just like Rin didn't.

I shoved that thought away.

Focus on Titus. He needs this, just as much as I do.

"You won't go too far."

Please fill me, please make me forget Rin and how this is probably going to hurt and how I almost lost Cassius. Make me forget everything. Please. Just for a moment.

I knew it wasn't healthy to keep using sex as a distraction. But right now, if I didn't find a way to let everything go and focus on Titus, he might not be able to mend his connection with his beast.

"Promise me you'll make me stop," he— no his beast growled.

"I promise." I knew neither he nor his beast would go too far and seriously hurt me beyond what I could heal. From the tension in his body, I was afraid he wouldn't go far enough.

Proving my fears right, he dipped in with a barely-there kiss. It was nothing like the wild forceful one we'd had before in the aerie, and it wasn't going to do anything to heal the damage in his soul, or drive everything out of my mind... or satisfy my aching desire inflamed from kissing Rin.

Before my mind could jump back to Rin, I brushed my fingers across the rough red-gold stubble dusting Titus's cheeks and tangled them into his dark red hair so I could draw him closer and deepen our kiss.

He rumbled low in his throat, the sound deliciously

primal and masculine, but he didn't take my cue and his body remained tense with the effort to hold himself back.

"Titus," I murmured against his lips. "You have to let go and stop fighting your beast."

"I know but—"

"No buts. You're not going to break me, I'm not glass, and I'm not afraid of him."

His life force heaved against my senses, sharp, desperate, wild, and scales slid up his neck again.

"You should be." He sucked in a quick breath, forcing the scales back under his skin then cupped the back of my head and pressed his forehead to mine. "He's angry. Angry at being locked way inside me and angry that you need *them* as well." His trembling increased, the extra point of contact with our foreheads not helping to calm his soul. "And he's angry that you branded Rin and not me."

My throat tightened, even as my need for Rin rippled through my core. "I'm angry about that too. But we'll get the Heart and fix that."

I drew back just enough so I could look him in the eyes. I let him see how much I desired him, all of him, how much I needed that something in him that I also needed from the others, and how determined I was to make this right.

"Stop fighting your beast and stop holding back," I said. "I've been fantasizing about this from the moment I first saw you. Thinking about our kiss back in the aerie has been driving me crazy."

I captured his lips, releasing my desire for him, determined to show him how much I wanted him and that I wasn't afraid, despite my concerns for his size.

He rumbled again and—finally!—kissed me back. His hand on the back of my head held me close as he raked his tongue against mine, making my whole body throb with need. He kissed me with the same wild, desperate passion he'd had when we'd been back in the aerie and when we'd been attacked in the Winter Court, and I gave in, letting it overwhelm me.

There were no thoughts of Rin or fear about Titus entering me. There was just pure need, surging and whirling, sweeping through the remnants of my backlash and mixing with my life force.

This was what I wanted, what I needed.

God, yes.

But Titus jerked back, making my thoughts stutter and my fears start to rush back in.

No. Don't stop.

He groaned, his expression was tight with pain and his body tense. He was still fighting his beast when he should have been accepting it and trusting it, still trying to control it.

"Let him out. It's okay." *You need him to heal and I need him to forget. Please.*

"I know." He squeezed his eyes shut and took in a deep shuddering breath, but it did little to ease the tension in his body.

"So what are you waiting for? It's the only way you'll be able to properly reconnect your soul." Well, not the only way. Having sex was the way shifters of the same species helped each other. For vastly different species, those with no sexual desire, or those rare patients who'd been newly infected with lycanthropy, the alternative was slow and steady. A process that took weeks, sometimes months or years.

We didn't have that kind of time, and Titus and I shared a sexual desire. I could help heal his connection with my body.

And he could help steady my soul, something that, as an angel, I wasn't supposed to need.

"Just let him out."

He snorted, smoke curling from his nostrils, but his body remained tense.

Nothing I could say was going to make him let go. He'd been holding his beast in for so long, he feared that part of himself. Which meant I was going to have to force his beast to take control, show the man that his beast wasn't just mindless and wasn't going to hurt me.

Please, God, let his beast still have some kind of control.

"For goodness sake. If you're not serious about having sex, I'll go back to Hawk," I said, trying to get a rise out of his beast—not the safest thing to do but really my only option.

His eyes narrowed, and a hint of his red-gold scales reflected the lamp light along the side of his neck, but his body remained tense, his will still keeping Titus the man in charge.

Damn. Hawk wasn't enough of a threat to make his beast seize control. He'd already accepted that I needed to be with Hawk as well as him.

My heart twisted. I didn't want to push the matter, but it seemed he'd left me no choice.

I slowly ran a hand down my neck, into my robe, and cupped my breast, hoping, with my inexperience with seduction, that I still looked sort of sexy.

His gaze followed the movement, his pupils dilating, and my breath picked up with a mix of desire, fear, and regret at what I had to say next.

"Actually, I ache for Rin." Which, God, I did. *And I'm not going to think about.* "I'm going to go to him."

I stood, but Titus snarled, grabbed my wrist and yanked me back down to the bed. Scales rushed up his entire neck and into his stubble, and he bared his elongated canines at me.

"No," his beast growled, his tone sending an inappropriate shiver of desire racing through me.

Yes, let it go.

"You're mine."

"Prove it," I growled back, shoving him with all my might.

Don't fight him. Let him take over. Trust him. Trust me.

He toppled onto his back, only because I'd caught him off guard, and his eyes widened in surprise.

I straddled him, digging my fingernails into his chest, and leaned close, my lips almost, but not quite, brushing his. "Prove it," I repeated.

His beast rumbled at my challenge, grabbed the back of my head, tangling his fingers in my hair, and smashed our lips together.

He fully controlled the kiss, tilting my head to get the angle he wanted so he could completely possess me. My body ignited, every nerve suddenly sensitive, and my mind went gloriously blank. There was just the sensation of being overwhelmed and my desire fueled by the ferocity of his shifter's life force. And his life force was wild and strong, man and beast surging, blending, breaking apart.

Titus the man wanted control, but his beast right now was too strong.

He wrapped his other, powerful arm behind my back, yanked me close, and rolled us over.

"Mine," his beast snarled, pinning me with his pelvis, his large erection grinding against my clit and sending the whisper of a climax through me.

Oh, yes.

I tried to rock my hips in response, but I couldn't move against his weight. He pulled back and looked down at me, his expression pure sexual hunger, making me shiver in anticipation. Scales now ran across his collar bone, over his shoulders, and across the tops of his pecs. I scratched my nails across his skin, the scales still soft like flesh, and drew another rumble of desire.

"Mine," I snarled back.

At my word, his life forced swept into a whirling vortex inside me, his battling threads merging into a blazing, ferocious power for a second before breaking apart again.

Crap, he'd had it.

He just had to trust himself. Something he used to do. He'd been born a shifter, his soul had always had those two halves and, like all born shifters, he had a natural connection between them.

Did that mean our connection was strong enough for

me to help him heal? If it wasn't, it wouldn't matter if I slept with him or not.

Except everything within me screamed that wasn't true. That I could heal him. That there wasn't just something in his life force that I needed. That he, like the others, was mine.

"Mine," I snarled again, and with an instinct I didn't know I possessed, I sat up, grabbed his head, but instead of kissing him, I bit him between his neck and shoulder. Hard.

His life force snapped back into that merged vortex, both man and beast joined in reaction to me biting him, because by doing so, I'd claimed him like many predatory shifters claimed their mates.

With a growl, he grabbed my hair at the scalp, jerked my head back, and captured my mouth again in a bruising kiss that shattered all breath and thought. His other hand pushed inside my robe and roughly kneaded my breast as his erection ground against me with the hard promise of where we were headed.

And God, that was exactly where I wanted this to go.

My body was on fire with sensation. Every nerve turned on, all my senses locked onto him, his merged wild life force, his hand in my hair, and his other hand rough against my nipple. His hot breath rushed into my mouth and washed over my cheeks, and all I could do was let go, like I'd told him to do, and give in to it all.

"I knew you were my soul's mate," he snarled against my lips, and he shoved a thick finger into my already slick heat.

I gasped and bucked at the sudden invasion. But he

didn't let up, possessing my mouth with a ferocity that sent me reeling and pumping his finger inside me, hard and fast, twisting my need tighter and tighter.

Oh God, yes.

My breath grew ragged and he shoved in a second finger, adding to the pressure and friction, then a third, stretching me. His thrusts were hard and fast, verging on painful. Then he ground his thumb against my clit, and my muscles clench tight around his fingers, my orgasm sudden and powerful, drawing a cry of pleasure.

"Mine," he growled, and he withdrew his fingers, opened his fly, and pushed his large erection inside me before I could fully register what he was doing.

My whole body tensed at the sudden bite of pain. Oh God, he was too big. I needed more time. Then his life force blazed inside me, and that piece of my soul that needed him clicked into alignment. It sent an aftershock of my orgasm rippling through me and relaxed my muscles to better accommodate him.

Titus gasped and jerked his golden gaze to mine. His pupils were fully dilated like a human's, but both man and beast were looking at me, his eyes filled with shock and awe and desire.

Then his desire overwhelmed everything else, and his life force inside me surged. I was wild and ferocious, just like Titus. My desire for him was stronger than my worry or pain or anything else.

I locked gazes with him, snarled at him, and dug my nails into his chest, drawing blood.

He snarled back, grabbed my hips, jerked himself out

and thrust back into me in a forceful stroke. Glorious friction and pressure filled me, and he did it again and again.

I cried my pleasure, dug my nails into his forearms, and bucked into his powerful strokes. His breathtaking, powerful life force roared inside me, and my full-body glow writhed around my body like a sea caught in a powerful storm. We crashed together, two primal beings, connected in spirit, our souls aligned, gasping and moaning and growling, and our gazes locked.

His pupils slitted again and his canines extended, the wild desire in his eyes feeding my own need. He was mine. This was right. And oh my God, it felt amazing.

My whole body roared with a consuming rush of wild life force and sensation. I couldn't catch my breath and I didn't care. This was the passion I'd ached for, and this was Titus fully embracing who and what he was.

God, he was mine. Just like the others were.

Mine mine mine.

The muscles in my core seized and another climax tore through me. It ripped a scream from my lips. My glow burst into a brilliant white light that lit up the entire room, my eyes rolled back, and stars exploded behind my lids.

With a final, powerful thrust, Titus roared his own release and sank his teeth into my shoulder, making my soul sing. He'd claimed me, marking me as his, and I was going to bare his mark with pride...

And not think about what might happen when my brand made me fall in love with Rin and Rin alone.

CHAPTER 17

CASSIUS

MY FIRE SEARED THROUGH MY VEINS, BOILING MY BLOOD, AS my desire and fear and anger raged through me. Flames poured from my hands onto the concrete patio around my bare feet and I didn't bother trying to hold it in.

I wouldn't have been able to no matter how hard I tried.

The best I could hope for was to contain it enough to not burn down Voth's hotel... which somehow we'd gotten to.

I was afraid to ask what had happened. The last thing I remembered, I'd been injured and Amiah had been screaming and running into the middle of the battle with Deaglan's shadow fae, and then a blazing agony had sliced through my throat and my life had gushed from my severed arteries. I'd collapsed and all I could think about was protecting her and that I'd failed. I'd had one job and I'd failed.

It didn't matter that I was still alive to continue fighting for her. Deaglan was still out there and she was still in danger. That, and everything within me was screaming that Titus wasn't in control and he was going to hurt her. I shouldn't have agreed to them having sex.

Why the hell had I agreed?

Except she'd had that look in her eyes, the one that said it didn't matter what I said. She was going to do what she wanted, regardless of the consequences, and the only way I'd be able to stop her was if I tied her down.

She'd had the same look when she'd run into the fight and I'd told her to get back to safety, and again in the office when she'd walked right up to Titus, who'd been shaking with his beast's fury, and had pressed her body against his.

Still, I should have tried harder to make her see reason, forced her to wait until he was at least in control.

God, all I wanted to do was wrap my arms around her and protect her.

Except that wasn't *all* I wanted.

I bit back a scream of frustration and my fire surged around me, shooting high above me before I could hold it back.

Shit. We were supposed to be hiding. I had to hold it together, or at least hold it together enough that I didn't give away our position.

But God damn it, I couldn't just accept that I'd never be able to give her what she needed like Titus could—like he *was*. Right now. Only the odds weren't good that I'd even be able to touch her again. Not unless I could fix whatever inside me was broken or my magic was permanently taken away from me.

That was what really made me angry. It should have

been me up there with her. I was the one who'd been in love with her for a hundred years. We weren't just friends any more, we were lovers, and I'd treat her the way she deserved, with reverence and adoration.

But I couldn't. I couldn't even get close to her, and I knew she also desired passion. It had been obvious in the way she'd melted into Titus's ferocious kiss in the cavern in the Autumn Court.

But even if I was mistaken and she didn't want the intensity of a shifter's passion, she still would have had sex with him. It wouldn't have mattered what she wanted at all. He needed her. Even I could see his connection with the beastly half of his soul was broken and knew that the best and fastest way to heal that was through sex.

And, as much as I wanted to pretend it wasn't true, I also knew she needed him, needed to make her own connection with his soul... or—how had she put it?—his life force, just like she'd connected with me.

Which, if I couldn't get my magic under control or get rid of it, was never going to happen again. And none of that mattered if we couldn't get the Heart and remove her mating brand.

I was going to lose her forever.

I'd already lost her.

The brand she'd said she'd had removed, that she hadn't wanted and had been afraid of, had already taken her from me.

Fuck.

My fire roared around me again and ignited my robe.

Fuck!

Fuck fuck fuck.

I heaved at my power, yanking the flames out of the fabric before I ended up naked. Again.

This was a nightmare. My only hope of getting Amiah back was getting the Heart and given that Deaglan had nearly killed me, I had serious doubts all of us were going to survive another confrontation. Not to mention, I was losing the instinctual control over my fire that I'd been born with that protected my clothes, which made me less than useless to Amiah. It made me dangerous.

I needed Bane to freeze or pull out my fire. It was the only way. Just for a little while, just until we could figure out how we were going to deal with Deaglan, because without my fire I couldn't protect Amiah.

God, I'd never wanted to be the Salamander again, but it seemed he was all that was left of me, the wild, angry force of nature bent on brutal justice for the murder of my youngest brother. Once we had a plan, I could point myself at the Shadow King and stop fighting my magic.

A part of me was relieved at the thought. My battle with myself would finally be over. It had been twenty-five years of struggling, my hold getting weaker and weaker, and I couldn't hold out much longer. I was broken and no one could fix me. This, at least, was a way to protect the person I held most dear.

We'd still need to figure out a way to stop Deaglan from taking my fire… although I had a horrible suspicion that if I truly gave in to the firestorm raging inside me, Deaglan wouldn't be able to take all of it.

My flames billowed around my feet, rolling toward a potted tree, and I heaved it back in.

Please, God, let Bane have figured out what Deaglan had done to take my fire and be able to repeat that. I just needed to hold out long enough for one last confrontation with that monster.

Except I hadn't seen Bane in the office when Titus and the hybrid had been fighting over Amiah.

The hybrid.

Her mate.

My throat tightened and a gust of wind swept sparks from my fire drifting into the night sky. Bright angry specks against the darkness.

Why couldn't it have been me?

Hell, why couldn't it have been any one of us? I'd even have accepted Bane as her soul mate.

But not a complete stranger who'd tried to kill her the instant he'd seen her back in the park ring when we'd first found Titus. She didn't deserve that. She hadn't deserved anything that had happened to her in the last few days.

Except if her magic hadn't locked onto Titus and she hadn't been accidentally leashed to him, she never would have realized the truth about herself.

I'd never heard of an angel needing to connect with someone through sex, which meant she never would have even known to ask until she realized what was happening, and even then, she might have been confused. She wouldn't—

My thoughts stuttered. Could she make her connection with anyone? She'd said she'd been waiting for her soul mate and hadn't realized she'd needed to connect through sex.

Did that mean she hadn't had sex until we'd fallen in with Bane and Hawk?

I had no idea if that made things better or worse. If she could connect with anyone then my death wouldn't affect her nor Bane and Hawk going their separate ways. She could happily carry on with Titus or replace us. But if it was just the four of us, she was fated for more heartbreak. Even if I survived, she'd still lose Bane and Hawk—

And none of that mattered because her soul was bound to the hybrid.

God, I couldn't allow that. I had to get Faerie's Heart and fix this for her... maybe it could even fix me.

Hope squeezed around my heart and I shoved it as deep down inside me as I could. I couldn't afford any doubt, anything that made me hold back. That could mean Amiah's death. I had to fully embrace my power and let it consume me if that's what it took to keep her safe. If I survived what was coming, then I could hope.

And the first step to saving Amiah was coming up with a plan, which meant I needed to gather the others. I couldn't do this alone and they *were* going to help Amiah even if I had to force them to.

Except even if everyone agreed to have that conversation on the patio, I still needed help with my fire, and that meant finding Bane.

I sucked in a steadying breath and imagined myself surrounded by ice, but that did nothing to cool my flames.

My fire snapped and hissed. The breeze picked up

more sparks, twirling them into the sky, and a pillar of flame shot up, following it.

God damn it. Ice. Cold. God damned frozen things.

I wrenched the pillar back into me, making the inferno inside me burn hotter, and clenched every muscle in my body, determined to keep it in. I could do this. I had to do this.

I mentally seized the fire rolling across the patio and dragged it back inside me, adding to the inferno burning my skin then yanked in the flames around my hands.

The effort left me panting with a searing pressure that threatened to tear out of my chest, but now only smoke billowed around me. And that was going to have to be enough. I was barely holding the flames in, gathering up the smoke was going to be too much. I could only pray I wouldn't set off any fire alarms.

Better yet, I should just open the door and call for Bane, get hm out here on the patio and relieve some of this pressure. Then I could sit inside like a normal person and have a non-normal conversation about the night-mare Amiah was caught up in.

I opened the door to go back into the suite and was met with moaning and grunting punctuated with cries of pleasure.

Good Lord. Was that Amiah having sex?

My pulse leaped in a wild tattoo and my heart squeezed at that thought with a churning mix of fear for her and jealousy directed at Titus, and my fire exploded over my hands.

God damn it.

I jerked back onto the patio, letting the door close and

shutting out the sound—the lack of noise an indication that a sound block spell had been cast on the suite.

I fought to heave my fire back under my skin, but I couldn't concentrate. All I could think about was how it sounded like he was hurting her and—

Movement through the bank of floor-to-ceiling windows caught my attention as Hawk strode into the living room from the kitchen. He held a full, white, plastic bag and was headed for the stairs, but his gaze met mine and he changed directions.

"A change of clothes," he said, opening the patio door and holding out the bag.

Amiah screamed again and I couldn't tell if it was pleasure or pain.

Except Hawk had said the moment she stopped enjoying sex with Titus he'd put an end to it. And I trusted him to take care of her. He might have been a lot of things, but he'd proven I could trust him and he'd sworn he'd protect Amiah.

So if he wasn't running upstairs, that meant he was still getting sexual energy from them and she was all right... or at least emotionally all right. I wasn't sure about physically.

My fire flared and I backed away from him, not taking the bag, afraid I'd set the clothes on fire before I had a chance to change into them. "How can she be enjoying that?"

Hawk's expression darkened and he stepped fully onto the patio, letting the door close behind him. Guess he wasn't happy about what he was hearing, either.

"It feels like she's riding his essence," he said. "I don't

know how she's doing it. That's an incubus or succubus thing, but her desire right now has the same edge that a shifter's does."

Of course it did. Because if she needed to connect with him, whatever it was that was inside her would help her do it. It was the only explanation... since I didn't want to accept that she wanted that kind of sex. If she did, I'd never be able to give it to her even with my magic controlled or gone.

I sagged to my knees in the middle of the patio, needing to sit but not trusting that I wouldn't destroy the patio furniture. "Whatever it is she needs from us is helping her."

"That would be my guess," Hawk said. "It's making this first time with him and his larger-than-she's-accustomed-to cock enjoyable."

My fire surged, rushing up to Hawk's feet and making him jerk back with a yelp. I didn't know if he meant that to also mean that she didn't have a lot of sexual experience or just that Titus was big and she probably hadn't ever had sex with someone as... well endowed—and thanks to his shifter magic destroying his clothes, I'd seen him fully erect, and he was very well proportioned.

I gritted my teeth and heaved my fire back as best as I could.

I couldn't do anything for Amiah right now. I couldn't even touch her. I needed to get my God damned fire under control, and then I needed to stop Deaglan for good.

"Where's Bane?" I asked through clenched teeth. "I

need him to try to rip out some of my fire before I burn this place down."

Hawk's expression darkened even more, and he dropped onto the edge of one of the three black couches and rubbed his face. "He's down for the count until we can deal with his demonic magic infection."

He's what?

"He's infected with demonic magic? When the hell did that happen?" Although that would explain why he wasn't as magically powerful as he should have been. A man who I knew had teleported an astounding ten people shouldn't have been struggling in the last couple of fights as much as he had been.

"He said something about the Hellfire Queen and an archnephilim."

That had been my brother and his mate's last battle, where I'd been next to useless in protecting him. That also meant Bane had been struggling since before this whole mess had started.

"Every time he uses magic it gets worse and that last battle with Deaglan and then escaping his apartment—" Hawk ran a hand down his face again. "I know you're struggling, but we can't do anything until we can get that shit out of him."

Movement inside the suite caught my attention again as Bane, wrapped in a fluffy white robe, staggered to the top of the stairs. He looked horrible. His complexion was gray and I could see him shaking from all the way out on the patio.

He clutched the railing and took a trembling step

down, but his leg didn't support him and he crumpled, tumbling forward.

Hawk and I jerked to our feet, but we weren't going to be fast enough to stop his fall—and I was now fully engulphed in flames again and more likely to set the suite on fire if I ran inside.

Then a dark figure swept up behind him and grabbed his arm. He yanked Bane up, jerking him to his body, and wrapped an arm across his chest to support him.

The hybrid.

Hawk bolted inside and the hybrid's gaze snapped to him.

"We should get him back in bed," Hawk said before the patio door slid shut.

Bane raised a trembling hand and shook his head.

The hybrid didn't say anything and didn't move. His expression was hard and void of any kind of emotion, and it made my fire heave and blaze hotter.

This was who fate had bound Amiah to. This emotionless monster—

No. Amiah didn't think he was one. She'd said he'd been tortured by Deaglan, had been his slave, and he did just save Bane from falling down the stairs.

Except that didn't make their soul bond right. She didn't know him. She didn't love him.

And I wouldn't be able to free her from him without Bane, and Bane was in serious trouble.

CHAPTER 18

TITUS

I clung to Amiah, my cock buried inside her, my teeth in her shoulder, and a wild new energy rushing through my body. It snapped through my soul and wrenched at my two disconnected pieces, a mix of my own shifter nature and the strange powerful magic that had flooded me the moment Amiah had screamed her release.

I hadn't thought her power could get stronger. I'd entered her and whatever it was that she needed from me —from all of us—flooded me, connecting our hearts and souls. It had filled me with absolute certainty that she was mine and I was hers, and nothing else in that moment had mattered.

And then she'd come and my soul had ignited. I was on fire, filled with strength and power. Her power. My power. A power from someplace else, someplace that called to both halves of my soul and wove both man and beast back together into a balance that had been missing for centuries.

This. This was how I was supposed to feel.

I'd forgotten how steady my soul used to be, how strong. Now, even in my human form, I could feel my dragon's fire warming my throat, a sensation I'd lost when my soul had started to separate.

I wanted to shift, spread my wings, soar into the sky, and roar the news of my mate for all to hear. I'd never felt stronger than in that moment, our bodies and souls joined. I'd never been more certain of who and what I was, and I knew exactly what my purpose was: protect my mate.

Mine.

Forever and always. And all of me, not just my beast, was positive she was more than just my mate, more than what I could give her soul, she was my soul's mate. We were fated for each other.

It was the only way she could have mended my soul so easily. Because she hadn't just eased my turmoil, she'd face my raging beast without fear and completely steadied him. Only my soul's mate had that kind of power.

And even though she wasn't a dragon, I'd been unable to stop myself and had marked her as mine.

Of course, much to my surprise, she'd tried to mark me as well... which was what had gotten the whole thing started.

I didn't know what had possessed her to try—and I didn't want to accept it was just to make my beast take over, even if it had been. Pushing me over and drawing my blood with her nails would have been enough for him to seize control of our body, especially given how tenuous my hold had already been. But then she'd bitten me. I hadn't stood a chance.

My control had shattered and my beast had fully taken over, his passion without restraint, not caring that she wasn't a dragon and couldn't withstand a dragon's full strength.

And now I could only pray I hadn't hurt her too badly... since I wasn't even sure exactly what I'd done.

This hadn't been what I'd wanted for our first time. I'd wanted to draw it out, bring her to climax again and again, and when I couldn't take it any longer, I'd wanted to savor the feel of slowly sliding into her slick tight sheath and watching her eyes roll back in pleasure

But my beast had wanted to claim her, *needed* to claim her, and it had been denied for so long our passion made anything other than ferociously taking her impossible.

"Oh wow, Titus," she moaned, and another, smaller, orgasm swept through her, making her muscles clench around my cock again and her full-body fae glow flare even brighter.

A pressure in my chest, the fear that I'd seriously hurt her, that she was now afraid of me, and that she hadn't enjoyed that, released, and my beast rumbled against her shoulder, her blood trickling between my lips. *Mine.*

Oh yes, mine, I agreed and the power in my soul surged.

She was amazing. I couldn't believe she'd enjoyed that, wasn't crying in agony from how rough I'd been.

My thoughts tripped at that. My teeth were still in her shoulder.

Shit.

I shouldn't have bitten her, not sinking my canines in all the way. She wasn't a dragon. She didn't heal like a dragon.

Shit shit shit.

I drew my teeth from her flesh and raised my head up, my gaze instinctually jumping to hers, and I was drowning in her stunning blue eyes.

Her angel glow blazed bright, brighter than when I'd carried her into the bedroom, although that was probably my imagination since she hadn't had enough time to recover her magic, and she captured my soul, my whole healed soul.

The love and warmth and acceptance in her gaze wrapped around me and my heart thrilled. There was no fear or pain and anger at the fact that I'd hurt her. She embraced all of me, my large, dangerous body and my wild primal soul. She was incredible.

And the pain I'd seen in her eyes back in the aerie, that fear that there was something broken inside her that she didn't understand, was gone. It was replaced with certainty and strength and I could sense something deep inside her starting to awaken, something empowered by connecting with me... and the others, and—

My pulse skipped a beat. Crap. I'd claimed her. Would my beast accept her having sex with the others even though I *knew* she needed them, or would he see that as a challenge to his claim?

But my primal nature huffed at me. She needed them as much as she needed me and that made them a part of her. That was who our mate was.

The love in her eyes deepened as if she saw me come

to that shocking realization, and she raised her hands to cup my cheeks, but stopped before making contact and frowned. Her fingers were bloody.

Her gaze jumped to my shoulders then my arms and my chest, taking in the marks she'd scored in my flesh, and her expression turned shocked. "Did I do that?"

I chuckled and my beast turned the sound into a satisfied rumble. "Oh, yeah. It could only have gotten better if you had claws." And much worse because I did have claws.

I slid my gaze down her stunning body, taking in her delicate figure, and my cock, still inside her, started to harden again.

But a whisper of fear chilled my desire as I reached the swirling gold lines of her mating brand on her hip. It pulsed with power, proclaiming that she wasn't mine, she wasn't even Seireadan's, Hawk's, or Cassius's. It didn't matter what I knew to be true in my soul. Her brand said otherwise.

And there was no way I was going to accept that. She was mine and I'd never let that monster touch her again... even if he had helped her ease her backlash... which meant maybe he wasn't a monster?

I bit back a growl. I had no idea what to think about the hybrid, and really, that was a worry for later.

"Are you okay?" I asked, my voice gruff. I couldn't see any bruises or scratches, save for my bite, and she wasn't crying, but that didn't mean I hadn't hurt her.

She shifted as if testing her body, taking more of me inside her and softly groaning with pleasure. "I'm good. I don't know how. I should be black and blue and very raw because... well..."

A gorgeous soft blush blossomed on her cheeks and I grew harder, drawing another soft moan of desire from her.

"Because?" I prompted.

"Because you're bigger than I'm used to," she said, her voice breathy.

I slowly drew myself halfway out of her and her eyelids fluttered shut, her lips parted on a soft moan, while my dragon preened at the thought that I had something the incubus didn't.

"But—" she groaned.

"But what?" I leisurely pushed back in. She felt incredible, better than I could have imagined and my five hundred year drought had nothing to do with it. She was mine. This was right, the way we were supposed to be, and this time I was going to give her the slow, sensual lovemaking that she deserved.

She gasped and dug her nails into my forearms, making my beast rumble in pleasure.

"But my body is fine and some of the power Rin took to relieve my backlash has already been restored."

I drew halfway out again and she bit her bottom lip, only partially keeping in another moan.

"Just give me a minute to stop my bleeding," she said, even as her hips curled up, urging me to push back in.

My beast snarled at that, half in anger at itself for biting her and half because it didn't want to stop, even for a minute.

Somehow, I resisted the urge to push back in until she

told me she was ready. She'd already made love with me for me. This time was all for her. But my instincts urged me to dip forward, making me tremble with the effort to hold my cock still, and I gently licked her front puncture wounds and cleaned away her blood.

It was pure dragon instinct, although I was sure there were other shifters who had the same compulsion, and as weird as it might have seemed to an angel, I reveled in the action. Licking her wounds without thinking meant my beast and I were one again, that I was in touch with all of my soul not just fractured parts of it.

Her magic warmed her flesh under my tongue and the power of the connection she'd made with my soul flared again.

"God that feels so good." She opened her eyes and captured me body, mind, and soul again. "You make me feel incredible, and strong, and ferocious."

"Because you are." I couldn't understand how she didn't think she was strong. She was one of the strongest people I'd ever met. She was willing to do anything to protect us despite the dangers. She hadn't hesitated to heal Cassius even though I was certain she knew she'd get burned and that she wouldn't have any magic left to heal herself. She gave and gave and gave to anyone and everyone from her soul and heart, from the very essence of her life force.

And somehow fate had decided I was hers.

Because I would give everything to protect her, to bring her joy and pleasure.

I pushed back inside her, drawing a low throaty

moan, as someone—soon to be a dead man if he didn't leave right now—knocked on the door.

I dipped into kiss her, my lips a fraction from hers, when whoever it was knocked again.

"Hey, guys," Hawk said through the door.

"Go the fuck away. If you know what's good for you, you'll leave," I snarled, my lips curling back and my canines extending even though he couldn't see me.

"Oh, I'd love to keep riding your sexual energy, but Bane is up," Hawk replied. "He doesn't look good and I don't know how long he'll remain conscious. If you want to participate in the plan to get us out of this mess, now's the time."

"Tell him to suck it up. We're not done." I glanced at Amiah, who gave me a soft smile. "I want to make you feel strong all night."

"I want you to," she whispered, cupping my cheeks between her small palms and drawing my gaze to hers. "God, I want you to. But Sebastian knows this situation better than any of us, and I won't allow Deaglan to hurt any of you again. You deserve to be free."

She gave me a sad soft smile and my heart clenched. She wasn't free. She was trapped in a soul bond with the hybrid and claimed by the Winter Court.

And Seireadan was the only one who could possibly fix that.

"Okay," I said, my voice gruff.

"Guys?" Hawk asked. "You in on the planning or not? Cassius will be pissed if he thinks I didn't invite Amiah."

"We're coming," Amiah called out, even as she shifted her hips taking me deeper inside her and drawing a soft moan of pleasure. "We just need a few minutes to clean up."

"Well you're not *coming*," Hawk said, his tone turning playful. "And I'd hate to leave you hanging. Let me give you a hand so you can finish off... again quickly."

"No!" I wasn't going to have him take over when it was finally my turn... even if my turn was being cut short. And hell, I could be quick without the incubus's help. She'd get at least one more orgasm before we left this bedroom. I captured her lips in a hard, fast kiss that made her dig her nails into my shoulders. "You're not coming in here. I'm perfectly capable of satisfying my mate."

"Oh yes, you are," she breathed.

"Hey," Hawk said, "it wasn't a criticism. I bet you she's lit up like the sun she's so satisfied. It was an offer. For both of you. You need to wrap it up quick. She's ready to go, but you could use a boost if you're going to come again. And after half a millennium of celibacy— You deserve to come again."

Well, I did, and it sounded like a great idea, but— "You're just trying to share my time with Amiah." It was bad enough I had to share her body with them. I wasn't going to also share the time I got to have sex with her.

"Nope. Although don't get me wrong. If you want to share? I'm game for that."

Amiah bit her lip on another moan, but I couldn't tell if it was Hawk's words or her slowly moving hips, inching me in and out of her channel that was heightening her arousal... although I had found her with Hawk and Sebastian when the second key had been empowered, and she'd been glowing with satisfaction, so I know she enjoyed having more than one of us at the same time.

"Right now, though," Hawk said. "I just need to touch you, give you a boost, and leave."

"Would you like that?" I asked her, but I wasn't certain if I was asking about just getting a hit of Hawk's magic or having sex with her and Hawk. And could I do that?

Her muscles trembled around my cock and she stilled and sucked in a breath, trying to control her climax. "I don't care if you want to have sex with me and the others at the same time, but let Hawk give you another orgasm. I want to feel you come inside me again."

Her words made my balls tighten. That was a request I desperately wanted to honor.

But I didn't want Hawk in the room and I certainly didn't want his help. She was mine and this was my time with her.

"Tick tock, guys," Hawk said.

"Let him help you," she said, capturing my gaze with hers, her love and need clear in her eyes. "Come again for me, Titus."

I bit back a growl. How could I say no to that?

"Fine. But know that I don't need your help getting off," I called out to Hawk.

"Again," Hawk said, "not a criticism on your prowess, merely a comment on your limited time."

He opened the door and his gaze leaped over us lying on the floor, me pinning Amiah's small fragile body beneath me and blood from Amiah's scratches streaking my body. For a second I was afraid he was going to be furious that I'd hurt her, then he flashed his wicked smile, making Amiah softly moan with his power.

"Hey, gorgeous," he purred, crouching by her head. "I see you've figured out what really gets a predator shifter going. Are you okay?"

"Really? You're going to ask me that?" she said, her voice breathy. "You already know I'm better than okay."

He rolled his eyes at her. "Yeah, and I have no idea how you are from all the racket you were making. I'm surprise the room isn't destroyed what with dragon boy here finally releasing his beast."

"Ha ha. I have some control," I said since there was no way in hell I was going to admit I'd been terrified that I'd hurt her. "Now can we get on with this? I have a mate to satisfy."

Hawk's expression heated. "Yes, you do."

He grabbed my shoulder and without warning sent a blast of hot sensual magic exploding inside me. It roared through every cell in my body then shot into my cock. I was instantly hard, so hard it hurt, and before I realized what I was doing, my hips thrusted forward even though I was already buried inside Amiah.

She took it with a quick gasp, her blazing fae glow rippling up her body with the impact and her eyes widening just before they rolled back and she released a deep moan that made my balls even tighter.

"God, you're gorgeous," Hawk said, the desire in his eyes deepening as he slid his gaze down her body to where we were connected. But instead of looking upset, his need deepened and his hellfire swept across his cheeks. "Man, I know joining in is out, but you sure I can't watch?"

"Hawk—" His magic inside me surged and my attention snapped back to Amiah as I slid myself out to the tip and thrust back into her. She was so tight and slick and felt so good and Hawk's magic had me already on the edge. And as much as I'd wanted slow and sensual for our second time, I was going to come hard and fast. Again.

Another surge and I slid out and thrust back in. This time Amiah curled her hips to meet me and we crashed together, my hold on myself starting to slip.

I gritted my teeth. I needed to hold it together long enough to make her come first. Whatever I did, she had to come again. This time was supposed to be for her, and it didn't matter what Hawk did. He could stay or leave or, hell, join in, so long as he didn't get in my way.

A growl rumbled in my throat and I thrust again, harder this time, and once again she met me, moaning her pleasure, and fueling my shifter's passion.

Mine.

Mine mine mine.

I thrust again and again, our pace leaping from fast and steady to frantic. Amiah met me every time, gasping and moaning and bucking beneath me, just as wild as me, and Hawk's magic twisted me tighter than I'd ever been before.

I pounded into her, barely conscious of ensuring my grip wasn't too tight and my claws didn't extend. My own need to release raged through me, but I hung on, clinging to the need that I needed to hear and feel her release first.

And then she cried out and tensed. A look of pure bliss filled her expression and her fae glow blazed so bright it was almost blinding. Her contracting muscles clenched tight around me and I released my hold on myself.

Stars exploded behind my lids, and every muscle in my body contracted with a powerful orgasm fueled by Hawk's magic that filled me with sensation all the way down to my soul.

Mine.

Amiah's connection within me surged, and Hawk's magic sent another eruption screaming through me, and my soul roared it certainty.

She. Was. Mine.

And it didn't matter that Hawk was still in the room, that his hellfire licked across his cheeks with his desire for her or me or both of us, or that I'd ridden his power to pleasure Amiah. He was a part of my mate.

He was mine, too.

They all were.

I didn't want to have sex with them, not without Amiah, but my beast had made up its mind and that shocked the hell out of me.

They were mine. They were also my soul's mate.

CHAPTER 19

SEBASTIAN

Sweat dripped down my back, coming, only in part, from the muggy night air, and I huddled on a couch on the patio, the demonic magic inside me slicing deep into the very essence of my being.

God, I shouldn't have gotten out of bed.

Hell, I wished I hadn't even woken up. Except if I'd waited for the agonizing acidic burn of the demon magic inside me to ease up, I'd have never woken, let alone moved again.

Which, at the moment, seemed like the best idea ever.

Except if we were going to get out of this mess, we needed a plan, and I was the one who knew the most about what the hell was going on.

"Hawk said they were done," Cassius growled from the far side of the patio, fire dripping from his hands onto the wide concrete tiles as if he'd given up on trying to fully contain his magic. "How long does it take to get someone?"

The demonic magic surged, making me suck in a sharp breath. "Give them a minute to clean up."

And for Amiah to heal herself.

Which I wasn't going to say out loud, even though I was sure he was thinking the same thing. From the moaning and crying and roaring that had been coming from the bedroom when I'd woken, Titus's beast had to have been fully released, and even if by some miracle Cassius had accepted that Amiah wanted to have sex with all of us and he had no right to stop her, he'd never accept sex that hurt her.

Hell, I was shocked by it as well because I was pretty sure she didn't get off on pain.

And maybe she didn't.

She knew the fastest way for Titus and his beast to merge back together was through sex, and that he needed to release his beast and trust it on a soul deep level. She'd do whatever it took to heal him, even if that meant enduring some pain. And even if she didn't make the same connection with Titus that she did with me and Hawk, she'd sacrifice her body to save him.

Although I was pretty sure she'd connect with Titus, and that she'd connected with Cassius when they'd had sex.

Except if she did need something from the four of us, how did that explain her mating brand awakening and forming a bond with Rin? Was that fate just being fucked up? Or did she need him as well?

And why.

That was what really bothered me.

I had no idea why. Why did I want to be bonded

with her despite still being certain that I never wanted to be soul bonded with anyone? Ever. There was something about her, something that was fucking with my mind, and I really hated when things fucked with my mind.

The demonic magic surged again, and I bit back a groan.

Jesus. I also hated things that fucked with my body.

All I'd wanted was to be left alone. No Winter Court, no fucked-up head games, and no expectations. I didn't want the throne. I never did, and things had been great. I'd made a good life, had no obligations, and could buy all the books I'd wanted.

And then I'd gone and helped.

I was such a fucking idiot. If I hadn't stuck my nose in where it didn't belong, if I hadn't cared so damned much about this realm, I wouldn't have been infected.

But I did give a shit and letting the Hellfire Queen take over would have ruined my perfect life.

Which had really just been a fantasy, because Faerie had always been fated to shove its way back into my life. I was a royal and that's what Faerie did to royals. I'd been an idiot to think I could have escaped it. And yet the idea of dealing with this mess with the Heart and Deaglan— because the only way out was through—and leaving all this shit behind made my pulse race.

Because it wasn't the mess I didn't want to leave. It was *her*.

I liked what she, Hawk, and I had. Hell, I didn't care if Titus and Cassius wanted to join in, just as long as I could keep her. I loved her.

Which was probably more of whatever she was that was fucking with my mind.

The demonic magic flared again and my vision darkened, forcing me to suck in ragged breaths to stay conscious.

And yet a small part of me said it wasn't, that I wasn't being influenced by her magic, that I was genuinely in love with her and my behavior was perfectly normal for an idiot in love, while another part didn't give a shit. The connection she made with me when we had sex didn't just go one way. I'd felt it too and every time we had sex it got stronger and made me feel stronger in spite of my demonic infection.

I still didn't want her brand. Really. But I certainly didn't want to give her up.

I glanced at Rin.

Why the hell couldn't it have been me?

I clamped down on that thought. I didn't want it to be me. But if it hadn't been me then what we had would still be gone.

A spark of hellfire popped from Rin's right eye, the only indication he was alive and conscious... well, undead and conscious. He still wore his all black assassin's garb that was probably still coated in blood, and stood at the edge of the patio's conversation area, staring into the living room. Except I couldn't figure out if he was watching for Amiah or not... like Cassius and I were.

I also had no idea what to make of him. He still showed no emotion. I think the most I'd ever seen from him had been when he'd been straddling Amiah in my clean room and that had been pure desperate hunger. I hoped to God, for her sake, that he'd open up. Amiah might have been cold and in-control when we'd first met, but now her heart was fully exposed, her emotions clear, and she lit up with passion. All that wonder and confidence was going to vanish if Rin couldn't muster any outward desire for her.

I also had no idea if any of us trusted him, and wandering around free didn't mean anything. There wasn't any place in the suite to lock him up. And hell, from his body language and the fact that he stood halfway across the patio from me, it was clear he didn't trust us, either.

Except he hadn't had to catch me before I fell down the stairs. Which didn't necessarily mean anything. It could have just been a moment of weakness when Amiah's brand had overwhelmed him and forced him to do the right thing, or his hope of lulling us into trusting him before he killed us and dragged Amiah to Deaglan.

God. And at some point Amiah was going to have to sleep with him.

The thought made my insides churn, increasing the demonic magic's burn.

Of course, I didn't know what had happened between Amiah activating my teleportation spell on my circle and waking up here—which from the Quarter's skyline had to be Voth's hotel.

Maybe Rin had opened up. Maybe one of the others had gotten a better read on the man.

"They're taking too long," Cassius said, drawing my gaze away from Rin and the living room and back to him. "I'm going to get them."

The angel's expression was tight with a pain that almost looked as bad as mine, and his fire roared around him, shrinking and billowing as if caught in a wild storm. I had no idea how his robe or the plants around him hadn't caught fire.

He sucked in a noisy breath and most of his fire vanished, leaving only tiny flames flickering from the back of his hands and smoke curling around him. Except his body shook so hard, likely in his attempt to control his fire, the smoke around him undulated.

He was one fucked up mess.

The demonic magic billowed again, stealing my breath for what felt like an agonizing eternity but was really only a second.

And so was I.

"Just wait," I gasped. "You're going to hurt yourself trying to control your power like that."

"Well I need to figure something out until you can deal with your demonic magic infection."

If I *could* deal with it.

Something else I didn't want to say out loud, because everyone would freak if they knew there was a chance the demonic magic had already severed my connection to Faerie and I couldn't be saved.

Amiah most of all.

God, I hoped I was wrong. Except my fae glow was gone and I couldn't feel Faerie's magic inside me or sense my always-there connection to the realm.

Movement at the top of the stairs caught my attention and Amiah, wrapped in a fluffy white robe, stepped onto the first step.

She was radiant. Literally. I'd never seen her unnatural fae glow so bright before. It created a white nimbus around her like that of the angels depicted in the humans' art, and her expression was joyous... and a little dazed. She'd thoroughly enjoyed her time with Titus. Which was a relief, because Titus still needed more time with her to properly reconnect the two halves of his soul and she'd make herself do it even if she was now afraid of him.

But there was also something more to her glow. The power radiating from her that always pressed against my senses because of my magical sensitivity felt different, and I could sense it even with her on the other side of the suite. It had changed when the Winter Court had claimed her and now was ever-so-slightly different... or was it just that the Winter Court's power was starting to break free of the spell Karthick had cast to block it?

God. It was bad enough we barely had any time before my mother recast her tracking spell and found us again. I had no idea how she'd managed to recast it so quickly in the first place. But Karthick's spell on Amiah should have lasted longer than a few days. We should have had more time.

Titus, in a pair of beige shorts, and with water from his hair, glistening on his massive, muscular chest followed close behind her. His power was strong and sure again, not stuttering and fractured, and a pressure in my chest eased—and was quickly replaced with a painful surge of demonic magic.

His essence hadn't felt this steady since before the last time Faerie's Heart had awakened and he'd lost his kin. I was pretty sure his realignment was still fragile, but this was the first step he'd needed to take. A step I wouldn't have been able to help him with even if I hadn't been infected with demonic magic. No, he'd needed Amiah and fate had thrown those two together.

And was now tearing them apart.

Hawk stepped into sight—still wearing his beige shorts and blue T-shirt. His essence was back to full power as well. Except it hadn't been when he'd left to get Titus and Amiah, which meant he'd gotten more sexual energy while he'd been up there, he'd probably encouraged them along for a little more.

He was someone else fate was fucking over.

And God damn it, it pissed me off that even when I got rid of this infection, I wouldn't be able to help them.

Halfway down the stairs, Amiah's gaze landed on me and her angel glow flared, her joy sharpening into seriousness.

She hurried the rest of the way down and across the living room, moving as if she were in perfect health, and my heart skipped a beat.

She was okay, and with her power at full, Titus hadn't seriously hurt her.

Thank God.

Cassius jerked forward a step as she opened the door, his fire rolling up his forearms before he sucked it back in and backed up the step he'd taken.

Rin also shifted toward her then froze as another spark of hellfire snapped from his right eye and drifted to the patio, the only indication that she affected him as well.

"We have to deal with this infection," she said, sitting on the couch beside me, cupping my cheeks between her cool palms, and urging me to look at her as if she could do something about the magic trapped inside me... which she couldn't.

A weak flurry of frozen sparks rushed from her hands into my face and a hint of fae magic fluttered inside me.

Okay. Maybe she could help me.

Except she could only transfer magic. She couldn't remove the infection because as a being from the Realm of Celestial Light, she had no way of connecting with the demonic magic.

I slid my gaze to Hawk, who'd sank onto the couch opposite me, his gaze on Amiah, a strange soft yet still heated look in his eyes—another one of us who was also a fucked-up mess.

"Any word from Sargos?" I asked him as Titus picked up Amiah, pulling her hands away from me.

My heart stupidly clenched at the absence. Jeez. Yes, I was in love with her, but so was everyone else and Titus's realigned soul was still fragile. He needed to hold her more than I needed her touch.

But instead of moving away, Titus took Amiah's seat and settled her in his lap with her arms around her, and she reestablished contact with me, interlacing our fingers.

"You're going to Sargos?" Cassius asked, more flames rolling up his forearms. "Are you insane? He's responsible for the deaths of at least four JP agents."

"Then it's a good thing I'm not an agent." The

demonic magic surged, but another small flurry of fae magic sparks rushed from Amiah's hand into mine.

Cassius glared at me. "We can also link him to human and super trafficking and the deaths of a dozen more supers."

"And he's the only one close enough to get here on time that can get this shit out of me." Another agonizing surge. "Trust me," I said through gritted teeth. "I'd rather not risk drawing his attention, but I have no choice."

I'm running out of time. If I haven't already.

Cassius's smoke thickened around him. "You don't know what Sargos will charge."

"Does it matter?" Amiah asked. "Sebastian can't carry on like this."

"It matters because Sargos could ask for one of us as payment, not just Bane." A burst of fire shot from his body into the night sky. "God damn it," he hissed and yanked his flames back into his body. "I will *not* let anyone take you again."

"Sargos won't know about her," I said.

"You honestly believe he won't find out about her?" More fire rolled up his body.

"He won't because the fucking brand is going to take her out of my life," I snapped back.

Titus rumbled and tugged Amiah closer to his body and the muscles in Hawk's jaw tightened.

Amiah squeezed my hand and she met my gaze. For a second, I was drowning in a glowing blue sky, my soul captured by hers and the hope I saw in her eyes. "Not if the Heart can remove it."

Out of the corner of my eye I saw Rin shift a step closer.

The Heart could fix this.

Holy shit, the Heart could fix this!

I cupped her cheeks and captured her lips in a quick, hard kiss. "I'm an idiot. Of course the Heart can fix this."

"Which doesn't solve the issue of Sargos," Cassius said.

"Who hasn't even called back," Hawk pointed out. "Sargos or not, we're running out of time."

"How much time?" Amiah asked, fear creeping into her expression.

God, I wished she hadn't asked that. I didn't want to confess to her that there was no time. I needed to do something now if I still had a connection with Faerie. It had been torture watching her grieve Cassius. I didn't want to put her through that with a real death. Of course, Amiah and I barely knew each other. Maybe she wouldn't be heartbroken over me like she'd been with Cassius... and I didn't know what made me more upset, the fact that she'd be all right if I died or that she wouldn't be.

"Not much," Hawk said before I could figure out an answer.

"There's got to be something we can do, some way we can buy you time." Amiah's angel glow flared, revealing her worry. "I thought I could help and give you fae magic like I did back in your apartment, but it doesn't look like I'm giving you anything, and your pain isn't getting any better."

I offered her a sad smile. "You're giving me some, just

not very fast and the demonic magic is consuming it as soon as it enters my system."

"Then tell me how to give you more. I did it before. I don't know how, but I did. It was after we had sex. You said—" Her eyes widened. "You said you got it when I came. It has to be the connection I form when we have sex. It lets me transfer more magic to you faster."

Hawk sat forward. "If you don't cast anything, another transfusion could keep you going for a day, maybe more."

"How much do you want to believe I won't have to cast something in the next twenty-four hours?" I shot back.

"Maybe you'll get to Sargos in time," Titus said, his voice gruff. "How powerful is he? There are four of us and you were powerful five hundred years ago. I bet you're more powerful now."

"Alone, we could take Sargos," Cassius said, "but he has a small army. Even if we fight them off, he'll just send more men after us."

"Then we recall the main team," Amiah said, her expression grim. "Essie can pull demonic magic out of demons, and it's her magic. Surely she can pull it out of Sebastian. We'll have to turn ourselves in for a disciplinary hearing, but she can get back here in about twelve hours."

"Except if you turn yourselves in, you might not be able to go after the Heart," Hawk said. "What happens when the next key is empowered or when the Winter Court starts calling you back?"

Amiah shivered. "We'll deal with it. At least no one will be dead or one of Sargos's slaves."

Except I didn't know if she could deal with it. The last time a key was empowered she couldn't breathe, had been freezing, and Titus hadn't been able to find the key without her.

If we couldn't get the key, we couldn't get the Heart.

The demonic magic surged again and so did a trickle of her fae magic.

"You can't call the JP," I forced out.

"We have three options," Cassius said. "Nothing—"

"Not acceptable," Amiah interrupted.

The light in Cassius's eyes flared. "I agree. Which leaves us with going to Sargos or calling the JP."

Rin shifted a little closer and another spark of hellfire snapped from his eye.

"I can do it," he said, his voice so soft I could barely hear it.

Everyone stared at Rin and I mentally slapped myself. Of course Rin could pull the demonic magic out of me. That was what he did. Except—

"Can you pull out just the demonic magic?" I asked. It wouldn't be helpful if he also pulled out all of my fae magic. Although that might kill me faster than the slow fade I was looking forward to when my connection to Faerie was severed.

"Demonic magic is sticky. It'll take some fae magic with it, but I don't know how much." Rin's gaze darted to Amiah then returned to me. "Your highness will have to replenish yourself first."

Meaning I needed to sleep with Amiah.

CHAPTER 20

RIN

I WAS FOOLISH TO HAVE AGREED TO HELP. I DIDN'T KNOW IF I trusted Prince Seireadan or any of them, and I didn't trust the desperate aching desire I had for Princess Amiah, but I certainly didn't trust the Shadow King.

Even if the odds were good that Prince Seireadan would enslave me and that Princess Amiah couldn't free me from our unwanted soul bond, I had to take the chance. Because there was no chance anything good would come out of the Shadow King getting Faerie's Heart.

Except the only way for Prince Seireadan to get the Heart was if I removed his demonic infection. Something I was certain I could do. It just wasn't going to be easy, and I suspected it'd be painful. And that could incur the prince's wrath. Something I'd been trying to avoid since I'd realized escape while trapped in the soul bond was impossible. Right now was the freest I'd been since before I had been murdered, and there was a slim chance that I'd be completely free. I wasn't going to screw that up by drawing the attention of one of Faerie's fickle royals.

"So I guess we should—" Prince Seireadan jerked his chin toward the lavish, black, white, and gold living room that was almost as opulent as the Shadow King's rooms. "You know. Get it on."

"Oh, how romantic." Princess Amiah rolled her eyes at him, adding to the evidence that even if they weren't married, they were close. No one rolled their eyes at a royal from Faerie. It was too dangerous, and I'd seen people pay with their lives for less.

"Sweetheart, you already know there's nothing romantic about me." He flashed her a wicked smile, but the sharp angry magic I could sense inside him snapped and his expression twisted tight with pain. "Fucking hell."

"Come on." Princess Amiah tried to pull out of the dragon's hold, but he held tight, and even if she fought with everything she had, she'd never be able to break free. With a sigh she raised her gaze to meet his. "You have to let me go, Titus."

"I know." Titus heaved a heavy sigh.

"She's not just yours," the angel said, smoke billowing around him. We hadn't been introduced, but I'd over heard them calling him Cassius, just like I'd overheard them calling the dragon Titus. "At least you can hold her."

"*She* won't be any of yours if we can't get the Heart," she said, her gaze flickering to me, capturing my soul within their blue depths before she jerked her attention away.

Except looking away didn't release me. I burned with a need I'd never experienced before, a cruel unwanted yearning to pull her out of the dragon's arms and kiss her again even though I knew it would be a mistake that could enrage the prince.

It had been a mistake to kiss her that first time.

It had been a mistake to even offer to ease her backlash.

Now I knew what she tasted like, her lips and her magic, and I hadn't gotten nearly enough.

I shouldn't have said anything, shouldn't have spoken up when she'd stepped into the office.

But I'd been starving. I was still starving, and not just for magic. I hadn't been able to trust anyone since Deaglan had bought me, and while His Majesty had granted me a sexual release from time to time there'd always been strings attached to remind me of my place.

And everything within me said I could trust Princess Amiah, I needed Princess Amiah, I was lost without her. With her I would be free, even though we were trapped together.

Except that was just another prison. One she didn't want either. That much, at least had been clear. With my enhanced hearing, I'd heard her tell Cassius how horrible the brand was and that it hadn't been fair that she was stuck with me when she was in love with all of them. She hadn't lied to me back in Prince Seireadan's clean room when she'd said the brand would make her love me and fall out of love with them. I just had to hope she'd meant what she'd said in the garage, that I wasn't their slave or prisoner.

"So if any of you want to keep me, Sebastian needs to get rid of his infection." She gave the dragon a firm, fast kiss.

With a huff he released her and she slipped from his embrace and held out her hand to Prince Seireadan.

"Shall we... get it on?" she asked.

Now he rolled his eyes at her, making jealousy that I shouldn't have been feeling twist around my heart.

They were so comfortable together, so relaxed, something I was sure I'd never have with her... not that I wanted that. That was the brand making me desire a relationship with her. And yet it wasn't just her. They were all comfortable with each other, like close friends—something else I'd never had and never would—and none of them treated Prince Seireadan like they should and he didn't seem to care.

With a groan and a sharp surge of his magic that drew a strangled gasp, the prince stood and staggered into Princess Amiah.

She caught him, wrapping her arms around him and letting him lean into her. "God, I wish I could take your pain," she murmured into his ear.

"I wouldn't let you," he whispered back. "You already carry too much."

My hellfire heaved inside me and I mentally knuckled down, holding it back. I couldn't show how I felt. That was a weakness that could be used against me. But it was clear he was in love with her. If they weren't already married, something I still questioned even though she'd said they weren't, they would be soon. They already had the Winter Court's blessing.

"I don't carry enough," she replied. "You guys keep doing things for me."

"Yep, and going to keep on doing it," Hawk said, pulling Prince Seireadan out of her arms and supporting him. "Let's get him up to bed."

Princess Amiah held open the patio door for Hawk and the prince, then followed them across the living room, taking a part of my soul with her, while I fought the rest of me that urged me to follow.

"I'm ordering food," Titus announced. "You want anything?" He glanced at Cassius, who frowned at him.

"Didn't you already eat?" Cassius asked.

Titus flashed his canines at him, his expression pure male satisfaction. "I worked up another appetite."

"Really? You're going to push my buttons, too, like Hawk and Bane?" Cassius glared at him then dipped his gaze to the fire rolling over his hands, making Titus's cocky expression vanish. "Can you guys please stop rubbing it in?"

"When Seireadan gets his magic back, I'm sure he'll be able to help you," Titus said. "And then *you* can work up an appetite."

Cassius's eyes widened in surprise and his angel glow flared. "You mean that? You don't see that as a challenge for her?"

"She's my mate and she needs you. So you're my mate, too," Titus huffed as if it was obvious, which it definitely wasn't. "Do you want food?"

More smoke billowed around Cassius and he narrowed his eyes. "I'm not having sex with you."

"Good, because I'm not having sex with you. Food?" Titus asked again.

"Don't bother. I'm just going to end up burning it right now."

"Okay." Titus opened the patio door, and his gaze slid to me despite me trying to stay still and unnoticed, and his expression grew sober. "There's a change of clothes waiting for you, too. Deaglan has a new shifter on his team and it would be better if you weren't smelling like blood."

I gave him a slight nod and followed him inside. I couldn't tell what the hierarchy was between the other men and didn't want to risk pissing off Prince Seireadan's right hand, not until I had a way to escape—which wouldn't happen until I was no longer bound to Amiah. And while Titus might have just escaped the Shadow King's prison and was the least likely to be in charge of this group, that didn't mean he wasn't.

He led me back to the kitchen and handed me a white crinkly bag with black material—presumably clothes—then opened the room service menu and scanned the listings.

I didn't wait to see if he'd offer me more blood. He hadn't been the one who'd done it the first time. That had been the incubus... who I also couldn't figure out. Princess Amiah had said she loved him, but the prince had kissed him to save him back in the cavern. Was Hawk the prince's right hand? He'd taken over when Prince Seireadan had passed out.

So far, with the exception of Princess Amiah, who was

being influenced by our bond like I was, Hawk had been the most welcoming, and Titus the least.

The dragon had barely looked at me since we'd arrived, and I didn't know if that was because I reminded him of the Shadow King and his imprisonment or because his beast had chosen Princess Amiah as his mate, which made our soul bond a huge problem.

It was actually shocking that he'd given Cassius permission to sleep with her or that he hadn't fought harder to keep her from having sex with the prince. Sure, she'd said she was in love with all of them, but that didn't mean it went both ways, and I'd heard that dragons were extremely possessive.

Another sour band of jealousy wrapped around my non-beating heart. I wanted that acceptance with them... with *someone*. I wanted someone I could trust, who I could finally, after five hundred years, let my guard down with. But it didn't matter that my soul was saying I could trust them.

That was the brand.

Because *she* trusted them.

The best I could hope for in the situation was that I could stay unnoticed until all of this was over and then sneak away.

Except that was only if they could get the Heart.

Which meant it was in my best interest to do whatever it took to ensure the Heir to the Winter Court's throne got the Heart and the Shadow King didn't.

With a new determination that I hadn't felt in a good couple hundred years, I headed up the stairs to take a shower and change. But the moment I reached the top step, my gaze was drawn to the door at the end of the hall.

It was slightly ajar as if someone hadn't been paying attention when they'd shut it and the latch hadn't caught.

"You sure this is a good idea?" Hawk asked, my heightened hearing easily picking up his soft words. "He hasn't tried to kill us or summon Deaglan, but that doesn't mean he won't. I'm not comfortable with him feeding on you."

I tried to go into the first bedroom, not caring who'd been in it last, but I couldn't stop myself from creeping toward the end of the hall.

"You were going to let him feed on you," Princess Amiah said.

"He can feed on me because I can take it," Hawk replied.

"Yeah right," the prince said. "He needs to feed and you think it doesn't matter if he kills you because you're not as useful as I am."

I reached the door, peered inside, and my essence stuttered.

There she was, a radiant goddess, standing perfectly framed in the crack with her back to me, her fae glow so bright I couldn't tell if there were lights on in the room or not. Her long blond hair, still damp from the shower she must have taken after sleeping with Titus, hung loose, the ends just starting to curl, and her magic, still a little wild, her backlash not fully calmed, rushed inside her like waves in a light wind.

I knew peeking in was a bad idea, that I'd be punished

if they caught me, and with Prince Seireadan lying on the bed, his head in sight, there was a good chance I'd be caught. All it would take was a glance at the door. But I couldn't help myself. I was drawn to her whether I wanted to be or not. My soul cried to be with her in every way possible, spiritually, emotionally, and physically.

And God, I wanted to be in the room with her, to feel her mouth against mine, her pulse racing with the same aching desire that raced through me. I didn't care how she took me. She could keep her relationships with the others. I wasn't possessive like a dragon. I'd sleep with her alone and I'd sleep with her with them. I just needed to be with her.

The thought made my cock start to stiffen and, with far too many years of experience, I focused on the still nothingness in my heart and relaxed my body's reaction, making my burgeoning erection slip away.

"Is that true?" the princess asked, opening her robe and letting it slide to the floor, pooling around her feet.

Oh, God.

My cock went instantly hard again and the urge to storm into the room and take her squeezed in my chest. I *had* to join with her. Everything in my soul screamed at me to be with her, finish what fate had started and seal our connection.

Because of the brand.

I struggled to get myself back under control. The Shadow King would have devised a cruel humiliation if he'd seen me get hard without permission while he was having sex.

Hawk stepped into sight behind her, brushed her hair aside, and pressed his lips against the back of her neck.

My hellfire heaved inside me and heated my eyes.

I dragged my thoughts back to my inner stillness. I was dead. I was perfectly still. I was a calm pond, its water still like glass.

A ripple shuddered through my mental pond.

Calm. Like glass. I had to regain control of my body. The incubus might know how I felt—and he'd probably tell the others—but I couldn't let it look like I was going to act on my desire.

Because they weren't *my* desires.

"If we can get rid of Bane's infection, he can fix everything for you," Hawk murmured, his lips teasing her skin and drawing a soft sigh. He glanced past Princess Amiah at Prince Seireadan. "And I can take it. You can't. I've got more magic between taking too much and being dead than you do."

"Which is why you're going to watch him and my magic levels and the second it looks like he's taken too much of my fae magic or he actually gets rid of the source of the infection and is still feeding, you make him stop." The prince propped himself up on his elbows, his expression serious. "And I don't care how, so long as you don't kill him."

Which meant I was going to have to be careful... or expect an attack that I wouldn't be able to defend myself from, because fighting back would only make them think I still meant them harm. I'd already made the mistake of fighting back when the dragon had attacked me after my too-brief kiss with the princess. Instinct had kicked in and I'd just reacted. And while there hadn't been an immediate punishment, that didn't mean there wouldn't be one.

And it would be worse if Prince Seireadan saw me hard for his wife.

I had to leave. Get into one of the bedrooms and lock the door.

But I couldn't make myself move or even look away. My essence was locked onto her in a way that terrified me. My desire hadn't been this intense when she'd accused me of killing Cassius and collapsed. I'd seen her naked body then and hadn't gotten hard.

Except then I hadn't kissed her or tasted her magic. Now I'd had a torturous tease of her that only added to the pressure of our unwanted bond.

"Maybe it won't come to that," Princess Amiah said, sitting on the edge of the bed and laying a hand on Prince Seireadan's ankle. "I don't know if the brand is affecting him in more ways than desiring me, but he didn't have to help me with my backlash."

More ripples undulated through my mental pond.

"Don't forget he got something out of that, too," the prince replied.

I tried to close my eyes, but I couldn't stop watching.

The demonic magic in the prince snapped, sharp and hard against my senses, and he collapsed back on the bed with a groan.

"Fuck." He squeezed his eyes shut. "I don't want to admit that I'm not up for this, but—" Another snap that twisted his expression. "I have no idea if I'm up for this. It certainly isn't going to be anything to brag about."

Princess Amiah gave him a sad, soft smile. "You don't have to worry about impressing me." She slid her hand up his calf and past his knee, pushing aside the edge of his robe and revealing the curl of a thick tattoo running up his thigh.

So the prince hadn't just inked glyphs into his arms and torso. He was completely covered. I didn't know if that meant he wasn't as powerful as everyone believe because he needed the spells already set on his body, or if he was that powerful and wanted to use his magic as efficiently as possible. Efficient magic use meant he could go longer and cast more complicated spells, and that would make him incredibly dangerous.

"You've already impressed me," she said, her voice turning husky.

A wave swept through my mental pond and my cock grew harder.

Calm. Still. I am the nothingness inside me.

"I know what you're capable of and I know once we've treated this infection, we'll go back to our—" She caught her bottom lip in her teeth for a second, sending another wave sweeping through my stillness. "We can go back to our arrangement."

"Yeah," he replied, as the demonic magic inside him surged. He clutched the comforter beneath him, clenched his jaw against a groan, and squeezed his eyes shut.

"Now." She straddled his legs and tugged open his robe. He wasn't fully erect but I was sure that had more to do with the pain and not how he felt about the princess.

"Let's get some magic in you and relieve a bit of this pain."

He reached for her, urging her to come to him, but instead of crawling up his body, she dipped down and ran her tongue slowly up his cock, making it rise to attention.

Any hope of controlling my erection shattered. She'd just dropped a massive boulder in the center of my pond, sending the water crashing inside me. My cock throbbed for her attention and it took everything I had to just stay where I was.

That was what I had to focus on now. Staying put. I wasn't going to be able to control my body's reaction and I wasn't going to be able to turn away.

But I sure as hell couldn't go into that room. I just had to endure. I'd endured worse. I could endure it now. Because if I didn't screw this up, there was a chance I could finally be free.

CHAPTER 21

AMIAH

I RAN MY TONGUE UP SEBASTIAN'S ERECTION AGAIN, AND focused on the anticipation of driving him crazy. I couldn't think about his pain even if it sliced against my senses. The only thing I could do to help was give him an infusion of my fae magic.

Except the small connection I now had with him just by touching him wasn't enough. We needed to be fully connected and to do that, we needed to have intercourse, and neither of us were ready for that.

"Oh, fuck," he gasped. "That really wasn't a one time deal."

I glanced up at him, the pain in his eyes making my heart clench. "Are you really surprised?"

"Sweetheart, you're still an angel and this is very unangel-like behavior," he said.

His pain surged again, slicing into both of us, and I fought to not show how it was affecting me. He wasn't Cassius, but I didn't want to risk him trying to stop this. It was the only way I could help him.

He drew in a ragged breath as the surge passed. "I keep waiting for you to come to your senses."

Still? Really? Was he trying to push me away?

That didn't make sense, not with what he'd said before I'd healed Cassius. He'd implied there was something more between us than just our arrangement.

But then that had been before he'd seen Rin straddling me in his clean room, and had been reminded that there couldn't be more between us—at least not until we got the Heart. And even if we got the Heart, there was still a chance I'd never be free.

My pulse stuttered with the realization of what he was doing. He was trying to push me away to protect me.

Being in love with him and the others would only make everything harder for me. It was already tearing me up that my body desired Rin, and I knew it was going to shatter me when I realized I'd fallen out of love with them.

But his plan was stupid. I wasn't going to stop loving him or any of them because of the fear that my brand would make me fall out of love. I wasn't ever going to stop fighting for us until I'd tried everything possible to keep them. Even knowing that eventually Sebastian would want to go his own way. But our separation had to be his choice, not because of the cruel fate forced upon us.

"You're not going to get me to take it back. I love you just as much as I love Hawk and Cassius and Titus." I wrapped my hand around his now full erection and drew it up to my lips. "I know you can't make a commitment. I don't expect you to and I don't expect you to love me back."

"Amiah—" he started, but I captured his gaze, stopping whatever he was going to say. He didn't have to apologize for who he was. I'd been trapped before—I was trapped now in my bond with Rin—I wasn't going to force that on anyone, no matter how much I loved them. *Because* I loved him.

"We have an arrangement. And until you say we're done, I'm going to enjoy you in every way that excites us." I slid him into my mouth, savoring his low throaty groan, this one clearly from pleasure.

His pupils dilated, and I gave myself to the sensation of him in my mouth. He was harder than when I'd first grasped him, full and thick, and his life force, weak and straining against the darkness, thrummed against my senses.

I slowly slid him out, my hand following my lips, then pushed him back in. His groan deepened and the sound rolled through me, making me wet.

God, I loved that sound, loved that look in his eyes. I didn't know how he did it, but I always felt as if I was the only woman in the world for him when we made love. I knew it was a lie, that there'd been lots of women and there would be a lot more, but I didn't care. It made me feel as if I was free to do anything, that he wouldn't laugh at me if I made a mistake or didn't know something, and I didn't have to maintain any kind of control. I could just be me with him.

"Next time you slide him out, swirl your tongue over his tip," Hawk said as he climbed onto the bed and knelt beside me.

Sebastian's gaze jumped to him, and I obeyed, teasing

him with a fast flick, making his gaze snap back to me and his erection flex beneath my hand.

Hawk leaned close, his lips against the divot behind my ear, his warm breath sending a shiver of need racing through me. "Harder."

Sebastian's erection flexed again at the suggestion.

I slid him out and roughly swept my tongue over his tip. Sebastian's eyes rolled back as his hips rose, telling me what he wanted.

"Now relax your throat so you can take him deeper," Hawk murmured, his breath sending another shiver racing through me as he slid in a curl of his seductive magic. It unfurled, soft and small, in my core, just a whisper of what I knew it could be, and melted away some of the tension still in my body, reminding me that I needed to relax not just my throat.

I dipped in, taking Sebastian deeper than he'd ever been before, drawing another throaty groan, but his demonic magic infection snapped, turning his groan into a strangled moan.

My heart clenched, and I struggled to concentrate on feeling good, on the sounds he was making, on the heat building within me. If we couldn't get the Heart or it couldn't free me, my time with him was limited, and I didn't want fear ruining what could be one of our last times together.

Not to mention if I couldn't transfer enough fae magic to him, Rin might not be able to save him.

My pulse stuttered with fear, and I slid him out, raked his tip with my tongue, and took him back in, trying to distract him from the pain and myself from my worry.

Sebastian's breath picked up and he clenched the comforter. The icy brightness of his life force grew a little stronger, and I clung to that. It was proof I could help him, that I could give him enough magic to survive.

"Amiah," Hawk murmured, jerking me from my thoughts back to the bedroom. "Stop concentrating. You get to enjoy this too."

The curl of his magic grew a little stronger and he teased his fingers over the invisible seams between my shoulder blades where my wings emerged.

Hot, sultry need burst in my core, overwhelming any other thoughts. God, it was just a whisper of a touch. It could have been an accidental brush if I hadn't been positive Hawk had known exactly what he was doing. But it was as if he'd sucked on my clit and shot a blast of magic into me, making that sensitive bud throb and activating every nerve in my body.

I released a deep throaty moan around Sebastian's erection, I wouldn't have been able to hold it back if I'd tried, and he slipped in a little deeper.

"Oh fuck," Sebastian groaned.

"Not quite yet," Hawk chuckled. "But if you want her to keep going, you're going to need to give her a hand because I plan on seriously distracting her."

My pulse lurched in a rapid tattoo, his words skyrocketing my anticipation, and he brushed my wing seams again, twisting my need tighter.

Sebastian tangled his fingers in my hair and I realized I'd stopped what I was doing, all my thoughts lost to the aching need inside me.

"Do you want to keep going?" he asked, his gaze dipping to his erection in my mouth. "With me, I mean."

I rolled my eyes at him. Of course I wanted to keep going. This was on my list of things to try. I wanted to know what it felt like to pleasure him with my mouth while I was being pleasured, wanted the press of bodies and the thrum of their life forces. I just hadn't expected it to be so... distracting.

Hawk teased my wing seams again, and another moan escaped me, but I managed to maintain enough thought to answer Sebastian by sliding him out and back in again.

I could do this. I just needed to concentrate.

"Jeez, gorgeous. Stop thinking," Hawk chided, giving my seams a firm rub, shooting more sensation straight to my core. "You're supposed to be enjoying this. Trust us. We've got you."

Sebastian's gaze jumped to Hawk and he gave a tight nod. They'd agreed on something and I had a feeling it was to blow my mind and make me come screaming.

And I had absolutely no problem with that.

"Now let go, and let us make you feel good," Hawk purred.

He rubbed the seam behind my right shoulder blade again as he swept his other hand over the swell of my rear and traced a finger through my wet folds.

Oh, yes. I just needed to let go. Every time I gave in to them during sex, I'd felt amazing. They had me. I was safe with them. If I really thought about it, I'd always felt safe with them.

A pressure in my chest released and I let go. I could

worry about my bond, about getting the Heart, about facing off against Deaglan, about keeping my guys alive, about all of it later. Right now, there were just the three of us and the amazing sensations rushing through me.

Sebastian's grip in my hair tightened, holding me steady and drawing my attention back to him, his pale gaze capturing me. The desire burning in his eyes turned me on even more. This wasn't an act. He craved me as much as I craved him, and he drew himself halfway out of my mouth then pushed back in again. His expression and the friction against my lips and tongue were unbelievably erotic. I wanted him to make love to my mouth, wanted to watch him lose control and shatter, and I wanted to taste him.

My muscles clenched at the thought, and Hawk pushed two fingers inside me, adding another point of erotic sensation. All fear of Sebastian's condition, all sense of pain vanished. There was just him and Hawk, their hot and cold, dark and bright life forces thrumming against my senses, and my throbbing desire. I reveled in the feel of Sebastian's fingers in my hair, his body trembling as he slowly pumped into my mouth, and Hawk's fingers sliding in and out of me.

My need twisted tighter and my breath grew ragged. God, it felt amazing. I wanted to be like this forever.

Then Hawk swept his other hand from my wing seams over the swell of my rear, and teased a suddenly slicked fingertip around my anus.

My breath stalled, everything within me stalled, focused on that one point. I'd read about this and the sensitive nerves there, and I ached to try it, just like I'd ached to have Sebastian in my mouth, to have both of them capturing me between their bodies. So far everything about sex had been so much more than I'd imagined and my body vibrated in anticipation. Then Hawk slowly pressed his fingertip inside me, sending a heated pleasure rippling through me that had nothing to do with his magic.

Oh, wow. Oh, yes. I released a long low moan around Sebastian's erection.

"Fuck me," Sebastian groaned, slowly pumping back into my mouth.

No. Fuck me. Please.

I pushed my rear back, encouraging Hawk, trying to tell him—as if my moan and his ability to sense sexual energy wasn't already enough—that I wanted him there, wanted more, wanted what it meant, both of them at the same time.

I dipped my head down, bumping Sebastian against the back of my throat, and Sebastian's fingers dug into my scalp, his body shaking.

His erection was as hard as steel in my mouth, but somehow he managed to keep his slow pace, in and out. Hawk matched it, slid his fingers in and out of my rear and folds. The sensations were overwhelming, hot and tight and building an incredible pressure inside me as their life forces grew stronger and whirled around my heart.

Sebastian's thrusts grew faster, his breath just as ragged as mine, his control starting to slip. "I don't know how much longer I can hold on," he moaned.

"Just a little bit more." Hawk slipped the fingers

between my folds up to my clit. He stroked the sensitive nub as he slid a second finger past the tight ring of muscle in my rear, joining the first, stretching me,

Oh, yes.

Need snapped through me, and my muscles started to contract with the promise of an orgasm, and cruelly, wonderfully, breathtakingly, Hawk captured my release with his magic and held me on the edge, torturously close but not able to fall over.

"Not yet," he purred. "Neither of you."

Sebastian's breath hitched and his head tipped back. "You're fucking cruel."

"Am I really?" Hawk asked, working his fingers inside me and teasing my clit, twisting me so tight I was going to shatter the moment he released me. "I don't believe for one second you're not enjoying this."

"Asshole," Sebastian groaned, and he pulled himself out of my mouth, and tugged me up his body. Hawk shifted in behind me, his fingers still stretching and teasing, and making me tremble with need, trapped on the verge of an explosion.

I fought to keep my gaze on Sebastian, but my eyes kept threatening to roll back, my body desperate for the mind-blowing release twisting in my core.

"Oh, sweetheart," he murmured, brushing a lock of hair out of my eyes, the touch tender and warm even though his gaze was still scorching. "I don't think I'll ever get tired of watching you fall apart."

He captured my lips in a searing kiss, one hand tangled in my hair, holding me close, and the other aligning himself with my opening.

He buried himself inside me with a slow, glorious thrust and the icy brightness of his life force flared inside me. My soul clicked and his magic swelled around my heart, more powerful than the last time we'd joined. This time I was the ice and the vast power. Just like I'd been the wild ferocity when I'd connected with Titus and an inferno with Cassius.

His eyes widened as if he felt the new strength in our connection, then the tip of Hawk's thick erection pressed against my rear, and my thoughts scattered. All I could think about was how Hawk was going to make this feel amazing, and with a seductive swell of his magic to turn the bite of pain from his size into a breathtaking hot throbbing, he slowly breached my entrance.

This time my eyes did roll back. I couldn't stop them. The sensations were overwhelming.

Beneath me, Sebastian's trembling increased, but he managed to hold both of us still, waiting for Hawk to fully enter me.

And slowly, oh so slowly, Hawk pushed inside, using his magic to help me adjust. He felt enormous, both of them did, and every nerve ending inside my body ignited as he sank deeper and deeper in, until his flesh was pressed tight against mine.

God, it felt so good. I was panting and mewling for release and they hadn't even done anything yet.

That thing in my soul clicked again, and Hawk's fiery darkness surged through my veins and entwined with Sebastian's life force around my heart. I was darkness and sex and ice and power. My already bright fae glow grew brighter, rolling up and down my body with my pent-up need.

Then they started to move, slowly, finding their tempo, the friction and fullness twisting me tighter and tighter. I panted and moaned, my fae glow rushing around me, a lake in a wild storm, revealing just how much I was enjoying myself.

Sebastian's grip in my hair tightened, twisting my head to the side, and I caught a glimpse of Hawk driving into me, which would have made me come if his magic hadn't been holding me back. His hellfire licked his cheeks, his expression was a mix of awe and bliss.

The guys' breaths quickly grew as heavy as mine and each thrust became stronger. Their life forces swelled, roared around my heart and through my veins, and I knew in my soul that they were mine. I didn't know why I hadn't branded them, but I knew without a doubt they were mine. Even Sebastian. There weren't going to be any other women in his future, not because I'd force him to make a commitment to me—I doubted he would regard-less—but because we were fated for each other. It didn't matter how much I'd wanted to control my fate, meeting him, meeting all of them had been inevitable.

They were mine. Always.

"Oh, God, Amiah," Sebastian cried as he thrust hard and tensed. His fae glow ignited as brightly as mine, his eyes rolled back and his hips arched off the bed, burying him deeper inside me as his orgasm tore through him.

Hawk released his hold on my desire, and a tsunami of bliss pounded into me. Glorious sensation tore through every cell in my body, ripping a scream of pleasure from my lips and tensing every muscle. Stars exploded behind my lids and the sense of Hawk and Sebastian's life force overwhelmed me, powerful, entwined light and darkness, ice and fire.

Far away, I felt Hawk tense behind me, crying his own release, but the waves kept crashing over me, again and again, spinning me until I melted into an amazing, bone-less, darkness.

I didn't know how long I drifted, but when I woke, my cheek was against Sebastian's chest, his white flesh, marked with all his mesmerizing tattoos, radiant.

We'd separated, all three of us, but he had his arms around me in a tight embrace, and Hawk was pressed against my back. Cold in front, hot behind, and the memory of them driving into me.

Another smaller orgasm rushed through me, drawing a moaning sigh of pleasure.

"No kidding," Sebastian said. "I'd thought holding back an orgasm was something only fucked up incubi or succubi did, but damn. I don't think I've ever come that hard, and from your scream," he said to me, "I don't think you have, either."

"I don't think I've ever gotten a hit that strong," Hawk murmured, his words slightly slurred as if he'd gotten too much sexual energy.

I shifted in Sebastian's embrace so I could check Hawk's eyes.

He gave me a heart-stopping smile and kissed me before I could get a good look, but it didn't seem as if he were ODing, just a little intoxicated.

His kiss made another rippling orgasm tease through me and I released a soft moan, savoring the sensation.

But as much as I wanted to just lie there in their arms, the whole point of this was to heal Sebastian's infection.

I turned back to him, concentrated past my orgasmic haze, and checked his life force. He still battled the darkness trapped inside him, but the spark of fae magic embedded in every cell in his body, just like it was currently embedded in mine, was stronger, brighter, and icier.

It called to the icy power inside me, urging me to open myself up to it.

A chill shivered down my spine and Hawk shifted closer, pressing more of his ever-so-slightly too-hot body against mine.

"We should check with Rin to see if I've given you enough magic," I said.

"A part of me really hopes you haven't." Sebastian pressed his lips against the top of my head, giving me a tender kiss. "But it would be best if I recovered what this demonic shit has been blocking before my sister and Deaglan find us again. I don't want to have to channel raw magic in our next fight if I don't have to, and it's going to take time for me to add power to my glyphs and replenish my internal well."

Another chill raced through me, this time setting off another soft aftershock of orgasm.

Oh, wow.

"We should give Amiah a little more time," Hawk said, his warm breath caressing my neck. "It's probably not safe to stand yet. You were barely out for a minute and my magic usually knocks you out for longer than that."

Except as much as I wanted to keep cuddling with them, Sebastian was right. It was dangerous to not heal him as soon as possible. So many things depended on his magic, the most important being his survival.

"If you two are fine, go without me. I can join you when I'm ready."

Sebastian glanced over my head at Hawk. "How much do you believe that? The moment we step out of this bedroom, you're going to try getting up."

I opened my mouth to deny that, but Sebastian cut me off with a hard, fast kiss.

"Don't bother denying it," he said. "You're too damned stubborn to not try."

"It's one of the things I love about you," Hawk added.

I shifted, squeezing in between them so I could prop myself up on my elbows and look both of them in the eyes, as another shiver swept through me.

"You're probably the only one," I said. "I have a feeling the rest of you have already sided with Cassius and have decided I'm too fragile to do anything."

Sebastian snorted and his life force surged against my senses sliding a thin thread of ice through my veins. "He did let you and Titus go at it. I have no idea how he managed to stay on the patio with all the noise you were making."

"Pretty sure we just made a lot of noise too," I said.

Another icy thread swelled inside me and Hawk was starting to get too hot to lie beside.

"Yeah, but they all know it's because of me," Hawk

said as I carefully sat up so I didn't make myself dizzy. The absence of his body heat sent gooseflesh rushing over my skin, and I didn't know what was worse, being too hot or too cold.

Hawk put his hands behind his head and swept his gaze down my body, desire rekindling in his eyes. "I want you to have the best experience possible. First times only happen once."

"Yeah, but now she'll be expecting that every time," Sebastian said, his life force swelling again... except now I wasn't sure if the ice was coming from Sebastian, it seemed sharper, colder than he'd felt before.

"Pretty sure I won't notice if the next time is half as good. That was so much more than I'd dreamed it would be."

"You dreamed it, hunh?" Hawk's lips curled into a dark wicked smile. "Any other dreams you want to tell us about?"

"We'll there's—"

The ice inside me exploded into a ferocious storm, and God, it wasn't Sebastian, it was the Winter Court. With horror, I realized I hadn't just been feeling his life force, but his connection with the court as well. And through him, it had found its way into me.

"Amiah?" Sebastian frowned and something popped behind me.

"Oh, shit." Hawk jerked up and reached for me, but a powerful frozen wind jerked me off the bed and yanked me across the room into a portal.

Sebastian screamed and one of his glyphs lit up, but

the air around me thickened with magic, plugged my nose and ears, and poured down my throat.

The Winter Court was taking me back to Faerie whether I wanted to go or not. And this time, I would be without my guys.

Don't miss the next book in the series!

FATED RESOLVE
Angel's Fate: Book Five

She bargained everything to save the men she loves. Now the debt is coming due.

The Winter Court is not through with me. I've been sucked through a portal and spat back out into Faerie, where the Winter Court howls for me to wrest control of its magic from the Winter Queen. Much as I want to—need to—I can't.

My soul and body are nearing my breaking point. If I can't fulfill my promise to the Winter Court to find it a new queen, it'll take the next best option: me. Whether I can survive its magic or die trying.

As my guys push themselves beyond exhaustion to find me and I fight to get back to them, the heat of my unwanted soul bond grows stronger, calling me with the ferocity of a siren's song toward my fate.

But even as the rest of me cries for the men I love, fate be damned, I'm desperate to come up with a plan to find Faerie's Heart before my own freezes to a stop. A plan that will save my guys from themselves, because they'll sacrifice everything to get me back.

OTHER BOOKS BY TESSA COLE

THE NEPHILIM'S DESTINY SERIES

Destined Shadows, prequel story

Destined Darkness, book 1

Destined Blood, book 2

Destined Fire, book 3

Destined Storm, book 4

Destined Radiance, book 5

THE ANGEL'S FATE SERIES

Fated Bonds, book 1

Fated Winter, book 2

Fated Fear, book 3

Fated Despair, book 4

Fated Resolve, book 5

Fated Heart, book 6

www.ingramcontent.com/pod-product-compliance
Lightning Source LLC
Chambersburg PA
CBHW020346180626
46812CB00001B/358